I Heart Ed Small

by

Shirley Johnson

I Heart Ed Small

Copyright 2012 by Shirley Johnson

Cover Art Copyright 2012 by Craig Johnson

This book may not be reproduced in part or in whole without permission

ISBN-13: 978-1478318095

All Pink Floyd lyrics used with written permission by Roger Waters 10/17/12 : "Breathe", "Fearless", "Green is the Colour", and "Echoes."

CHAPTER ONE

I was at the neighbor's, Mrs. Small's, when Mama collapsed. I was eating a foot long hotdog and drinking a very cold and very strange new soda pop; new to me at least and strange to me as well as it was a Fresca, when Mama collapsed on our old black linoleum steps going up the stairs to our second floor.

I had been out in our back yard playing with my Drowsy babydoll when I saw Mrs. Small head out into her garden to pick snap beans. I had been shooed out of my own house by my own Mama so she could get the laundry ironed and folded and put away without me under foot.

As I sat out in the back yard with the hot sun burning off my long blonde bangs, I watched Mrs. Small walk out into her snap beans wearing a wide straw hat and carrying a basket lined with calico cotton.

Mrs. Small had a son who was a teenager. The word teenager was synonymous with good-for-nothing smart aleck in our house. Mama said he was probably going to turn out to be a hippie. Daddy said he wouldn't be nothing but a layabout draft dodger, and you could take that to the bank. Mama said to never look a hippie in the eye. They were all apt to be crazy and unpredictable. Mama always reminded me when we were out and about on our errands, for instance say at Tolly's grocery store that if we saw any men with long hair and beards that I should not look at them because they were apt to go nuts. At least that's what Mama always said and she would pull me away.

I of course always turned like Lot's wife to see the hippies on the verge of going crazy. If they were behind us, and 'apt to go crazy' I thought one of us should keep an eye on them as we beat a retreat to the Kleenex isle. But all I ever saw were men with long hair and beards who dressed in a lot more casual clothes than my parents did.

Following Mrs. Small out into her snap beans served two purposes. According to Mama, Mrs. Small's son Ed was on his way to becoming a hippie and I was curious to study him from the safety of Mrs. Small without Mama being around. And two, I was hot and thirsty and lonely for someone to talk to. I knew if I followed Mrs. Small around the garden that eventually she would offer me a cold pop, and I knew she wouldn't mind keeping me company and talking to me. Mrs. Small was a friendly sort of woman with mousy brown curls and large light blue eyes who always called me 'dear' and who always had patience for me.

    I followed Mrs. Small into her garden and helped her pick snap beans. In return she cooked me a foot long hotdog (She even had foot long buns.) and gave me that strange cold can of Fresca. We only bought tall glass bottles of Pepsi at our house.

    And so I was at Mrs. Small's, sitting on her dead husband's black lunch box so I could reach the table, when my Mama collapsed on the black linoleum of our stairs.

    I didn't go home for an hour. I stretched out eating my hot dog in hopes of catching a glimpse of Ed. I wondered if I stared in his eyes long enough if he'd go crazy. But he never did come out of his room and I never did get a glimpse of him.

    Finally I walked home sun burnt from picking snap beans and full of Mrs. Small's hot dog and Fresca. I walked from their side porch to our back porch thinking maybe Mama would let me plug in my electric toy iron and help out with Daddy's hankies. But instead I found her lying on her side on the stairs next to two baskets of ironed and folded laundry. Her blue eyes stared wide as if she saw something between the banisters that frightened her.

    I ran back over to Mrs. Small's and ran on in the house without knocking. But I didn't find Mrs. Small at the kitchen table. I found Ed. Sixteen year old Ed with his long legs stretched under the table and his head of long golden brown tangles. And it was Ed who I took back to help my Mama. But it was too late.

**

It wasn't easy going through life with the double nickname 'Baby Hunni'. My parents named me Katharine. Katharine Hunnicutt. But I was never called Katharine, or Kathy, or Katie or Kat. I've always been "Baby." Baby with the long, white blonde hair and the sun burnt cheeks.

I was the baby. The baby out of large family of many cousins. I was a baby in my own family when my mother died of a heart defect when I was six. I wasn't a baby in the technical sense of drinking from a bottle and crying a lot. Though I did cry a lot after my Mama died. But I wasn't a baby in the sense of wearing a diaper and not being able to do the simple things for myself. My mama had toilet trained me at two and half. That I remember. But I was a baby in the sense that I still very much needed my Mama. I needed someone to love me and to care for me.

I didn't even know she was ill. She wasn't. Not in a "we can cure you and make you better" sort of way. I didn't even know a mama could die when her baby girl was only six. She had a minor heart defect that made her heart-beat run completely off its tracks and off into a wild rhythm till it slammed to a complete stop when she was carrying two baskets of laundry up the stairs to the second floor on a hot day in July. She just collapsed and she never got up again.

I remember driving way out in the country to the funeral. I didn't get to ride with my Daddy in his truck. His brother Fritz, the one with the five kids, rode with Daddy in the truck. I rode in Fritz's International Harvester Travel-all with the five cousins. The oldest of Fritz's kids, Frank, drove. He was nineteen. I was six.

I was the baby of all the cousins and there were many more than just Fritz's kids. All these cousins and aunts and uncles called me "Baby". They didn't mean it in a "You're just a baby," way. They meant it in a "We're all eighteen or so and you're our sweet baby cousin." "Baby".

I was so happy to find my Daddy at that country funeral home. I was even more happy that he seemed just as happy to have found me. He picked me up in his arms and passed by all the aunts and uncles and cousins in their Sunday finest. I thought he was taking me somewhere special.

"Where's Mama?" I asked him. "When's Mama coming?"

"She's already here Baby," my Daddy said, as a fat tear rolled down his sunburnt cheek.

"She is Daddy?" I asked him and reached out and touched his blonde flat-top haircut with my hand. I thought it was odd he didn't have his CAT hat on. He always wore that every day and I liked saying it back then, "CAT hat."

"Yes, Baby, she's been here," he whispered. He spun me around in his arms and leaned me over a little. There was my Mama in a long box full of white pillows with her eyes shut and her mouth pulled down rigid like Howdy Doody's on that terrible show that scared me. Her eyes were closed. I couldn't see her big beautiful blue eyes. Her jet black hair was curled tightly all around her head like she just came from the beauty operator's.

"Mama," I called and reached for her. She had on her bright blue faux suede church pantsuit, the one she ordered from the Blair catalogue. It was the fancy one, the one she waited for weeks to arrive, the one she made me promise to not tell Daddy how much it cost. I reached out to touch the soft blue cloth but Daddy pulled me away before I could fall out of his arms and onto her.

"Now you go with Aunt Clementine, Baby, I'll see you later on," my Daddy said and took me to another room in that large house that was a funeral home, way out on the prairie on the western edge of Illinois. He took me over to where my aunt and my two cousins were.

"Baby Hunnicutt," my tiny Aunt Clementine leaned down to me and held out her arms, "Come to me Baby Hunni," she said. She had the same big blue eyes as my Mama. And I ran to her and hid my face in her skirts and cried.

I went home from the funeral home that afternoon with Aunt Clementine and her twin sons Allen and Jeffrey. Allen, the shorter and stockier twin drove Aunt Clementine's long, green '64 Olds DeLuxe. It smelled of minty Rollaids that Aunt Clem chewed all the time for her ulcer.

Jeffrey, the tall lanky twin helped me climb in the backseat with him. I cuddled right up to him and snuggled my face into his soft flannel shirt. Jeffrey was the twin that always looked after me and played with me when Aunt Clem babysat me. Allen always had his nose in a book and ignored me. Jeffrey patted me on my back as Allen adjusted the rear-view mirror and backed us out of the gravel parking lot and pulled out onto the county black-top road and headed back to La Rue.

"You okay back there little Baby Hunnicutt?" Aunt Clem called gently over the front seat. I didn't answer.

"I think she's asleep," Jeffrey whispered to his mom.

"What are we going to do, boys?" Aunt Clem always talked to her boys as if they were adults instead of being only sixteen-year olds. Her husband had left her while she was still pregnant with the twins and I think they had been taking care of her and looking after her as soon as they came out, if that makes sense.

It was quiet in the car and Jeffrey shifted around a bit to crank down the window a crack. I smelled smoke from his cigarette as I lay across the bench seat with my face on his lap. I chanced a glance up at him. He was looking out the window, squinting into the afternoon sun and smoking silently. The wind from the open window whipped his long golden curls out from behind his ears and lashed them across his eyes.

"Light me one, Jeff," Allen said from the front seat. I glanced another peek up at Jeffrey and watched him take a last inhale before flicking his cigarette out the window. Slowly, and with purpose, he cranked the window back up and retrieved a box of cigarettes from his shirt pocket and lit two smokes at the same time from one match.

"Mom?" Jeffrey asked as he leaned forward. He handed her the cigarette and she passed it on to her other son as if she were passing him a dead mouse or something just as revolting. I wondered if Daddy would be mad if my church dress smelled like cigarette smoke. Mama would have been mad because it would mean she would have to wash and iron it before I could wear it again. But Mama wasn't coming home. And she would never have to do laundry again. Which reminded me of finding her collapsed next to the laundry baskets on the stairs. I remembered running back to Mrs. Small's, and finding Ed at the table eating a sandwich, his long legs stretched out under the table and his mussed up long golden brown hair tucked behind his ears. He looked startled to see me. His eyes were light crystal blue with black pinpoint pupils that always felt like they burnt my flesh when he looked at me.

"What?" he asked and pooched his lips out at me quick as a blink.

"Mama!" Was all I could bark out at him. And I grabbed his hand and pulled him to my house.

"MOM!" he yelled as I yanked at him and pulled him to my house. "MOM! Baby Hunnicutt is taking me somewhere! Get out here!"

But now, lying in the back of the big green car I was thinking of how Mama would never have to do my laundry again. She was never coming home again. They were going to drive her away later tomorrow and Daddy said I should just go home now with Aunt Clem.

Now both Allen and Jeffrey had their windows cracked and the warm summer country air whipped around in the car and dried my tears on my cheeks just as fast as they rolled out. Jeffrey wiped at one with his thumb. His touch stung my cheek with its heat and my eyes popped open from where I lay. His blue eyes were studying my face. His hair was blowing every which way. My own long blonde hair was straight and pulled back tight in an elastic. Jeffrey's was almost long enough to do the same. I watched his curls as they blew from one side of his face to the other. My eyes stopped crying as they followed his whipping hair. He surprised me by breaking out in a huge smile. He had crinkly lines at the corners of his eyes.

"You're gonna be all right Baby Hunni," he whispered down to me as if it were a secret between just the two of us.

Allen heard him from where he gripped the wheel up in the front seat.

"Did he even tell her?" Allen asked. His own long blonde curls were held tight to his head from being brushed back with generous amounts of Aunt Clem's Dippity Do hair solution.

"Mom? Did he tell her?" Jeffrey asked.

"I don't think so boys."

I knew they were talking about me but I didn't understand. I looked up at Jeffrey's face and caught him with a serious look for a second. But when he noticed me watching him, he sucked in his lips and made the fish face at me. He goggled his huge blue eyes and broke out in a wide smile. Fish face usually made me laugh but I was too busy looking at his huge dark blue eyes. Eyes just like Aunt Clem's. Just like my Mama's. And the tears began to flow again.

"I want Mama," I croaked to him over the wind whooshing through the car. He pulled me close to him.

"You're goin' home with us. And when we get home, you can hold Pink, my new lizard I found down by the trestle." He wiped my tears with the cuff of his flannel shirt and held me close all the long ride home.

I was lightly asleep by the time we rolled up the alley to the back of Aunt Clem's small white bungalow. Jeffrey passed me out the car door to Allen who carried me up the stairs of the front porch.

"We're home," Aunt Clem said to no one as she unlocked the door.

CHAPTER TWO

Monday morning I was still at Aunt Clem's and faced the dilemma of what was to become of me while Aunt Clem went to work.

"Is Daddy coming to get me soon?" I asked Aunt Clem while eating my sausage links at the kitchen table. Jeffrey turned around where he was at the stove frying eggs and more links. Allen sat at the table reading a paperback with little bearded men on the cover and a dragon on the back. Allen looked from me back to Aunt Clem.

"Well, Baby Hunnicutt, your daddy has work today, so he won't be coming to get ya."

"Oh. Don't you have work too, Aunt Clem?"

She was drinking instant coffee out of a small white china cup and had on a camel colored pantsuit that was the same color as her coffee. Her platinum blonde curls were arranged perfectly and held back with two brown combs.

"Well yes, I have to go to work at that wretched place but the twins will be here. And they can walk you over to Mrs. Small's if you'd rather be there."

Aunt Clem only lived a few blocks or so from my house and Mrs. Small's. I didn't know how to answer or respond to her.

"Can we have the car, Ma?" Jeffrey asked from the stove as he tucked his hair behind his ears.

"What for?"

"It's hot out. We thought we'd take Baby to the pool." Allen looked up from his book to see how his mother would answer. Aunt Clem looked from Jeffrey, to me, to Allen and back to Jeffrey.

"The Rush-La Rue Pool?"

"Yes Ma. Ed will come too. We'll all keep an eye on Baby." I stopped chewing and stared at my aunt while I waited for her answer. I used to always see the Rush-La Rue Pool Club from the highway when we'd take a drive over to the college town with Mama and Daddy and I always wanted to go there. Mama said it was too deep for me and probably unclean to boot. So we never went.

"You'll be the one to drive?" Aunt Clem asked Allen.

"Of course, woman! You think I'd let that knucklehead drive? I'd let Baby drive before I'd let him or Ed drive."

"Ok. But keep a close eye on Baby Hunni and don't let her get a sunburn. And don't let her go in that locker-room alone, and don't let her swim alone. And don't let Ed drive no matter what."

"Yes!" the twins both cheered together.

"One a you's has to take me to work and pick me up at five. Don't forget!"

"We won't."

"And for garsh sakes don't let Baby Hunni in the deep

pool or go off the diving board. Just because you boys are crazy don't go getting' her," she trailed off as she shook her head and thought of all the ways the twins could get me in trouble of some sort.

Allen jumped up to take her to work before she could give out more warnings and rules. Jeffrey slid an egg on my plate and sat down to eat with me. He had a cigarette dangling out of his mouth as he cut up his eggs.

"Not even 7:00 and you're already smoking!" Aunt Clem shouted at Jeffrey as she came back through the kitchen one last time, tying a silk scarf under her chin. "Put it out. Baby Hunni is trying to eat for crying out loud!"

"Yes Ma, 'bye Ma, see you later Ma," Jeffrey said as he shooed her out of the door with his cigarette behind his back. After Aunt Clem and Allen left I looked at my cousin and said, "But I don't have a swimsuit or any floaties. I need a floatie."

"I reckon it's time we got you some clothes, Baby Hunni, and I bet you'd like your toys too."

I looked down at the giant t-shirt of Allen's I had on like a dress. It said YMCA on the front and some other words I couldn't read. I'd worn it all day Sunday and slept in it Sunday night and now here it was Monday and I still had it on.

"We'll scoot over to your house and pack up your things before we head out to the pool. Don't you worry, Baby Hunni."

"Ok. Here's the plan," Allen stated as soon as he slammed in through the screen door after taking Aunt Clem to work. "First we need to wake up Ed. That'll be your job," he looked at Jeffrey who was swirling the eggy plates with the scrub brush in the sink and had another cigarette hanging out of his mouth.

"Secondly," Allen said, as he held up his two fingers and licked his lips as if thinking hard, "we need to break into Baby Hunni's old house and get all her things. Third, we need to go to Cloyd's and get some snacks and things for the trip."

I looked from Allen over to Jeffrey at the sink. I was worried about what Allen said about breaking in to my old house. I was worried about taking Ed with us swimming. Mama had always said to stay away from him.

When I would hear the lawn mower running over at the Small's I would always fly out onto our porch to sit and watch him. He had a big head of long matted golden brown hair and when he mowed the grass in his cut-offs and old tie-dyed shirt he always tied a bandana around his forehead to keep his hair out of his eyes.

Mama would find me out there watching Ed mowing back and forth across the Small's front yard and make me come in. She said he was apt to cut off his own foot because he mowed barefoot for one thing and he goofed off too much for another thing.

If she didn't come get me and make me come in, I'd watch him mow the entire yard. He'd stick his tongue out at me every time he made a turn near our side of the yard. I didn't get scared when he pulled faces or stuck his tongue at me. But sometimes, after he'd stuck his tongue out at me three or four times, his face would split open into a huge smile and he would shake his head and laugh at me over the noise of the mower. When he would do that I would get scared and run inside and fly up to my room and watch him from my window up there from behind the curtain.

Thinking about the long ride to the pool with Ed in the car made me afraid. I was afraid he would smile at me and that maybe that was what hippies did right before they went crazy. He had big white teeth. He looked like the wolf in Little Red Riding Hood just before he snapped his jaws and tried to eat her.

"What's the matter Baby Hunnicutt?" Allen asked me. I didn't answer.

"We won't get in trouble for breaking in to get your things. We won't actually break anything. Your dad won't even know we were in there."

This thought made me more worried. If we broke some part of the house Daddy would be very mad. Why couldn't we just go in the front door?

"Don't worry Baby Hunni, Ed will know how to get us in," Jeffrey patted me on the back as he went to the room he shared with Allen. The twins packed up towels and Coppertone and changed into their black swim trunks. Allen ran down to the basement and came back up with a Styrofoam cooler.

"We'll have to get ice at Cloyd's, no way Ma's got enough in here," he said as he poked his head around in the ice box above the fridge.

"All right, Baby Hunni, let's roll!" Jeffrey clapped me on the back and took my hand and led me out to the car. I sat up front between the twins.

"First stop, wake up Ed. And that's your job," Allen said as he pointed at Jeffrey.

"I know, I know."

Allen steered the big car around the curves and down the few blocks to Mrs. Small's. It was strange pulling into the drive to the house next to my own. I hadn't been to my house in two days but it felt longer. I was still wearing Allen's YMCA t-shirt that was as long as a dress and I still had on the same underpants I'd worn on Saturday. We pulled up the long gravel drive to the Small's little house.

"Ed," Allen said and pointed at the door. Jeffrey got out without a word. I started to follow him. Allen lightly grabbed my arm.

"I wouldn't Baby Hunnicutt. Ed's not nice when he first wakes up."

My eyes widened at this.

"He likes to cuss a lot when he first wakes up and sometimes he don't have on no clothes." Allen looked at me right in the eye. He had the same dark blue eyes as Jeffrey. I sucked air in with a whistle and longed to see my Mama. Allen misunderstood.

"Disgusting, right? Not even in his skivvies. You just stay out here with me, Baby Hunni."

"Ok."

"Here it is almost nine and that boy is still in bed. Sheesh." Allen shook his head back and forth. His golden curls lay in waves and sprung out from where he had pushed them behind his ears.

"So Baby, how are we gonna break in and get your things?" he asked as he looked up at my house. The upstairs had two windows that stuck out from the slanted roof. The one on the right was my room.

"We'll go right up there," Allen pointed as he looked up at the window. "See, the window's open. Just have to get the screen off."

Just then Ed came out on the porch. His hair was all fuzzed up on the back of his head and the rest of it was long and hung in his face. He was rubbing the corners of his eyes with his fingers and yawning. He had on white swim trunks and nothing else. He came out to the car and collapsed on the back seat.

"Shit. It's too early," he groaned.

"Language, Ed, language."

"Fuck. It's too early."

"Ed. Curse again and I'm gonna have to split your lip!" Allen threatened. He whipped around in his seat and tried to grab Ed but missed.

I covered my ears with my hands and closed my eyes up in the front seat.

"Where's Jeffrey?" Allen asked.

"Ahh geez, he's inside with Mom. She's giving him stuff for the cooler. Frescas and bologna sandwiches."

"Frescas? Yuck. We'll get Pepsis. But first we gotta break in Baby's and get her clothes and things."

"Ugh," was all that came from the backseat. I ventured a peep over the seat at Ed. He had both palms pressed into his eyelids and his bare feet were on the back of the front seat. He had long toes and the tops of his feet were brown. His arms had a farmer's tan.

"Come on Ed, let's get a ladder." Allen opened his door and held it open for me to follow.

So they broke into my window and went into my room to get my things. I wanted to go too. I wanted to see my room and my things but they wouldn't let me go. They made me stay down in the yard with Ed who shouted up instructions on how to take the screen out without destroying it. Ed sat on the grass with his elbows on his knees and his hands in his hair, rubbing his head.

"Get Drowsy!" I called up to Jeffrey as he followed Allen into the window. I jumped up and down in my YMCA shirt.

"Get Drowsy? What the hell does that mean?" Ed mumbled to himself. I ignored him and took a couple of steps away from him.

"Get my Road Runner jammies!" I called up to the empty window. I missed my room and my things.

"Look out below!" Jeffrey called and dropped a big pillow which made a dull poof when it landed near Ed and shot flowered underpants out on the grass. Ed peered out between his fingers. His crystal blue eyes locked on mine for a second and I turned away scared to death of him. I ran and picked up the pillow and peeked inside. Jeffrey had stuffed a pillowcase with underwear and t-shirts.

"Bombs away!" Jeffrey called again and another pillowcase poofed down near Ed. This one had shorts and dresses in it. They were all balled up and would be a wrinkled mess.

"One swimsuit coming down!"
I looked up and watched Allen sail my swimsuit out the window like tossing a Frisbee. I watched as the sun caught its colors as it spun near the treetops and I waited for it to drift down to me.

"Wheee!" I called as it floated down. It was my new swimsuit from Montgomery Wards that Mama had gotten me for my last birthday back in June. It had different colored squares all over it that looked like stained glass.

"Whee!" I called as I spun around with it in my arms. When I got done spinning I saw Ed had his head up and a huge smile spread across his face. His teeth were very white in his tan face and he had a dimple in his cheek and a dimple in his chin like a bad guy on t.v. would have.

I stopped spinning with my swimsuit and stared at him.

"What?" he demanded and he pooched his big lips at me just for a second.
I didn't answer.

"You're a strange kid," he said and shook his head and pressed his palms into his eyes one more time. I looked at the top of his head. He had a part in his tangled-up hair that ran from his forehead in a zig-zag back to the back of his head where his hair was a birds' nest from sleeping on it. If I had hair like that Mama would have yanked me half bald with the brush. I wondered why Mrs. Small didn't take care of Ed's tangles.

"Baby Hunnicutt, look who I found," Jeffrey called as he climbed down the tall ladder with one hand, his bare toes gripping the rungs as he came down with Drowsy in the other hand. He waved her at me from up high. The morning sunlight danced in Jeffrey's eyes and the breeze pulled his curls this way and that.

"Here ya go Baby," he said as he handed me Drowsy. I immediately pulled her cord and heard her ask, "Can I have a drink of water?" in her sing-song whine. I pulled her cord again to hear what else she'd say but she only asked for water again.

"Oh Jesus, are we gonna hafta listen to that possessed doll all the way there?"

I flashed a mad glare at Ed and pouted at him. He stuck his face at me and pooched his lips out at me even bigger than mine and then broke into a huge smile. The sun flared in his messed up hair as he rolled onto his side and slowly got up on his feet.

"You're a funny little kid," he called over his shoulder as he opened the door to the car.

"Yeah? Well you're, you're," I stammered as I pulled Drowsy close to me and looked back at my house as Allen and Jeffrey carried the ladder back to the Small's garage. "You're a," I trailed off as I thought of my Mama coming out on the porch to tell me to get away from Ed and how she'd never be able to make me get away from him again.

"What? What am I?" Ed asked from the car. He was grinning as he looked at me. I focused on his bad-guy dimple on his chin and then looked down at his bare feet.

He batted his eyelashes at me and grinned and waited to hear what I had to say.

"You're just a crazy hippie!" I yelled. And that sent him into fits of doubled up laughter.

"Get in Baby Hunni. What's the matter?" Jeffrey asked me as he got in the front seat.

"Climb on in, Baby," Allen said to me and held the back door open for me. Ed was still giggling and laughing as he scooted across the seat away from me.

"Come on now, get in. We're going to Cloyd's and then off to the pool!" Jeffrey beckoned from the front seat for me to get in the back. I got in and Allen shut the door behind me.

"Wait!" I hollered.

"What?" all three boys asked together. I looked over at Ed. His eyebrows were pointy on his big forehead as he pushed his hair behind his ears.

"What?" he asked as he untangled a strand of hair from his pinky and looked at me with those pale eyes.

"You gotta pee, cousin?" Allen asked from the driver's seat.

"No. I need a floatie. A floatie," I emphasized with my hands.

"Well Baby Hunni, maybe they'll have one we can get you at Cloyd's," Jeffrey said as he reached back to pat me.

"No. Wait," Ed looked at me and pooched out his lips like he was thinking hard. "Wait," he said as he looked at me with his ice blue eyes. "I got something." He got out of the car yelling, "Mom! Mom!" as he went into the house. Two minutes later he rolled a big black tube out of the side door from the basement and came over to my side.

"Here kid, get out a minute. You can sit on this for the ride over." He put the huge black inner tube on my seat and hoisted me up on it. It gave me a tall, bouncy seat.

"We ready now?" Allen called out his window at Ed.

"No. You dumbfucks forgot the cooler," Ed looked over his shoulder at Allen and began to run away towards the house, his hair streaming out behind him. "It's still inside!" he shrieked as Allen sprung from the car and bounded after him with his fists clenched. Allen's black trainers slapped up the porch stairs after Ed. He was yelling threats on Ed's skull for swearing in front of me.

"Get him! Get him!" I cheered and bounced up and down on my inner tube.

"Better run boy!" Jeffrey whooped and hollered from his window.

And so after a bit Allen and Ed emerged from the house and loaded the cooler into the trunk. We replaced the Frescas Mrs. Small had packed with Pepsis that Allen got on credit at Cloyd's Market.

"You guys each owe me a dollar for four pops. I ain't havin' it all taken out of my pay-check."

"A dollar?" Ed complained. "I'm only gonna have three. How's that equal a dollar?" he shouted out into the wind of the open window as we turned onto the highway.

"You're helpin' pay for Baby Hunnicutt's share. Penitence for all the swears."

"Well shit mother fuck."

My eyes got huge and my mouth popped open as I looked at Ed. He was now sitting with his big bare feet pulled up on the seat Indian style and was sticking the back of his head out the window. The back of his hair was flying around high above his head. A huge lopsided grin broke out on his face as he looked at my reaction. I covered my open mouth with my hand as I bounced on the black tube.

"I like to cuss Baby Hunni," he said to me as he reached over and pinched my knee. I slapped his hand. His pinch left a red mark on my knee and I tried to rub it away.

"Ed. I'm gonna dunk your scrungey butt soon as we get in that pool," Allen threatened in the rearview mirror.

"I reckon that'll be the first time water's touched that hair in weeks," Jeffrey laughed as he struck a match and lit a cigarette in the front seat.

"Bite me!"

"That pool filter won't know what hit it after Ed takes a lap or two!" Allen laughed.

"Screw you Goldilocks!" Ed grumbled and sat back as near the door as he could.

"That's two, Ed, two," Allen warned.

"Pass the smokes."

Jeffrey tossed back a red and white box over his head to Ed, who didn't have to roll up the window in order to light it. Ed looked sour and pooched his lips out. He put his feet back up on the seat and rolled his eyes over to me. I was beginning to get sweaty where I was sitting on the black tube. The sun was streaming in my window and my shoulder burned from it.

"Smoke?" Ed asked me as he held the box towards me. I pulled back from it like it was a snake.

"Huh Ahuh!" he laughed with his lips rolled back over his teeth, "Where's this kid's smokes, Jeffrey?"

"Oh. Yeh. Here, Baby, we got you your own." He passed a small red and white box to me. "Just till you're older Baby," Jeffrey said and smiled at me.

I tore the wrapping off and took out a candy cigarette and smiled back up at Jeffrey. Jeffrey and Allen always bought me candy cigarettes from Cloyd's when they'd walk me down there in the wagon when Mama used to pull me over to visit Aunt Clem.

"Need a light?" Ed held a book of matches towards me.

"Go away."

"What? What I'd do?" he asked and stuck his lips out. He pulled a big pout, the kind Mama would have said you could have tripped over. But he didn't hold the pout long. He grinned at me and batted his eyelashes at me and smoked his cigarette as I sucked on my sugar one.

I bounced on my inner tube and smiled at Jeffrey up in the front seat. And then I smiled at Allen when I saw him looking at me in the rearview mirror. I was thinking of him dunking Ed and I smiled even bigger.

"Goldilocks," Ed said and shook his head. "Goldilocks twins get all the smiles from the girlies." I looked at Ed. He was sitting criss cross again and sticking the back of his head back out the window.

We spent the day at the pool. Jeffrey pulled me out to the deep end in the inner tube.

"Now don't go and tell Ma we pulled you out here. You're perfectly safe out here Baby," he assured me from where he treaded water. "We can't keep an eye on you over in the baby pool."

"Don't wanna go make Ma shit herself with worry now," Ed imitated Jeffrey and quickly dove under the water.

"You bastard! OH! Sorry Baby," Jeffrey shouted and dove in after Ed. Jeffrey was long and lean but not as strong a swimmer as the compact and muscled Allen and couldn't catch Ed before he got to the edge. Ed pulled himself out of the pool and trotted over to the diving board, his hair long and slick and dripping down his back.

"Watch me Baby Hunni!" Ed called from the diving board.

I watched the three of them play and wrestle in the deep end and when I'd get too hot Allen would let me sit on his back while he swam around. The pool wasn't very crowded and the twins and Ed were the roughest playing boys in the deep end. I knew Allen wouldn't let me fall off. There were several girls sitting with their legs in the water on the sides but none of them ever got in.

Late in the afternoon we had our Pepsis and our sandwiches while we sat on lounge chairs together. The boys all chugged down their three Pepsis in a row. I watched in awe as they raced to finish them and I giggled as they tried to out belch each other.

We were having fun when three teenage girls in bikinis walked up to us. I couldn't stop staring at how they were almost naked. I wondered how their parents could let them wear those suits outside of the house.

"Hi Ed," all three of them said together.

"Hi Ed," Jeffrey and Allen mimicked them and burst out laughing and almost fell backwards off their lounge chair.

"Jeffrey, Allen," the blonde girl in the middle said as if their two names were just one.

"Hi Karen," the twins sneered and laughed again.

Ed just wiped his Pepsi mustache off on the back of his hand.

"Hey," Ed said, and then belched deep and long, "Scuse me. Hey, let me see your hair brush," he said to the girl named Karen. She was carrying a big, clear, beach bag and there was a pink hair brush in it.

"Sure Ed," she gushed and smiled and handed him the brush. I chewed on my sandwich and stared at her.

"Baby Hunni, scoot back here," Ed told me. I was sitting on the foot of his lounge chair, as far away from him as I could get without burning my feet on the hot pavement.

"Why?" I eyed him and continued to take bites of my bologna sandwich. The afternoon sun shone into his eyes and turned them a blue paler than the pool. Jeffrey and Allen were watching Ed in silence from where they sat on the lounge chair next to ours.

"Come on," Ed pleaded and scooted towards me while he still sat criss cross. "Your hair is a tangled mess," he said and reached out to brush my hair.

"Ahh!" I hollered as he got near my head. "No!" I shrieked and covered my head with my hands.

"Baby Hunni, it'll dry in a rat's nest if you don't brush it," Ed cooed to me.

"He's one to talk," Allen mumbled.

Ed reached out to my hair again.

"NO!" I hollered and hunkered over.

"Who is that, Ed?" One of Karen's friends asked.

"This is my daughter. We call her Baby Hunni. She's my *love*-child. Baby Hunni sweet as Honey."

Ed slapped me on the back and caused me to holler but it came out muffled because I was still curled over in a hump.

"Really Ed. Who is she?"

"We stole her," he whispered loudly. I whipped around to look at him and found him grinning with his wolf's teeth all showing and the dimple in his chin and in his cheek puckering. "Stole her at the county fair last weekend right in front of the tilt-a-whirl!" he nodded at the girls. Karen's mouth popped open.

"We keep her in a box in the corner of my room at night, don't we Baby?"

I started crying at this. I imagined being kept as some pet of Ed's in the dark in a little box like how Jeffrey kept his little lizard in a box with holes punched in the lid.

"Aw hell, don't cry," Ed looked at Jeffrey and Allen for help. "What the fuck?" Ed whispered to the twins.

"You knucklehead!" Allen yelled and jumped at Ed and the two tore off and jumped in the pool. Jeffrey came and sat behind me and started brushing out my tangles and when he was finished I was asleep on the lounge chair.

CHAPTER THREE

We spent many hot days at the pool that summer, the four of us. My Daddy came to visit me but he never did bring me back home. I lived with Aunt Clem and the twins.

"You're gonna stay with Aunt Clementine, Baby," he told me as he stroked my cheek with the back of his finger. He came to see me several times during the week after he got off work. He came in his work dungarees and safety glasses right from the assembly line. I ran out to his truck from where I'd been playing jacks on Aunt Clem's front porch and peeked into his truck to see if he'd brought me anything. But all he ever had in there was his black lunchbox and a red plaid coffee thermos.

"When can I come home?" I asked him as I sat on his lap on the front porch.

"I can't take care of you Baby because I have to work every day, see?"

I didn't see. Aunt Clem had to work too. I missed Daddy. Even if I was having fun going swimming with the twins nearly every day. I missed the bigness of my daddy. I missed being held on his lap. I missed being tucked in every night. The twins and Aunt Clementine tucked me in every night but it wasn't the same. It wasn't my own room and it wasn't my own bed.

A lot of times Daddy came by Aunt Clem's before she even got home from work. He'd find me out on the front porch with

Jeffrey playing jacks or paper dolls or looking at the lizard while Allen and Ed tossed the football around.

"Jeff, Allen," Daddy called to the twins as he came out of his truck. Then his face would turn stern, "Ed." It was a statement not a hello. He would look Ed up and down; Ed shirtless and shoeless in his shorts with his greasy long hair in his face and my Daddy would clench his fists.

Before he got up the walk I would leap off the porch to run into his arms. I never knew if he would be coming that day or not because some days he was too tired to come visit and some days he had to stay late on the assembly line. Since I didn't know if he was coming or not, I would bug Jeffrey and Allen all day if we were at the pool or away from the house, to make sure they got us home before time for my Daddy to be there. I didn't want to miss him. I wanted him to take me home. I wanted to see my things. I wanted to sit in the chair my Mama used to sit in. I wanted to see our kitchen and eat at the little pearly table. I wanted to sleep in my own bed. I didn't even have a bed at Aunt Clem's.

After a couple of weeks of staying at Clem's the twins assembled an old metal bed for me in their room. Aunt Clem made it up for me with an old pink and green quilt and soft yellow sheets.

"You can't sleep on the couch forever, Baby Hunnicutt," she said as she patted my head and pulled me into a hug. Aunt

Clementine always smelled like rich hand cream and puffs of expensive powder. I loved to bury my face in her clothes when she hugged me. "I know it ain't right to have you share a room with two sixteen year old boys but there's nowhere else to put you."

She let me go so she could go into the kitchen and make our dinner. I sat on my new bed and cradled Drowsy and resisted the temptation to pull her cord. I knew she was stuck on only asking for water.

My new bed was across the room from Jeffrey and Allen's bunk beds. The first few nights at Aunt Clem's she had made me a bed out on the couch. But I got scared out there and snuck into the twin's room and slept on the rag rug every night. Jeffrey said waking up every morning with me curled up on the rag rug was almost as good as having an actual puppy.

Ed and Jeffrey found the old metal bed-frame behind the Sycamore Shopping Center stacked in pieces against the dumpsters. Aunt Clementine overlooked the fact that they were digging around the dumpsters since it was such a great find.

They hauled it home and Allen sanded it and Jeffrey and Ed painted it white for me. Aunt Clem ordered a new mattress from Montgomery Wards for me and let me pick out a new pillow myself after I tried nearly all of them that were on the display at the store. The twins and Ed even helped try them all out too. The sales lady shot several sharp looks at us; especially at Ed, whose sun streaked hair looked more grizzled and tangled than ever, since it'd been three days since we'd gone swimming.

I still missed my own home and I missed my Mama more than anything. Even if everyday with the twins was an adventure. I even had some fun with Ed. I liked to hear him say bad words and watch Allen chase him around pummeling him in the ribs with his fists. It was fun to hear Ed shriek and holler and cuss some more as he ran around Aunt Clem's small front yard.

Some days Aunt Clem wouldn't let us go to the pool. She said I was getting too freckly. She told the boys they weren't putting the Coppertone on me enough. Some days Allen had to go to work at Cloyd's and Aunt Clem would not let Jeffrey drive us out to the Rush- La Rue Pool.

"Why won't she let you drive us out to the pool?" Ed groused from where he sat on the side of the stairs of Aunt Clem's wide front porch. "What the hell?" he grumbled as he put his head in his hands. He had on red shorts with blue trim on the edges and an old shirt with Mickey Mouse on the front. He was sitting with his knees drawn up and was barefoot as usual. "What the hell does she think we'll do? Run over to Rush and pick up some college women?" Ed was running his hands through his hair; trying to either mess it up or detangle it, it was hard to say.

"I dunno," Jeffrey mumbled. When Allen wasn't around he wasn't so hot to hang with Ed for some reason.

"That might not be a bad idea," Ed's head popped up and he eyeballed Jeffrey. Then his head swiveled on his neck over to me. "Why we always saddled with the kid?" He squinted at me hard like I was a pain in his side.

"She's little." Jeffrey shrugged. Both Allen and Aunt Clementine were at work for the day and Jeffrey was responsible for me.

"She's not yours. I mean, what the?"

"Don't. Allen's not around. But don't."

I glared at Ed. I knew there were times, many times when he didn't want me tagging along. There were many times I didn't want to be drug along with them. Like when they went to the pool hall where it was so smoky I could barely breathe. Where they would make me sit up in a high seat and watch them play pool for hours.

I put my head down on my arm. It was miserable hot and sticky humid and there was nothing to do. Jeffrey went into the house and left me alone on the porch with Ed.

"You seen Caesar recently, Baby?" Ed asked me. He was referring to his big tabby cat that usually hung out in their basement. I would stand in Mrs. Small's kitchen and strain my eyes looking down the basement stairs, trying to catch a glint of his green eyes. Caesar hardly ever came out.

Ed was waiting for me to answer. He had his head cocked sideways as he squinted in the sun towards where I was sitting.

"I can tell you how to get Caesar out," he said and smiled without showing his teeth.

I didn't say anything.

"You want to hear it, Baby Hunni?" He smiled sweetly again. I looked at his pale eyes and his wild sun streaked hair.

"Yes."

"Give me a piece of gum first," he demanded and held out his hand. He tilted his head back and looked at me under heavy lids as if he were bored.

"I don't have any."

"Liar." He grinned and held out his hand.

I didn't answer.

"You want to know, don't you?"

I got up off the porch where I had been playing jacks and took a stick of gum out of the pocket of my sundress. Allen was always bringing me packs of Juicy Fruit from Cloyd's. As I handed it to Ed his hand closed on my wrist. I tried to pull back but couldn't. He gave my wrist a gentle squeeze from where he sat and I looked him in his crazy blue eyes.

"You sit in his chair," he said to me as he looked me in the eye. His lips pulled together into a pucker for a second. "You sit in his chair," he said again and leaned his forehead toward mine. "He can always tell when someone is in his chair and he flies up out of the basement to kick out whoever is in his chair!" he whispered at me and let go of my wrist and popped the stick of gum in his mouth.

My heart beat fast and I was frightened and wanted to run inside but he was between me and the door.

"You want me to walk you over there? You want to hang out with my mom for the day, Baby?"

I didn't answer.

"You want to see if you can get Caesar to come out?" He grinned on one side of his mouth and winked at me.

"No." I pulled out another piece of gum and unwrapped it and put it in my mouth while Ed watched. Then I went back to my jacks and sat down to play more.

"Jeffrey, where the fuck did you go?" Ed called in to the screen door. "Where'd he go?" Ed asked me.

"I'm telling," I said and smiled at the thought of Allen chasing him around.

"Oh shit!" Ed clapped his hand on his mouth. "I'm going home. I can be bored at least in air conditioning there," he said and jumped over the porch rail and left. I watched him through the slats of the porch as he ran down the sidewalk.

That summer of '68 when I was six was one of the funnest summers I'd ever had, despite the sadness that hung on the corners of my life. That sadness would rear up at me at unexpected times and make me cry.

One Saturday I was watching the Flintstones with the twins while eating Alpha-bits out of empty margarine tubs for bowls and I smelled the hot starch of Aunt Clem ironing behind us in the dining room and began to cry. The smell of all that laundry reminded me of my last day with Mama; how I'd lingered extra long at Mrs. Small's, hoping I'd get a glimpse of Ed who was shut up in his room doing lord knows what.

From my seat between Allen and Jeffrey I glared over at Ed as he sat in the recliner with his big, dirty bare feet propped up, with his wide-open mouth full of cereal and milk dribbling down his chin. I glared at him in silence while Fred Flintstone's mother-in-law yelled at him on tv, while hot tears rolled down my cheeks as I smelled the freshly ironed clothes and missed my mama and blamed Ed.

"Huh! Ahuh!" Ed laughed at The Flintstones and spilled his milk down his stomach. "Shit," he hissed and looked over to see if Allen heard but instead froze when he saw me glaring at him with tears running down my cheeks.

"What?" he asked and pooched his lips out in that tic of his. "What'd I do now?" he asked and wiped the milk off his bare stomach and licked it off his hand.

"You idiot!" Allen looked from me to Ed and jumped up off the sofa and grabbed Ed in a headlock, causing him to spill cereal and milk all over his shorts.

"Shit mother-eff!" Ed squawked as he tried to get away from Allen and get out of the recliner and duck away from the Dutch-rubs Allen was applying to the back of his head.

"Greasy, little hippie," Allen grunted, "I ought to wash out your mouth boy!"

"Mrs. Rawlins! Mrs. Rawlins! Your boy is a killin' me!" Ed howled as Allen pulled him out of the recliner by his head and the rest of the Alpha-bits flew across the room.

"Boys! Boys! Get out of here this instant!" Little Aunt Clementine stormed the living room waving a wire hanger. "Cussing and fighting and throwing cereal everywhere!" She shrieked and she chased after Allen and Ed who were still hooked together.

Jeffrey wiped my tears with the tail of his t-shirt as I laughed and pointed with glee at Ed as Allen pulled him out to the front porch by his head.

The great, sad summer of '68 was drawing to a close, the end of August was upon us and we'd all be going to school the next week; me for the first time.

"Ma, we only have one week of summer left. Can we please have the car to go to the pool? We haven't been in forever," pleaded Jeffrey from where he stood at the stove next to Aunt Clem. She was heating syrup in a small pan for our pancakes.

"Get that lizard out of here, Jeffrey!" she shrieked and pointed at the lizard in Jeffrey's hands with her syrup spoon. "That thing ain't clean and don't belong in a kitchen!"

Allen looked up from his paperback. This one had several short, hairy men on the cover, grouped around a tall old wizard.

"Ma, Pink needs exercise," Jeffrey whined as the lizard tried to climb out of his hand. Jeffrey had to keep switching hands so the little emerald critter wouldn't get away.

"It's gonna end up in the syrup!"

"It's not," Jeffrey laughed and left to go put the lizard away.

"So, can we go? Can we have the car?"

It had rained for four days solid. That plus Allen having to work at Cloyd's had cut in on our precious pool time. The boys deposited me at Mrs. Small's house several days that week when they walked over there to pick up Ed and head out on their own adventures. They were tired of dragging me all over with them and they were tired of being stuck inside with me at their house.

I had Aunt Clem's old doll house that Allen brought up for me from the basement. And I had all the old furniture from when she was little. Allen and Jeffrey had gone in together and bought me a tiny doll for it from the Ben Franklin and that provided hours of entertainment for me inside.

But the boys had nothing to do in the house but watch hours of t.v. or watch it rain or get into wrestling matches with each other on the couch. If they didn't go drop me at Mrs. Small's and pick up Ed to go do something, they were bored. That was a long week. Mrs. Small was very kind and I liked to talk to her, but she was always trying to teach me games I didn't understand. Like Parcheesi. And Scrabble. I would lay my head right on the kitchen table at Mrs. Small's and wait for Jeffrey and Allen to come back to get me. I couldn't understand why they'd rather run around with Ed than me.

One morning Aunt Clem dropped me off at Mrs. Small's on her way to work at the denture lab. That morning I waved goodbye to Allen and Jeffrey as they sat in their cut-offs in the hot, muggy house, watching the Three Stooges while it thunderstormed outside.

When I got to Mrs. Small's Ed was still asleep and Mrs. Small was busy painting the trim in the kitchen.

"Go watch t.v. Baby. You shouldn't be in here smelling the paint, dear."

I went into their cold air-conditioned living room to watch cartoons. I sat and sulked on the couch for a while as it rained and thundered outside. I looked around for signs of Ed. His school picture from last year was on the table next to the couch. His hair was parted straight down the middle and his forehead looked larger than it really was. His eyes were half closed and he looked a little nutty in the photo with his maniacal grin and his ice blue eyes. I got as close to the photo as I could and examined his square teeth to see if they were as sharp as I always perceived them to be.

"You okay, dear?" Mrs. Small called from the kitchen, making me jump and ram my forehead into Ed's photo.

"I'm fine!" I called, as I caught the picture. I looked around for Ed. He was still holed up in his room with the door shut. He had a big sign on his door that said KEEP OUT. I looked around the living room and saw an old olive green chair next to the t.v. One I had never really noticed before. Walking over to it I saw it was covered in short cat hairs. Caesar's chair.

"Where's Caesar?" I called to Mrs. Small.

She stopped her humming. "Oh uh, he's under Mr. Small's bed, dear."

Mr. Small. He had died before I was born but I didn't know how much before and I didn't know how he died. I did know Mrs. Small talked about him like he was still around and Ed never talked about him at all. Not that I had had a chance to be around Ed much until this summer.

I walked down the hall a ways and peeked into Mrs. Small's bedroom. She had two twin beds in her room with gold chintz spreads on them. They were always made up perfectly.

"Can I go look for him?" I called out.

"Better not, dear." I heard her start singing about sending someone a kiss by wire while she painted the trim in the kitchen.

I glanced down the hall at Ed's door. I looked back at the kitchen but couldn't see Mrs. Small through the door.

"I'm using the bathroom," I called out to her and slunked down the gloomy hall towards Ed's room. I stood outside his door and listened. I cupped my ear up to the door and strained to hear if he was moving around or snoring. Nothing. Silence. I sat completely still and listened more and put my hand on the door knob. I had never seen Ed's room. I put my ear right up to the door and listened but couldn't hear anything over the pattering rain and the thunder that was coming in faster. Slowly I turned the doorknob, thinking I'd just take a quick peek, but just then the air conditioner came on with a whoosh and I jumped and let the door knob fly back into place and trotted to the bathroom, my heart going wild.

When I went back to the living room I eyed the green chair again. It was right next to the t.v. I guess the cat didn't care whether he watched t.v. or not. I looked around for Mrs. Small. For Caesar himself. Then I tiptoed over to the hairy chair and sat down. I had on my red and white striped shorts and a red shirt that said "JEANS JEANS JEANS" on it and my red and blue Keds. One said LEFT on the toe and the other one said RIGHT. Daddy had taken me to the Sycamore shopping center the weekend before and let me pick them out for school shoes.

I sat back all the way in Caesar's chair; my legs stuck straight out. I flicked my feet this way and that and rolled my eyes around the room. A Heckle and Jeckle cartoon played on the t.v. but I couldn't see it. Lightening flashed outside and thunder rolled and made me jump but no Caesar came out to claim his seat.

I sat there forever it felt. I sat through two Woody Woodpeckers, a Droopy, and a Chilli Willi Penguin and listened as the wind picked up and it began to rain harder and louder. The air conditioner turned on and I shuddered with a chill as my chin dropped down on my chest.

"MEOW!"

My head snapped up from where I'd dozed off and I saw Ed standing in the doorway in a very old pair of too small jeans. He pulled on a t-shirt with Mighty Mouse on the front and yawned.

"Shit, it's cold in here," he stretched and scratched behind his ear and padded over to the window near me. "If that had a been Caesar, you'd be dead," he said and poked me hard in the arm.

That was about exciting as it got at Mrs. Small's. I was so glad that the rain went away and that it was sunny again. Everyone's mood was improved with the sunshine.

"So please Ma, can we have the car?" Jeffrey begged.

"For heaven's sake go put that lizard away. Allen. Go get my pocket-book and take me to work so this kid will quit begging." Aunt Clementine sighed as she looked at me. "Baby

Hunni you're brown as a biscuit nearly from all the time at the pool. And look how long your hair has grown. Should we get it cut before school?"

"No, Aunt Clem, no," I said and covered my head with my hands. "I like it long."

"Oh Baby, ok. Just be sure to let Jeffrey brush it after you swim or we'll have knots on top of knots."

"Ma," Jeffrey said, coming back after putting his lizard away, "you should come with us to the pool."

"Yeh Ma, come with us," Allen chimed in as he got the car keys off the hook by the basement door.

"Come on Ma," Jeffrey said. The twins got on either side of her and picked tiny Aunt Clem up clear off the floor and carried her out the door.

"Someone has to stay with Baby Hunni!" she cried. After they carried her to the car Jeffrey came back in to help me with my pancakes. And after Allen came back home we went right over to Ed's.

We repeated the process that we'd done several times already that summer which would be Ed's, Cloyd's and pool. We'd done it so many times but Ed still cussed and complained about getting up early.

That morning I watched Ed come out on the porch from where Jeffrey had sat me up on the long hood of the green car. Ed pushed open the screen and stumbled out on the porch wearing cut-off Levis and a white t-shirt that was too small. He was shielding his eyes with the edge of his hand and frowning with his lips pushed out in a pout. He smacked his lips several times and stuck his tongue out far and yelled a strangled yawn.

"Arrrgh! Son of a bitch! I think it's going to be too cold to swim, you guys!" he yelled with his throat sounding thick and he plopped down on the top step.

"Baby Hunni, should I throttle him? Cuz I think I'm real tired of chasing him," Allen called to me from the front seat.

"Hmm," I thought about it. I looked at Ed sitting with his elbows on his knees and his head propped up on his hands. His hair had grown too and was almost past his shoulders. He had his lips pinched together and his head tilted back and his eyes half closed as he listened to hear if I'd send Allen after him for cussing in front of me.

"Should I, Baby Hunni?" Allen asked again from the car window.

"No. He looks too tired this morning."

Ed heard me pardon him and tilted his head up all the way to the sky as if trying to absorb some of the weak sun that was out.

"I'm gonna let that one slide this morning, Ed. You owe Baby Hunni one."

"You're just too lazy to get off your fat ass, you numb nuts," Ed croaked out and closed his eyes all the way and grinned.

I thought for sure Allen would go after him but he didn't. It was the end of summer and none of us felt too energetic. Jeffrey came out carrying the white Styrofoam cooler that was undoubtedly filled with bologna sandwiches and Frescas.

"Everybody in!" Allen called and honked the horn causing me to flinch. Jeffrey loaded the cooler in the trunk and Ed hoisted me down from the hood of the car so I could scamper around to my door and my seat behind Allen.

"Lazy ass," Ed sneered to Allen as he slid in the back seat.

Allen didn't reply to Ed, which was unusual. I looked at Ed and he shrugged his shoulders at me and didn't say a word. After getting Pepsis and a bag of BBQ chips at Cloyd's we hit the county highway for the Rush- La Rue pool.

"Ed?" Allen asked.

"What?" he answered as he gazed out at the cornfields. He had a cigarette hanging off his bottom lip. His eye lids were heavy over his eyes.

"You even bring swim trunks?"

"Wearin' 'em."

I looked at Ed. He was sitting cross-legged with his bare feet tucked up under him. He had on cut-offs and his thin white t-shirt that barely covered his belly.

"What's he got on?"

Finally Jeffrey turned around and looked. "Cut-offs."

"Gonna be too cold to swim I'm telling you," Ed said and flicked his cigarette out the window.

"They won't let you in with those on," Allen warned.

"They won't let me in if'n I take 'em off either," he answered and winked at me and I hid my eyes behind my fingers.

"You won't be able to even get in and watch us swim."

"Don't care." Ed ran his hands through his hair and scrunched at it and let it fall in his face. The boys were silent as we drove through the corn. I saw Allen give a stern look at the rearview mirror at Ed. But Ed was looking down and had all his hair in his eyes and was chewing on a piece of it.

My own hair almost reached my waist and was parted on the side and held back with a yellow barrette that Jeffrey had put in for me that morning. The ends of it were flying around in the breeze of the open windows. I took my barrette out and put it in the empty ashtray in the door and leaned over and ran my hands through my hair and scrunched it up and let it all fall in my face. I leaned over and let it hang there.

The sun went behind a cloud and goose pimples prickled my arms and legs.

"Too cold to swim I'm tellin' ya," Ed said. No one replied. I shivered from where I sat on my inner tube and scooted down inside it.

"Look at Baby Hunni!" Jeffrey laughed from the front seat. I looked up from hunching over and let all my hair hang in my face.

"She *is* Ed's love-child!" Jeffrey was having fits of laughter and trying to get Allen to look.

I looked over at Ed to see him push his hair behind his ears and come out from his meditation of the floor mat to look up at me.

"Huh! Ahuh!" he laughed with his lips pulled back over his straight, white teeth. "Her mama's off fighting in Nam while I stay home and raise the baby!" Ed guffawed.

"That don't even make sense," Allen said.

"Nothin' ever does, boy," Ed reached out and smacked Allen on the back of the head.

"Hey! Jackass! I'm driving!"

"Huh! Ahuh! Language Allen! Language!" Ed was doubled up and losing control of himself in laughter.

"It is too cold to swim, Allen," Jeffrey said as he blew smoke out his window.

Ed reached over to me with both his hands. "Here, Baby Hunni, let me," he said with a look of concentration on his face. His lips pooched out and his tongue stuck out for a second as he focused his pale eyes on me. He ran his fingers through my hair this way and that like long spider legs stroking the strands of hair into going the way he wanted them to go. Then he zipped his thumb down the middle of my scalp. "Part, part," he said as his eyebrows furrowed down and his tongue shot out again, "Part dammit!" he whispered and ran the edge of his thumbnail down the middle of my head from the front to the back again. "There we go." He sat back and observed me, reached over and tucked my hair behind my ears. "There ya go." He winked at me. "Now, you could be mine," he said with his hand cupping my chin. He smiled as I bounced up and down in the inner tube.

Allen passed the Rush-La Rue pool.

"Where you goin' boy?" Jeffrey asked.

"Too cold to swim, didn't you hear?" Allen asked.

I looked at Allen in the rearview mirror. He was grinning from ear to ear. No one said anything. Ed lit a cigarette and settled back in his seat and shut his eyes.

"Nancy boy back there might catch a chill." Allen hooked his thumb back at Ed. Ed's big foot flew out from under him and he kicked the back of Allen's seat but he didn't say anything or even open his eyes.

"So where we going then?" Jeffrey asked. He turned around and looked at Ed and I as if we knew. "You cold, Baby?"

"A little." I only had on my swimsuit and I had scrunched down into the hole of the inner tube as much as I could.

"There's the state park on the other side of Rush," Allen said. "They have swings and stuff. A picnic area."

No one answered or disagreed so we drove around the outskirts of the college town and headed over to the state park and picnic play area.

Ed was right. It was too cold to swim that morning. The sun kept going behind the clouds and when it did my skin would break out in goose pimples every time. We drove through the winding curves of the state park till we found the play area in the heart of the park, near the lake.

Allen and Jeffrey both only had on swim trunks. Allen was the only one of us wearing shoes and Ed the only one with actual clothes on. I had on my swimsuit with the stained glass squares on it, which was now faded from swimming so much this summer, and I was chilled. I ran from sunny patch to sunny patch into the sprawling wooded play area that was named Dragon Park. The center of the park had a stone dragon and the boys all ran and climbed on it.

I ran around going down the high metal slides on my own while the boys lounged on the dragon and smoked.

"Sitting on Smaug, burnin' a grit," said Allen as he patted the neck of the dragon from where he sat behind the great grey beast's head.

Jeffrey sat sideways on its ridged back and Ed lay in the curl of its tail near the ground. I kept getting stuck going down the slides because I only had on my swimsuit and the metal slides stuck to my bare legs. I was cold and cranky and bored because the boys wouldn't play with me.

"Allen," I called up to him from where I stood in the shade of the dragon's head, "come play with me." I wiggled my toes in the cold damp dirt while I waited for him.

"Awww, Baby Hunnicutt, I don't want to get down. Jeffrey?"

I walked to the side of the dragon and tried to scrabble up its fat scaly stone side but couldn't get any purchase and never got higher than three inches off the ground.

"Jeffrey," I whined as I reached for him. He was sitting with his long skinny legs dangling over the side and trying to blow smoke rings.

"Baby Hunni, you're too small to come up here," Jeffrey smiled down at me. His eyes crinkled and drooped at the corners. I pouted and walked back to the tail of the dragon where Ed lay on his back on the curl of the tail. He had his eyes shut and was blowing smoke rings up in the air without looking. I stood and watched him a minute in silence. His long knobby toes gripped the ridge of the dragon's tail and I walked over and poked the round ball of the toe next to his big toe. His eyes rolled open and were the same blue as the watery weak-sunned sky.

"What?" His lips puckered over his front teeth.

"Nuthin'." I walked off kicking pebbles with my bare feet. I was ready for a Pepsi and a sandwich but I didn't want to ask and be told no again.

I wished I was at Mrs. Small's playing Parcheesi. I wished Ed would have worn his swim trunks so we would have gone to the pool.

"What's got your pants in a bunch?" Ed asked. I turned around to find him following me as I wondered around the park. He followed me as I tottered down the balance beam with my arms out wide. He followed me to the springy animals and after I climbed up on the springy baby dragon, he straddled the horse and crammed his long bare feet into the stirrups, making his knees shoot out at odd angles.

"Yee haw! Ride 'em cowboy!" he yodeled.

"I'm gonna beat you!" I called as I rocked back and forth for a bit but I just didn't feel enthusiastic about it.

"What?" Ed asked when I gave up rocking. He looked down at me from his horse with his pale eyes that Mama had always told me to not look into. I had yet to see Ed go crazy this summer. Maybe I wasn't staring long enough because I was sure Mama had always said if I stared at hippies long enough they were apt to go crazy. I'd been staring at Ed off and on all summer and all he ever did was pout and cuss.

"What?" he asked again and let his hair fall in his face. "You in there kid?" He leaned over to look me in the eye.

"I'm hungry."

"Me too. We should eat. Let's get the cooler."

"Race ya!" I yelled and took off running. I didn't know if he was going to race me or not but I sprinted through the park on my bare tip toes, zig zagging through the toys, back to the gate.

"I'm catching up!" I heard him yell amidst a bunch of loose coughing.

Ed was almost level with me as we were approaching the see-saws.

"I'm gonna win!" I shrieked with glee at getting Ed to run with me and I jumped over the see-saw seat that was resting on the ground. I flew through the air and would have cleared it if Ed hadn't have smacked the other side of the see-saw, the side up in the air, as he jetted past it. I heard his palm whack the old green wood and I was stopped dead in the air with an upwards chock! of the sound of my teeth clacking together. My teeth came together hard on the edges of my tongue and I felt a hard popping in my lower front tooth. I saw the sky above me and tasted blood in my mouth and sat down on the cool packed earth of the playground as if I'd been dropped out of the sky. I looked up at the see-saw that had taken me out and my eyes rolled back in my head and everything went black and the world fell away from behind me as I wet my swimsuit and collapsed backwards in the dirt.

CHAPTER FOUR

"Baby Hunni? Can you hear me?"

I came up from the darkness and back to this earth hands first, not feet first. My right hand came up into the light first, though my eyes were not open to witness it. My right hand came up out of the darkness as it lay in a pair of hands with such fine bones it was like being held by two soft doves; warm and fragile.

"Baby Hunni? Baby Hunnicutt. Open your eyes for me, please." The doves pressed lightly on my fingers.

"Baby, open your eyes." The fingers on my left hand came up out of the darkness and were gripped firmly by hot, strong fingers.

"What are we gonna do, Allen?"

"Baby. Baby, open your eyes. For heaven's sake you're makin' Ed cry."

Something important was urging me to come up, to break through the darkness, to break through the weight pressing on my chest and my head.

"I think she's coming around."

"BABY! This is your cousin and I am telling you, OPEN your EYES!"

My head and shoulders came up out of the darkness next and were cradled by someone. Someone was holding me tenderly and I knew it was my Mama and that it was important to open my eyes and see her before she went away. My eyelids struggled to open and I tried to focus my eyes.

"Baby! Baby! Stay with us. Jesus Christ, you're workin' Ed all up, stay with us!" A firm squeeze of fingers pressed my left hand and woke my brain up. I looked to the left and saw Allen. His face glistened with sweat and his lips were pressed in a line.

The back of my head hurt and my teeth all ached. One of the bottom teeth felt so cold it hurt clear to my chin. My bottom lip felt huge to the point of bursting. I wanted to sleep. I felt the world falling away behind me.

"Baby! NO! Open your eyes." The doves were pressing my right hand. Someone's fingers were brushing my hair back from my forehead. Mama.

"Mama," I whispered to the right but I couldn't turn to look that way. Someone was cradling my head and that urged me to keep my eyes open. Someone was stroking my hair and my eyebrows. It was Mama. I rolled my eyes up to see her above me. It had to be Mama holding me. But it wasn't. It was Ed. Even upside down I could tell it was him. His hair hung in thick strands in his face above me. It was darker underneath than it was on top. I could see his dimple in his chin and his mouth was open and I could see the undersides of his white teeth and I could hear him breathing through his mouth. His eyes were glistening and red. My eyes were heavy and rolled shut.

"Baby, can you hear us?"

"Ed," was all I could say. I wanted to ask where Mama went and how did Ed get there in her place but all I could say was "Ed."

Hands continued stroking my hair. I felt the edge of a thumb nail go from the front of my forehead straight down the middle of my scalp to the back of my head and I whispered, "Part, dammit, part."

"See what you did? You done and went and taught the kid to cuss. Happy now?"

I heard Jeffrey laugh quietly and felt his thin hands cradling mine. I heard Ed suck in a heavy breath and I heard him snort back a thick wad of snot in his nose.

"Come on Baby, open your eyes for me," said Allen.

I opened them and focused on Allen and then used all my strength to turn to Jeffrey. His lips were pinched and twisted and there were lines on his forehead.

"Jeffrey?"

"Yes Baby?"

"I wet my pants." I pulled my hands away from the twins and covered my face in shame.

"It's ok, Baby." Jeffrey took my hand back away from my face.

"Ed knocked the piss plum out of you Baby, you couldn't help it."

"No, it's not ok. I want to go. I want my Mama!" Then I sucked in a great pull of air that froze my bottom teeth in pain and I let out a wail that caused me to shudder clear to my toes.

"Jeffrey," Allen commanded. "Go get me the big beach towel. Ed. Take off your shirt."

So the boys fashioned me a clean outfit out of Ed's t-shirt and then wrapped the big beach towel with the Quisp advertisement on it around my bottom half. Allen carried me to the backseat of the car. Jeffrey threw the inner tube into the trunk.

"How do you feel Baby?"

"My mouth hurts." I leaned out of the car door before Allen shut it and spat out blood.

"You lost a tooth!" Allen pointed.

"Where?" I reached for my mouth but was too scared to go past my busted and swollen bottom lip.

"You really do look like Ed's love-child now with that big bottom lip."

I looked over at Ed as he slunked into the backseat. His lips were pooked out and his eyes looked sad and watery. He reached over and tucked my hair behind my ear.

"I'm sorry, Baby." His icy blue eyes locked on my face. His bottom lip trembled.

"Where's my tooth?"

"I'll go see if I can find it," Allen told me. "Stay in the car with Ed."

I looked at Ed. He looked like a horrible mess. He sat there in his cut-off Levis and no shirt or shoes with his hair a big mess and really did look like the hippies Mama was always scooting me away from. He patted me on the hair.

"I'm sorry," he croaked. His throat sounded hoarse.

"I know." I opened my eyes wide and took in how shaken up and sad he was.

Allen and Jeffrey neither one found my tooth. Allen told me I must have swallowed it but that the Tooth Fairy could still come because he would stay up all night if necessary and tell her what happened.

We drove back to La Rue and straight to Aunt Clementine's place of work at the Denture Lab where she made false teeth.

"Ed, wait out here with Baby while Jeff and I get Ma."

"Ok."

My head hurt and my teeth hurt and I was upset about wearing a huge towel wrapped around my hind end like a skirt. Ed's t-shirt had a strange salty smell and wasn't long enough to be a dress and I had no underpants on. The worst part was I had peed my swimsuit in front of them all.

I looked at Ed and wondered if he would tease me about it later. He looked pale and he looked more tired than he ever did on any of the mornings when we woke him up to go swimming.

Aunt Clementine left work early and got in the back seat with me and Ed. She bought us cheeseburgers and Cokes and fries at the Dairy Freeze on the way home since we hadn't eaten all day. I had a big chocolate shake and large bag of salty fries. Ed showed me how to dip my fries in my shake and I ate them that way because my lip hurt too much to suck the thick shake through the straw.

Jeffrey and Allen didn't tell Aunt Clem exactly how I got hurt. But they did tell her I got hurt fairly seriously.

"We'll have to keep an eye on her all night boys, in case she has a concussion," she said while we ate in the car at the Dairy Freeze.

"I'll do it. I'm already gonna stay up all night to catch the Tooth Fairy when she comes, to tell her how Baby Hunni swallowed her tooth and how she should still get a quarter," Allen said.

"I'll help."

We all turned to look at Ed just as he dipped a handful of fries in my shake and shoved them in his mouth.

"What?" he asked with his mouth full of food. "I can sleep on the floor. I mean, I won't sleep. I'll keep watch with Allen.

He'll probably fuck up and fall asleep anyway," he said as he shoved half a double cheeseburger in his mouth.

"Language Ed. Language."

Ed tilted his big forehead down at me and smiled with a mouth full of shake and fries and cheeseburger, "Sorry Baby."

"S'okay."

The scariest part about getting hurt by the see-saw was when Aunt Clementine told us she needed to call my Daddy and tell him. I saw the boys all give each other looks but none of them said anything. I was too tired and my head hurt too much to care.

Aunt Clementine called him as soon as we got home and he showed up in his work jeans, flannel shirt and safety glasses when I was just getting into Aunt Clem's claw-footed tub. The boys were all watching a rerun of some scary program called Outer Limits and Aunt Clem was in the bathroom with me, soaping my back when he came in the house.

Aunt Clem's hand froze on my back when we heard him come in the front door. We both sucked in our breath and listened.

"Hello, Uncle Fitz." We heard Jeffrey address my daddy in a light-hearted tone.

"Hello Jeff, Allen. Ed? What are you doing here Ed?"

"What? Oh. Just watching t.v. Mr. Hunnicutt."

"Where's Baby? What's happened to her?"

It was silent for a second and Aunt Clem and I both swallowed hard.

"She fell down at the playground Uncle Fitz. She hit her chin hard and blacked out for a spell," Allen said.

"How'd she fall?"

Silence for two beats.

"Just running through the park too fast I guess. Knocked out a tooth and busted her lip and everything."

"Probably not wearing any shoes," my Daddy said in a deep grumble.

No one said anything.

"Well. Where is she? Where's Clementine?"

Daddy came back into the bathroom and watched as Aunt Clementine washed my hair. He checked over my busted lip and my gum where my tooth had been knocked out and then he even helped dry me off. He wrapped me in a huge rough towel and carried me out into the living room where the boys were now watching the Guns of Will Sonnett; which happened to be one of Daddy's favorite shows. Ed was kicked back in the recliner with his bronzed legs propped up and stretched out in his cut-offs without his shirt. His hair was a mangled, sweaty mess and his eyes were still a little puffy.

The twins sat apart from each other on the couch. They had changed into flannel pajama bottoms and white t-shirts.

Both twins had brushed out their golden curls and parted their hair on the sides.

Daddy carried me wrapped up in my big towel and sat between the twins with me on his lap. He glared at Ed while Ed stared at the t.v. with his eyebrows furrowed and his mouth half opened. The twins stopped watching the search for Jim Sonnett and looked from my Daddy to Ed and back again.

I sat on his lap for the whole program as he stroked my hair and held me tight. Ed looked at us once out the corner of his eye, but not for long. Eventually Daddy asked, "Where do you keep your jammies, Baby?" That was when he found out I was sharing a room with two sixteen year old boys and he exploded.

"She's fine back there with the twins," I heard Aunt Clem tell him in the kitchen in hushed tones. "She's perfectly fine back there. She's with them all day. They take good care of her."

"I should have never sent her here."

"She's doing fine. She doesn't cry much anymore. Those boys love her."

"What's Ed doing here? Is he here much?"

"No. And besides, he was all tore up about her being hurt. Can't you see that?"

"Why? Why would that layabout care?"

My ears pricked up at this. If she told Daddy that Ed was spending the night he was apt to go crazier than all the hippies at Tolly's Grocery Store. If he were to find out that Ed was the one that caused my injuries, Daddy was likely to cause great bodily harm on Ed no matter that Ed was only sixteen.

"He's a good kid. He's sensitive."

"I don't even think he's all there."

"Ed's a good boy, Fitzgerald." My aunt's tone was beginning to lose its hushed-ness and was starting to get louder.

"I wish I could bring her back home. I wish none of this had never happened."

"I know, Fitz, I know. I know you miss her," Aunt Clem said, her voice getting quiet again.

They talked quieter and quieter and I just got more and more tired. After putting on my Road Runner jammies I climbed into bed with Drowsy cuddled up tight to me and I went to sleep.

Allen and Ed woke me up several times that night and each time they accidentally frightened me with the flashlight shining up their noses and lighting up their teeth. They kept prying open my eyelids with their fingers and checking my eyeballs with the flashlight to see if I was concussed and I kept asking if the tooth fairy had come yet.

Finally morning arrived and with it the quarter from the tooth fairy. Except it wasn't just one quarter, it was three. I shrieked with delight as Ed cussed his favorite triune of 'shit mother fuck' and covered his head with a pillow from where he lay wrapped in a quilt on the rag rug.

CHAPTER FIVE

School was starting the next week and was faced with much enthusiasm on my part and with much grumbling on the part of the twins, and with complete indifference on the part of Ed. I was curious to see Ed in socks and shoes and a shirt and looked forward to school starting just to see that. I couldn't imagine his huge, tan feet in shoes.

But my mind was soon taken off Ed and his curious wardrobe or lack of one because for the first time ever I met a girl friend. Old Mr. and Mrs. Post who lived across the street from Aunt Clem brought their granddaughter to live with them just before school started. On Labor Day they brought her over to Aunt Clem's backyard while we were barbequing.

We had quite the gathering at Aunt Clem's; Daddy came over and he brought Mrs. Small with. Ed was already over. He had spent the night again, though no one said a peep about it to Daddy. Ed said the rag rug was more comfortable than his own bed. Allen said waking up to Ed curled up on the rag rug was more like waking up to a rabid cur than a real puppy.

Jeffrey was manning the grill in the backyard with a cigarette dangling out of his mouth, to the dismay of my Daddy. Allen and Ed were throwing the football around over everyone's heads. Ed actually had on socks and sneakers with his cut-offs and a Chicago Bears sweatshirt with the sleeves ripped off and managed to keep his language clean in front of my Daddy.

"Huh! Ahuh!" he laughed when Allen missed a pass and tripped over the cooler of Pepsis.

"Hey neighbor," Mr. Post called from the gate. We all turned to look.

That is when I met my first best friend. Mr. Post was carrying his granddaughter, a very small girl with long, silky black hair. She was pounding him in the chest with her small fists.

"Put me down Grandpa! Put me down!"

"Ok Petra, calm down."

He set her on the grass and she tottered through the gate and over to me on stiff legs, almost like a robot. I looked at her legs and she had shiny metal braces going from the insides of her shoes up to her knees.

"HI! I'm Petra! I'm going to kindergarten tomorrow. We're gonna be in the same class! We're gonna be best friends! You can come over after school and bring your Barbies and we can play!"

"Whoaaa, hide the Pepsi, that kid's all fired up already!" Ed had come over to see who was here. "Huh! Ahuh!" he laughed and spiraled the football to Allen. Petra stood stock still but her eyes grew huge as she eyed Ed as he leapt over my small lawn chair and caught a throw from Allen.

Petra shook her head like she was flicking something out of her ear. "Anyway, I'm Petra. I'm going to be living across the street with Grandma and Grandpa. I was on the MDA Jerry's Kids' Telethon this morning. I'm their local ambassador. I was born with Charcot-Marie-Tooth which means that..."

"Petra. Let someone else talk. Be polite." Mrs. Post with her permed, silver hair put her hand on her granddaughter's shoulder and gave her a light squeeze.

"My name's Baby."

"Baby? Is that your real name?"

"Yes. Of course it is. Well, it's what everyone calls me." I tossed my hair over my shoulder.

Ed stumbled back over to us and sat in my little chair with his legs stretched out.

"Baby, get me a Pepsi, will ya?"

Petra looked at Ed in fear. "Who is that?"

"Baby Hunni! I'm dying. Help a man out." Ed held out both his long arms wide and leaned all the way back in my little chair. I heard it creak. I hoped he didn't break it before I got to sit in it at lunchtime. Daddy brought it over this morning from the Ben Franklin as a special present for me. I looked around for my Daddy. He was still inside with Aunt Clem cutting up the cantaloupe. He'd been inside most of the morning ever since he saw that Ed was here already. I ran over to the box of cold Pepsis and brought one to Ed and handed him the bottle opener.

"Thanks Baby Hunni." He winked at me.

"What's your real name?" Petra asked as she walked closer to me on her stilty legs.

"That is her real name. Baby Hunni. She's my love-child." Ed reached over and put his arm around me and pulled me close. He looked at Petra with his ice blue eyes under heavy lids and then he smiled at me. He had sweat rolling down the side of his jaw and he had short, curly, springy hair growing down in front of his ears. He pulled a few strands of hair off his eye lashes with his fingers and leaned back a little from me and said, "What?" and pooched out his big lips at me. His ice blue eyes caught the sun and I stared into his black pupils and thought of Mama and how she would never have allowed me this close to Ed, ever.

Just then the back door slammed shut and my Daddy came out carrying a bowl of cut-up cantaloupe.

"Ed. Get out of Baby's chair."

"Yes sir." Ed let go of me and folded his long brown legs up and sulked off drinking his Pepsi.

"Hot dogs almost done kids!" Jeffrey called from the grill.

Petra and I sat together while we ate and she told me about all her Barbies. I listened intently because I had none. She held out her hand and ticked off on her fingers as she explained, "I have Twist n Turn Barbie, Stacie and Christie who are Barbie's best friends, Ken, who wants to be her boyfriend, Skipper – Barbie's little sister, and one mean GI Joe. He's a Green Beret," she said matter of factly as she took a delicate bite off the end of her hot dog.

"Jesus Christ. Who is this kid?" Ed asked as he sat Indian style on the grass with his four hot dogs on his plate and two bottles of Pepsi clutched in one hand. He didn't wait for an answer but leaned towards his plate and began shoving his relish and mustard covered dogs in his mouth. He also didn't see Mr. Post and Daddy glare at him. Allen and Jeffrey were shaking their heads and Mrs. Small had her head in her hands. I was looking at how the sun lit up the gold in his brown hair and made his head look like it was ablaze.

"So which Barbies do you have?"

I frowned and furrowed my eyebrows, "I don't have any. I have a doll house and a family for that." Allen bought me a little family of four to go with Aunt Clem's doll house the day after I got smacked by the see-saw and I loved them very much.

"Oh doll houses are for babies. Oh. Sorry."

I didn't know what to say and was saved from having to answer by Ed producing one his longest and deepest belches ever.

"Ahh almost satisfied but not quite," he smiled and looked up at everyone at the big table and at me and Petra at the small one. He had mustard on his chin near his dimple.

"What else you cookin' Jeffrey?"

**

The night before my first day of kindergarten I could hardly sit still on the chair as Aunt Clem combed Dippity-Do through my hair and rolled my waist length blonde hair around orange juice cans and secured them with rags.

"You'll have beautiful curls for your first day of school, Baby," she said to me.

We were all in the living room watching Jacques Cousteau. Allen and Jeffrey were on the couch in their jammies eating popcorn out of a giant paper sack and drinking Orange Crush out of tall bottles.

I was on a kitchen chair in front of the recliner while Aunt Clem rolled my hair. My school supplies were all packed away in the big vinyl carry-all Allen and Jeffrey helped pick out. It had a giant mushroom painted on a light green background. Ed had said it was "Trippy" when we bought it and I worried about it being too big for me to carry.

Allen and Jeffrey were going to walk me to grade school on their way to the high school. I would be going to morning kindergarten and coming home at noon everyday. At first I was very worried about being at Aunt Clem's alone every afternoon until she explained I'd be going to Mrs. Small's every day.

Aunt Clem would pack me a lunch box like an all day school kid, but I'd be taking it to eat at Mrs. Small's.

"That lunch is a waste of food, Curly-Locks," Ed said to me as he came in the door and picked a sausage link off my plate that morning. "Mom's gonna have lunch ready and waiting every day when you get there, just you wait."

"Hey bonehead!" Allen came into the kitchen and smacked Ed on the back of his head. "Get out of my seat."

"Did you shower?" Jeffrey asked Ed from where he stood at the stove pouring batter on the griddle.

"Shaved too," Ed replied as he stroked his chin. "Gotta make a good first impression on the women." He grinned and winked at me. His hair was parted straight and combed smooth for the first time I could remember. It looked shiny and soft and was flying about here and there without all the dirt to keep it plastered down.

"I'm not the only one looking to make a good first impression. Look at you Curly-Locks, Baby Hunni." Ed grinned at me and I squirmed and blushed. "We'll have to beat the boys back with a stick."

"Doesn't she look like a little Veronica Lake?" Jeffrey asked.

Aunt Clem had gently combed my big curls out this morning and they spiraled almost clear to my waist. Then she'd parted it on the side and put in a little butterfly barrette.

"Baby Hunni, Curly-Locks, my love-child. I should take you to school with me. You'd draw the girlies to me like, well, like bees to honey, Baby Hunni. Mrs. Rawlins, do you think I could sometime?"

"Ed, did you get concussed on your way over here? What the hell's gotten into you, boy?" Jeffrey asked as he sat down a stack of steaming pancakes on the table.

"What?" Ed smiled and took a pancake and rolled it up and shoved it in his mouth.

Jeffrey, Allen, and Ed walked me to my first day of school before going to the high school down the street. The other children oogled them and made a wide berth around them as they ran past us to class. I was the only kindergartner with a lunch box and many of the children stared at my little yellow school bus lunch box and at me before backing away from me. Ed rolled his lips back and growled and snapped his teeth at them just like the wolf I always suspected him of being. He sent children running and shrieking in all directions as the twins walked me up to Miss Pollock my teacher.

Miss Pollock looked very young. She had long, curly red hair pulled back in a loose pony tail. She had a huge smile on her freckly face and was wearing a short red dress with high polish black Maryjanes. She was leaning over and beaming at every child who came in the door saying, "Good morning, please find your name tag and take a seat at your table. Good morning, welcome to kindergarten. Please find your name tag and take a seat at the table."

"Good morning!" Ed said as he beamed at her with all his wolf's teeth out. He was a good five inches taller than Miss Pollock.

"Good morning," she said as her smile faltered. "Who do we have here?" she bent over to me as I fidgeted and pulled at the hem of my denim sundress.

"Well, this here's my love-child, Baby Hunni," Ed said as he leaned down and put his face next to mine and looked up at Miss Pollock and batted his eyelashes at her.

She immediately stood back up. "Baby Honey? Are you sure she's not in the afternoon class?"

I looked from Allen to Jeffrey. How could things go wrong on the first day?

"Uhhh, her real name is Katharine. Katharine Hunnicutt," Allen told Miss Pollock.

"And who are you?"

"I'm her cousin, Allen. This is my brother Jeffrey." The twins had on matching plaid shirts buttoned up all the way up and tucked into their khaki pants. Their blonde curls had been washed and combed out and parted on the side and tucked behind their ears. I looked over at Ed in his too tight, too short, faded jeans and his too small black t-shirt which I knew said, "You bowl me over", printed over the top of two bowling balls and a pin, because I had asked him at breakfast.

"Hmm," Miss Pollock pinched her lips together and looked at a clipboard. "Katharine Hunnicutt?" she asked me. I bit my lips and blinked back tears.

"Welcome to kindergarten Katharine. Please find your name tag and take a seat."

Allen and Jeffrey each took my hand and led me into the class. Ed stayed at the door with Miss Pollock, grinning like a madman. I refused to go two feet past the door.

"What's the matter Baby?" Jeffrey asked me. I stood rigid with my fists clenched around the handle of my new mushroom carry-all and bit my lips and shook my head. My curls boinged here and there behind me.

"Come on Baby, we're gonna be late to high school," Allen pleaded.

Ed came over and got down on his knees. "What's wrong, Baby?" I shook my head and clamped my lips harder. Allen walked on in the class and was looking at all the name tags. The other kindergartners were all staring at him, wide eyed.

"Found it. Over here," he called.

When I looked at my name tag it said something long that started with a K. It didn't say Baby.

"That's not my name. I'm not sitting there." I crossed my arms over my chest.

"Come on Baby, you're Baby at home but you have to be Katharine at school," Jeffrey pleaded.

"No."

Ed sat down in my chair and folded his long legs under the table. I watched as he reached over to the big basket of crayons in the middle of the table and pulled them all over to his spot.

"Baby, that is just what your family calls you. It's just your family nickname," Allen pleaded as he looked at his watch.

"No, it's not."

"Yes, it is."

"No, it's not. Ed's not family." I pointed at the back of Ed's sleek, clean head of hair.

"Ed's not right in the head either. Look at him. What's he doing?"

Ed was hunched over the table coloring and drawing something. The rest of the children at that table had all scooted away from him as far as they could go except for one little boy with a head full of curls was leaning over Ed's shoulder, trying to see what he was drawing.

"Ok! Finished!" Ed said and jumped up sending the little chair flying behind him.

"Ok, Baby Hunni, I think everything is squared away now. Come see," he said and held his hand out to me. I walked over to my spot and looked down to see that Ed had flipped my name tag over and written in curly letters:

Baby Hunnicutt

Ed's Love-Child

He also drew tiny flowers all around the edge of the name tag.

"Now we can git, and get Allen to school so he won't be late and won't ruin his chances of being teacher's pet. I wouldn't mind getting pet by a teacher, if the teacher looked like Baby's." Ed strolled up to the door past Miss Pollock and winked at her and turned around and waved to me, "Bye Baby Hunnicutt, my one, true, love-child. You'll always be Baby to me!"

That first morning of kindergarten was horrible. After it let out I ran all three blocks to Mrs. Small's, crying the entire way and headed right out to the snap beans to hide in the tall vines and crashed and fell right into Ed who was lying in the dirt in just his jeans, blowing smoke rings up into the air.

"Holy fuck!" he hollered and grabbed his head where I crashed into him and sat up. "Shit mother fuck! You scared the Jesus out of me! Ahh, sheesh it's just you, Baby Hunni. What're you doing out here? What are you cryin' for? Aww shit, I didn't mean to cuss at you. Come over here." He waved his big paw of a hand toward me to try to get me to come close to him.

I didn't move.

"What? What's the matter Baby Hunni?" He pooched his lips out at me for a second and furrowed his brow at me. The sun flashed on his pale eyes.

I had the worst first day possible. It started with the teacher insisting I answer to Katharine. But I had never been called Katharine so I never had answered to Katharine. I would be sitting there, tracing my name that Ed had written out for me, with my finger and not paying attention and Miss Pollock would call "Katharine" four or five times and I would just sit there.

The boy with the head full of curls raised his hand and said, "Ma'am, I don't think that's her name. Ma'am, I think she's called 'Baby', Ma'am."

"You must call me Miss Pollock, young man," the teacher scolded.

"Yes Ma'am," the curly boy answered and began to cry.

"Ma'am," Petra from across the room from where she had to sit, stood up as gracefully as she could with her leather and metal braces on her little legs, and piped up, "Ma'am I know for a fact she is named "Baby", that that is her God given name. Baby Hunnicutt in fact, though I don't really think that man with all the hair is her daddy, even though he tells everybody he is."

"Please sit down."

After a few more times of trying to get me to answer to Katharine, Miss Pollock finally gave up and began calling me Baby. It sounded like it almost choked her to do it, but she did it all the same.

I was thankful for the boy next to me for helping defend me and for Petra piping up too.

I thought the morning would go fine after that. And mostly it did except all the boys all had crew cuts and looked alike and I couldn't tell which one was Wyatt and which was Jimmy or Everett or Michael. But I did know all of them wanted to pull my boingy curls and I spent recess running from them till I fell and skinned both knees so bad I had to have mercurochrome from the nurse's office.

When I got back to Miss Pollock's class they were making pictures of flower baskets.

"Ahem, Baby, ahem, we are making flower baskets for Friday. What is Friday class?"

"Mother's Morning!"

"Friday is Mothers' Morning here at FDR Elementary. So please take your seat and begin work on your basket for your mother," she said and beamed her freckly smile at me.

"Yes, Miss Pollock." I shuffled to my seat. I didn't bother to tell her about Mama.

Now here I was in the beans with both knees skinned wide open and covered with mercurochrome, my beautiful curls pulled out long and I was covered in sweat and tears.

"That old Miss Polkadot mean to you Baby?" Ed asked. "She call you some other name all day?"

"No."

"What happened to your curly locks, Curly-Locks?" He cocked his head sideways and reached out and touched my limp hair.

I looked down at the dirt. "The boys." That was all I could say. I gathered myself up and felt the sting in my skinned up knees and took a breath and said, "The boys wouldn't keep their hands to themselves."

That was what Miss Pollock had said all morning when the boys would walk behind my chair and grab a curl and pull it out. "BOYS! Keep your hands to yourself!"

Ed stared at me with his half lidded ice blue eyes and pushed his big lips out far and inhaled through his nose. "They wouldn't would they?" he asked and grimaced.

I hoped he wouldn't be mad. Miss Pollock seemed very mad at me for the boys pulling my hair.

"Hmmph. Well. I'm gonna have a talk with them little shit-pokes tomorrow. Bunch of little snot-rags. We'll go early and you can point 'em out." He scratched his head. His hair was a dusty mess from lying on the ground and his chest was smeared with dust and grime as well. I looked down at his big tan feet in the powdery dirt and watched out of the corner of my eye as my butterfly barrette slipped down to the end of my hair.

"Baby Hunnicutt."

I looked up to see Ed shaking his head at me and pressing his lips together in a small grin. He walked over to me and took out my barrette. "You don't need that cussed thing." And he reparted my hair with his fingers, down the middle of my head and tucked it behind my ears. "Don't sweat it Baby. How about you let me have your lunch box and you go in and eat with Mom. She'll be wondering where you are. Sound good?"

"Sure." I started to walk away and then thought of something. "Why are you out here in the beans?"

"School was a drag for me too, Baby. They couldn't keep their hands off my hair either, so I cut out. I split for the day just like you." He smiled lopsided and winked and sat down in the dirt and opened my yellow school bus lunch box.

Ed and the twins had a talk with the crew cut boys the next day by the flag pole before school. Allen threatened to black every one of their eyes if he heard they'd touched one hair on my head. I wasn't even sure they were all from my class. They all had flat tops or crew cuts and all wore plaid shirts buttoned up high. Ed and the twins had rustled up everyone with short hair into the corner of the yard by the flag and gave them the warning while I stood behind Jeffrey.

Aunt Clem had curled my hair again and I knew the twins would be checking to see what state it was in when I got home from the second day of school.

I still hadn't said anything to Miss Pollock, or as Ed called her, Miss Polkadot, about my Mama not being able to come. When Friday came I was nervous and scared and sad all rolled up together. Everyone's mothers began to show at 10 that morning. I sat on my hands and looked around as if my Mama were only late and not gone from this world. When I turned to look at the door and saw my Daddy standing there in his flannel shirt and safety glasses, carrying his CAT hat in his hands I squealed and ran to him. Miss Polkadot scolded me but I didn't care. Daddy picked me up and kissed me and called me Baby in front of the whole class. "I know your Mama would have loved to be here, Baby. She would have been so proud of you, Baby Hunnicutt."

"See?" I heard Petra hiss to Miss Polkadot, "That is her name and *that* is her daddy, not that wild man with the hair, even if he says he is!"

School was much smoother sailing after Jeffrey, Allen and Ed set some ground rules with the boys, and after my Daddy showed up on Mothers' Morning and called me "Baby" in front of everyone all morning long. The other mamas kept smiling at my Daddy like they knew something he didn't. But he didn't care. He knew enough to not wear his CAT hat inside and he knew enough to be polite and say 'thank you' for my flower basket picture even though I had written on it "To: Mama, I LOVE YOU, Baby".

He wasn't a mama but he was all I had and I was thankful he was able to get away from the assembly line long enough to come to school. He held me on his lap all through Mothers' Morning and the other mamas didn't do that.

Afternoons from then on went smoother as well because every Friday I was allowed to go home with Petra to Mr. and Mrs. Post's. Petra and all her Barbies and man dolls taught me all sorts of confusing things and provided hours of entertainment.

I didn't even know how to work the tiny little dress off the Barbie till Petra showed me. Barbie's arms didn't bend at all and working off the long sleeves was a puzzle to me. Once I did get it off I couldn't stop staring at Barbie's breasts. I turned GI Joe over so he couldn't see.

"What's the matter, Baby?" Petra asked as she brushed Skipper's long straight hair. I didn't answer. I sat there with my mouth wide open. "Your hair is almost as pretty as Skipper's, Baby," Petra said and showed me how nice she'd brushed it out.

I poked at Barbie's hard breasts.

"What's wrong?"

"That's not like a real lady's," I said and poked one again.

"Yes they are."

"Nuh-uh."

"I've seen my mother's and they're just like that. Stick right out like that. That's what the men like." Petra looked at me with her dark eyes like she knew everything. And I believed she did.

Mr. and Mrs. Post would not let her come over to Aunt Clem's when Aunt Clem was at work and I was home with just

Jeffrey and Allen and God forbid Ed. Mr. and Mrs. Post did not like Ed and they asked me lots of confusing questions about him.

"Does he smoke a lot of dope?" Mr. Post barked at me at their kitchen counter one afternoon as Petra and I sat on stools eating Fig Newtons.

"He smokes," I answered between chewing my cookie and drinking my milk. "Him and the twins smoke but Aunt Clem knows. She doesn't mind and he doesn't offer them to me anymore, so it's ok."

"Damn hippie bastard," Mr. Post cussed as Mrs. Post led him out to the front room.

"But does he smoke grass?" Petra asked, her eyes wide.

"Grass? He just smokes red and white cigarettes from a box."

That fall Petra gave me an education the likes of which I would never have gotten in kindergarten from Miss Polkadot. Petra explained grass to me and as best as I could understand it was something hippies smoked that made them feel like they were floating above the earth. I didn't understand what was so bad about that and why everyone didn't smoke grass from time to time till Petra explained that it burnt their brains and made them spacey and made them always hungry.

I thought of Ed and how he always had his hand in my plate; how he would lie back in the backseat of the car with his shirt rolled up and pinch the skin on his stomach and cry out that he needed 'gut waddin' which meant a ton of cheap food from the Dairy Freeze. Maybe he was smoking grass. I'd have to ask him if he felt like he was high above the earth. Ed would tell me. I was his love-child, his Curly-Locks.

When I asked Petra how she knew all that she knew, she told me it was from her mother who worked in a diner that was really a honky-tonk.

"What's a honky-tonk?" It sounded like a goose of some kind.

Petra leaned in close to me and I could smell her spicy Dentyne she always chewed, "It's a dirty, wild tavern outside of town where women are loose and men get in fist fights over beer!"

It sounded like some place Ed would have been interested in.

"When your mother works at a honky-tonk, you learn all the good stuff," Petra told me dead serious.

That's how Petra knew about a real lady's titties as she called them. I didn't like that word. It made me shudder. Petra told me how her mother pushed hers up high as they would go before going to work. I frowned at that.

"Why would she do that? Don't they stick out like Barbie's already?"

"She pushes them up higher," Petra confided and pushed at her own flat chest with her two hands. I tried it. I had nothing to push either, but I still managed to hurt myself all the same. I still didn't understand.

"That's what the men like."

"Why?"

"I don't know. But that's what GI Joe always tries to do with Barbie." I looked at GI Joe laying face down and resolved to never touch him again. And I made a note to ask Allen and Jeffrey why men liked women's breasts. They would know. They would tell me.

I was learning so much uncompleted knowledge from Petra that I decided to take notes in my butterfly notebook of things to ask the twins and Ed. I was asking Petra for help on spelling my questions for the boys when she stopped spelling "high" for me and said, "Oh I wouldn't ask them any of this, they're teenagers!" she whispered and I realized she had the same bad opinion of teenagers as my Daddy did.

"Don't you see?" she asked me, "That's when people start doing all this stuff, Baby, when they're teenagers"

It sounded to me like the perfect reason for consulting the twins and Ed. If teenagers were the ones doing most of this, then who better to ask? I filed away my questions in my brain of things to ask at least Jeffrey, but I didn't tell Petra.

"Do you know why the boys always pull your curls, Baby?" Petra asked me one Saturday morning in October.

The boys still chased me at recess and threatened to pull my hair whether it was curly or straight. Often times I spent every recess running full blast from them while Petra stood stock still watching in her braces.

That Saturday morning I was jumping in the big piles of leaves that Allen had raked up in Aunt Clem's front yard when she asked if I knew why the boys did this to me. Allen had moved on to rake the back yard and Ed and Jeffrey were on the big front porch reading comics and drinking bottles of Mello Yello.

Petra was sitting on the sidewalk with her legs straight out and her leg braces shining in the sun waiting for me to answer.

"They're mean little booger-butts?" I asked as I jumped out of a big pile of leaves.

"Come here," Petra whispered and motioned for me to come over to her. I crawled out of the leaf pile, the knees of my Wranglers were damp from crawling around all morning on the moist earth.

"What?" I asked out of breath. My cheeks were cold and there were dry leaf bits stuck all over my red cardigan.

"They pull your curls because they're practicing for when your real lady's titties grow in," she hissed at me.

Jumping in the leaves wasn't fun after that. I thought Petra said that to me just to upset me because Mr. Post wouldn't let her jump in the leaves and she had to just sit there. She wasn't allowed to come up on our porch when Ed was there either because Mr. Post said he couldn't see her there. I had been going up on the porch all morning and taking swigs out of Jeffrey and Ed's bottles of Mello Yello and Petra was mad that she couldn't too.

Ed had said, "Hyper little piss-ant doesn't need any sugar anyhoo," to her and made her even more angry.

I thought of what Petra said about the boys at school and I touched one of my two-day old curls that had leaves stuck in it and I covered my chest with my other hand and thought about Jimmy Collins who lived across the street from my Daddy and the Small's and how every day, no matter how many Melvins Allen gave him, he would not stop pulling my curls. Little Jimmy Collins, Allen always called him. Snot nosed son of a bitch was what Ed called him. Harmless toss pot toe rag was what Jeffrey always referred to him as.

Jimmy Collins with his dark crew cut and his little glasses over his beady, black eyes pulled on my curls all day long. I told Allen every day about Jimmy chasing me all recess, and every morning before school we'd walk over to Ed's to drag Ed out of bed for school and then Allen would chase little Jimmy Collins and pick him up by his underpants and threaten to castrate him but it never stopped him. Getting his tighty-whities pulled up over his head wasn't high enough of a price to pay for pulling on my curls. According to the knowledgeable Petra, Jimmy was just biding his time till I resembled Barbie and then he'd be trying to grab me elsewhere.

"What about Kai?" I asked Petra from where I sat in the leaves near her on the sidewalk. Kai was the curly headed boy. He sat at the table right next to me and I would catch him all day simply holding one of my long blonde curls in his hand, rubbing it with his thumb. Kai was my good friend and I would have liked to have had him over to play but he rode the school bus. I think Kai would have given me a lot less to worry and think about than what my playing with Petra left me with.

"He's a boy right?"

"Yes."

"Well," Petra held out her palm to the sky, "all boys are all the same."

I looked at Ed and Jeffrey, both of whom were sitting on the railing of the porch reading Archie Comics. Ed and Jeffrey were both boys but were nothing alike.

Jeffrey collected little critters like his lizard. He raised tadpoles in a bowl in the summer and turned loose the frogs as fall came. He fed his toast crumbs to the sparrows in the back yard and he played dolls with me anytime I asked him. He was over six feet tall already and thin as one of the bean poles out behind Mrs. Small's.

Ed always looked like he just rolled out of bed or like he just fought his way out of a cloth sack as my Daddy would say. Ed was almost as tall as Jeffrey but wasn't delicate or thin. He had big knobby feet and hands as big as a man's. Aunt Clem said he looked like the wild man of Borneo. I wasn't sure who that was but it sounded like Ed. Ed needed to shave everyday but he didn't. He didn't bathe everyday and I think he only combed his hair with his fingers. He liked to brush my hair while I sat on the foot stool in front of the big chair and then he liked to mess it up wild while we watched Gilligan's Island.

Jeffrey always combed my hair on the side and put a barrette in it before school and often times Ed would take it out and re-part it on the way to dropping me off at FDR Elementary. He would re-part it in the middle and pocket my barrette in the front pocket of his too-small jeans. He must have had a whole collection of my barrettes at his house.

All boys couldn't be the same, I thought, and looked at Petra with doubt in my eyes. I thought of Allen, out back raking the leaves without being asked. No. Petra was wrong. Kai wasn't the same as Jimmy Collins. Kai never pulled my curls. He held them. There was a difference.

CHAPTER SIX

One November evening found us all in the front yard of Aunt Clem's goofing around when my Daddy rolled up in his truck. Petra and I were playing Barbies in her yard across the street. Mr. Post had decided he didn't want her anywhere near Ed, ever, not even in Aunt Clem's front yard.

Ed and Allen were in the front yard of Aunt Clem's throwing the football at each other as hard as they could; trying to hurt each other with it. Jeffrey sat on the rail of the porch and egged them on.

When Daddy rolled up I left Petra and her Barbies and her man-dolls who were always trying to get Barbie and her friends to take their clothes off, and ran back over to Aunt Clem's.

Jeffrey brought Daddy a glass of iced tea and we sat together on the porch and watched Ed and Allen trying to bean each other with the football. Ed looked almost normal in his plaid wool jacket even though his worn out jeans were much too small. At least his hair was clean. He and Allen nearly looked like average American kids; Allen in his blue and white letterman's jacket and sneakers with his blond waves combed back from his forehead. But then there was Ed with his two days growth of beard and his long wild hair and ice blue eyes; hamming it up in the front yard and calling for me to watch him.

"Watch me, Baby! Watch this pass!" Ed called to me as he threw the football as hard as he could right at Allen's head.

"Guess what Baby?"

"What Daddy?" I pulled my eyes away from the boys acting up with the football and looked up at my Daddy.

"Thanksgiving is coming up and I'm bringing you home."

Just as he said it, and just as I squealed with delight, there was a dull smack and a cry of pain in the front yard. We looked up to see Allen sitting on his hind-end and holding his jaw.

"Huh! Ahuh! I got you good boy! You see that, Baby Hunni?" Ed howled and jumped up and down in his hiking boots.

"You stupid sack of," Allen said out of the side of his mouth while holding his jaw.

"Huh! Ahuh! Language!" Ed shrieked as Allen got up and chased after him with the football. Ed ran clear around to the back yard with his clean hair streaming behind him. He circled the house, jumped the fence on the other side and hopped up over the rail on the porch and sat by me, breathing hard.

Daddy frowned at him. Ed brought with him a wave of sweat, cigarettes, and fresh air, all rolled into one.

"So Baby," my Daddy continued as Allen came up on the porch too, "I'll be bringing you home for Thanksgiving. What do you think?"

"Oh Daddy! I love you! I've been waiting forever to come home!" I threw my arms around him and gave him a kiss on the cheek. "I didn't think you'd ever bring me home! When's Thanksgiving? Can I go today? Now?"

"No, Baby. Next Thursday is Thanksgiving. I'll come get you Wednesday night and bring you over. You can sleep in your old bed." He put his arm around me and pulled me close. I was all smiles.

No one else seemed to be as happy with the news. Allen looked at my Daddy with his eyes slit. Ed had his mouth wide open and was staring at both of us. He blinked his pale eyes at me and furrowed his eyebrows and scratched behind his ear. He pushed his lips out in a big pout and hung his head and looked at his boots.

Jeffrey loped over and patted me on the head with his long fingers. "I'm gonna miss having you around, Baby Hunni."

"But, but, but, but Baby lives here!" Allen protested. He had a red spot on each of his cheeks besides the big red welt from the football on his jaw. He ran his strong tanned hand through his blonde curls; pulling his hair back from his forehead.

"Allen. Jeffrey." My Daddy held out his hands in surrender, something I'd never seen him do before, "It's just for Thanksgiving. It's just for the holiday and maybe that weekend. I can't have Baby at home all the time. I work." He looked at the boys.

Ed tilted his face up a little and rolled his pale eyes up to mine. His mouth was still in a turned down pout. Now it was me whose mouth was wide open. And it was me whose bottom lip set off quivering. I gathered all my courage because I knew my Daddy wouldn't listen to me at all if I were crying. "Daddy? Can't I move home?"

He smiled at me on one side of his mouth but didn't speak as he looked down at me.

"I stay with Mrs. Small till three everyday after school anyway. I'm right there! I could just come home afterschool and make your dinner!"

Now Daddy was smiling real big at me but it felt wrong. It didn't feel like a happy smile. Not happy for me at least.

"Baby, I need you to live here now, with Aunt Clem. She's your Mama's family. She's close by. We see each other lots," he trailed off and hugged me close.

Now Allen's face was entirely red and he was openly glaring at my Daddy. I'd never known anyone brave enough to glare at my Daddy. Jeffrey lit up a smoke behind us and with that Daddy stood up and put his CAT hat back on his blonde flat-top.

"Baby. Come here." Allen held out his hand to me. I was so used to listening to him I went right to him. "Let's go to Cloyd's and get some candy."

"YES!" Ed exclaimed from behind us and leapt plum over the porch railing, into the yard.

"Not you, knucklehead."

"Well I'm coming too anyway. Loan me some scratch, Allen."

"Go on, Baby," my Daddy waved goodbye as Allen pulled me down the walk. "See you Wednesday night, Baby."

"We'll bring her over Uncle Fitz, no need for you to come over and get her," Allen said and pulled me down the street by my hand with Ed loping along next to us on his long legs in his flood pants.

"I want some of them red hot dollars. They make my breath spicy!" Ed said out loud to no one.

***

The Thanksgiving of '68, my first Thanksgiving without my Mama was a mixture of sad and happy. I had mixed feelings about going home. I'd been living at Aunt Clem's since the end of July. It felt like a lifetime since we'd broken in and gotten my swimsuit and clothes that first time the twins took me and Ed to the pool.

Jeffrey and Allen walked me over to my house the Wednesday evening before Thanksgiving just as the sun was starting to slide down the sky. Ed was next door at his own house for once, sitting out on their small front porch strumming his guitar. He bit his lower lip with his square white teeth and waved at us with the pick in his hand as we walked by.

The twins didn't stop to chat. They took me right up to my house. I had walked the three blocks over to my Daddy's house on stiff legs the whole way.

"Is it so cold you're froze solid and can't walk?" Allen asked.

"You're walking like that kooky friend of yours, the one with the braces. What's got into you Baby Hunnicutt? You not looking to spend all Thanksgiving with all the other Hunnicutts?" Jeffrey asked me.

My dad's siblings and all of their families would be coming tomorrow for the big Thanksgiving celebration.

"What will you guys be doing?" I asked Allen and Jeffrey.

"We'll be right next door at Ed's. Ma's coming too," Jeffrey answered.

"Will you come over here for a bit?"

"I don't think so, Baby."

"I'll come over," Allen answered.

Jeffrey and I both looked at him.

"I want to make sure they're treating you right."

"What does that mean?" Jeffrey asked his twin.

The twins bickered till we got to my door and then Jeffrey hugged me goodbye and I climbed up in his arms. "Come see me tomorrow," I whispered in his ear. He kissed me on the cheek and sat me back down on the porch.

Allen hugged me and picked me plum off the porch.

"I'll see you tomorrow," he whispered in my ear, "save me some pie!" And he kissed me on the top of the head. I hugged him as hard as I could and I refused to let go till my Daddy opened the front door.

Walking through my own home after not being there since my Mama died was like walking through a museum to her memory. Daddy let me in the dusky house and I smelled all the old smells and saw all our old furniture and cried without making a single noise. Daddy wanted to pick me up but I didn't let him. I wanted to walk through the old house on my own. I wanted to touch all the old places where my mother had been.

I sat in her rocking chair and I held the pillow she had cross stitched, up to my face and inhaled her perfume and thought of her creamy white skin and her huge, midnight blue eyes. Daddy was always telling me I had the same eyes as her. Just like Aunt Clem and the twins.

I walked to the piano and hit the middle C quietly. Daddy stood behind me. I remembered rocking Drowsy and listening to Mama play Moonlight Sonata on quiet afternoons when the housework was done. Beethoven was her favorite. She would play Beethoven on the record player and iron baskets of clothes.

I ran my finger lightly on the library table in the hall and touched all the dusty little ceramic doggies she collected. The cocker spaniel with the ceramic newspaper in his mouth was always my favorite and I had always touched his head with my fingertip when I had lived here. But now his head was covered in dust.

The dining room had cobwebs on the lampshades of the overhead light and I didn't pause there at all but went on into the kitchen. The white and black kitchen glistened from my Daddy's military meticulousness. This was the room he spent most of his time in it seemed. He had moved the tv cart in here next to our little pearly white table.

For some reason I had really missed the little pearly table. Just seeing it made a lump grow in my throat. Our little table that only sat four; where the three of us had sat for six years, where I always dreamed of having a brother or sister to sit in my red high chair that was still in the corner was what I missed most about my house. But Mama and Daddy never got to have another baby and I hadn't gotten to sit at the table in months. That was where I wanted to sit and eat this whole time that'd I'd been at Aunt Clem's. It must have been where Daddy wanted to be too.

"Want to go see your room, Baby?"
I just nodded my head for my answer.

Halfway up the stairs I froze right where my Mama had collapsed. I looked down at the steps and recalled finding her there and running back over to Mrs. Small's and getting Ed. I remembered bringing him here in mute terror and pointing to my Mama on the stairs. I recalled Ed picking her up gently and carrying her to the couch. I remembered as if it were yesterday him putting his head to her chest and listening and how his ice blue eyes lit on mine and it was like the blinding white light of a lighthouse beam shining in my face, he looked at me with such fear in his face and such intensity in his eyes. He turned then back to Mama and put his two long fingers on her neck. Without turning away from her he said to me, "Baby, where's the phone?" with a waver in his voice.

I stood for several seconds at the middle of our black linoleum steps and the tears rolled down my cheeks.

"Where is Mama?" I asked my Daddy without looking up at him.

"She is in heaven, Baby, with Jesus," he whispered.

"But *where* is she?"

"She's in the Stone Valley Cemetery, Baby."

"I want to visit, Daddy."

"We will. In the spring. I'll take you."

Daddy settled me in my old room. I had no interest in looking through all my old things that got left behind when I moved into Aunt Clem's. I went right to bed. My only regret was that Allen and Jeffrey weren't snoring across the room from me. I'd even take Ed and his salty, sweaty, smoky smelling self on the rug over being in my dark room alone. It felt like a lifetime since I'd been in there.

Actual Thanksgiving was fairly happy. The house was packed with more cousins than can be listed. Daddy's brother, Uncle Fritz, not to be confused with Daddy who was Fitz came with his wife and their five children. Two of their children were grown and married and one had a baby on the way. Daddy's sisters Frances and Frieda and their husbands and between them their eight children, their chidren's spouses and boyfriends and girlfriends all came and it was more teenagers and young adults than I could keep track of. Having the house that packed with wall to wall people kept me from re-living old memories and I had a good time running between everyone's legs and getting lots of attention from all around.

Being the smallest I was of course sat at the kids' table which was the small pearly table, with the youngest of the cousins who were all the same age as the twins. But that was what I wanted, to sit in my old chair at my old spot at the little table.

Allen did show up later that day and pushed his way though all the clean cut cousins and the hubbub to find me by the piano listening to the girlfriend of one of the Hunnicutt cousin's playing Moonlight Sonata for me as I sat on the floor with my arms wrapped around my knees and I pretended for a minute my Mama was just in the kitchen helping all the aunts wash dishes.

Not too far behind Allen was Ed in a red, white and blue snowflake patterned sweater with his hair looking like he'd just fought his way out of a cloth sack, and lost; looking for leftovers and making a bee-line to the kitchen for a plateful of food. I remembered I'd never asked him if he felt like he was floating high above the earth and I smiled as I thought of Petra and her certainty that Ed was smoking dope.

Each Thanksgiving after that got easier. It became tradition to have it at my Daddy's house. Aunt Clem and the twins would always be next door at Mrs. Small's with her and Ed and I always thought that was a little odd but couldn't have told anyone exactly why I thought that. I guess I just didn't understand why I lived with them all year and they spent Thanksgiving next door. Though Ed could always be counted on to wonder in, late in the afternoon, in search of more food.

***

Growing up with Aunt Clementine, the twins, and Ed, I learned many different life lessons than what I would have learned if I had been brought up by Mama and Daddy. Growing up in Aunt Clem's house I was raised to believe that the war in Vietnam was bad; that our president was sending young boys over there by the planeloads and getting them killed by the Vietcong for nothing.

Growing up at Aunt Clem's I learned first hand that not just bad guys and criminals smoked and cussed, that sometimes good guys did too. I learned that dirty hippies weren't always drug addled nuts, apt to go as crazy as the violent Manson's.

I learned to root for the bad guys (my cousins and Ed) and to boo the good guys (the local beat cop) who threatened to turn all three boys into the draft boards as soon as they turned 18.

CHAPTER SEVEN

At age eleven I was still going to Mrs. Small's most days after school for her to watch me till Aunt Clem got home from work. Jeffrey, Allen and Ed were two years out of highschool and had better things to do with their time than babysit a eleven year old.

Allen was the assistant manager of Cloyd's and seemed to work around the clock. Ed worked most nights as a busboy at La Rue's one fancy restaurant, The La Pierre. Allen and Jeffrey both said it was a matter of time before he was fired. They were betting on whether it would be for his pilfering food or for lack of washing his hair. Jeffrey didn't have a job. He said it was pointless because they were all three going to be sent to Nam any day and that he was going to enjoy his time while he was still here, alive, and in one piece.

Mrs. Small's was not as much fun to go to after school as Petra's, even if Petra often times put worrisome ideas in my head. She knew things about life, about boys, about ourselves and our bodies that I hadn't even learned or been exposed to after all my time with the twins and Ed. I still spent my Friday afternoons at her house and they were usually enlightening even if they stressed me.

We were in her bedroom drinking Cokes and eating red vines while she looked through the phone book to see if she could find the numbers of boys from our fifth grade class.

"Ohhh, here's Kai!" she squealed as she lay on her pink chintz spread. "Call him!"

"Why?" I asked. I was sitting at her make-up table, braiding my hair with two tiny braids on either side of my part.

"Come on! I'm bored! Call him! Let's see what he's doing."

"He's probably not even home from the bus."

"You're so boring."

I didn't have an answer for that.

"Let's stuff our bras and sneak over to your place and see if anyone notices."

Petra swung her legs off her bed and pivoted on her braces over to her dresser and began pulling out socks. "Big socks for me, small socks for you," she mumbled to herself.

"Petra. I don't even wear a bra."

"You can borrow one of mine."

"I don't want to. Those are my cousins. They're old enough to be our dads. We're only eleven, we don't have boobs, end of story."

"They're not that old."

"They're twenty."

She could not stop looking out her window down at Allen and Ed. Petra had no interest in Jeffrey, who sat on the couch chain smoking and reading about the war all day.

I knew she wouldn't give up till we went over there. Mr. Post still wouldn't let Petra anywhere near Ed. But Mr. Post was due for his pre-supper nap any moment now and that is when she would sneak over to my place. I didn't feel like I was sneaking. It was after all where I lived, and those boys, Ed included, were the people who still took care of me for the most part.

I peeked out the window and looked down at the boys. Ed was sitting on the steps of our porch, strumming his guitar with a cigarette hanging off his thick bottom lip. He had has hair tucked behind his ears and he had on his clunky suede hiking boots with his faded highwater jeans. He also had on his white dress shirt and black vest from The La Pierre.

Allen sat behind him in a chair with a little table with his chess board on it. He had a book in his hand about chess and a cigarette dangling out of his mouth too. His blonde curls were pulled straight back into a pony tail and he had curly wisps hanging here and there.

"Ed is so dreamy," Petra swooned from where she balanced next to me at the window.

I didn't know how to answer that either. Ed was like a smellier, wilder version of the twins, who although he wasn't required to take care of me, usually pitched in more than Jeffrey and Allen combined. Sure he cussed and smoked and pinched me a lot and scared me from time to time because you just never knew what he was likely to do, but basically he was ok. He was just Ed.

"So are we going?" she asked me as she wedged socks down her shirt.

"I'm not doing that." I poked her in the sock.

"Don't you want breasts?"

"Not particularly."

"Why not?"

"I dunno. I never thought about it, I guess." I shrugged.

"You already have Jimmy Collins trying to cop a feel and you don't even have anything. You're so lucky," she sighed.

"How is that lucky?"

"The boys are crazy about you. Come on, you know it," she rolled her eyes at me.

"Jimmy Collins? He's just one boy and he's just a sick pervert."

"He's just doing a check to see if you started getting them yet. Once you start your period then he'll know they're coming."

"How will he know?" I asked and cursed myself and Petra too for how she gave out important information in half servings which always left me so confused and often times worried.

She had been telling me since we were small that men were crazy about women's breasts. But she could never explain why. Finally I had gone to Jeffrey when I was six and asked him why.

"Well," Jeffrey had answered, turning scarlet, "I reckon men just like them because they're something women have that men don't have."

I had looked at him blankly and so he had continued on with, "It's just something that gives men comfort, Baby. That's all."

I remembered furrowing my eyebrows at him in dissatisfaction like Ed was always doing with me, but I didn't press further.

Back then I was smart enough to figure Ed would have a better answer for me, but I wasn't smart enough to know better than ask him. And ask him I did. One Saturday afternoon when the twins and Ed, who were all finally seventeen years old, and who were yet again saddled with me, who was just six, snuck me in to see an R rated movie about drugs, hippies, hookers, and some tuff dude named Joe.

They smuggled me in and bribed me with popcorn and sno caps and a big Coke to see a movie that was definitely not a cartoon. I begged to sit on Jeffrey's lap because it was so dark and I couldn't see over the guy in front of me, but mostly because I was frightened of the gritty movie that I couldn't follow or understand. Jeffrey held me for much of the movie, till his skinny legs went numb from my weight and then he passed me off to Ed just as a naked lady in the movie was getting into a bathtub with a man. Just as she got in the tub, the man got out.

"Sweet Jesus, he's fucking nuts!" Ed exclaimed out loud as he ran his hands through his hair and stuck it up everywhere as if he were trying to yank it from its roots.

"Maybe he doesn't like her boobies as much as most men," I piped up trying to be helpful.

"Baby! Jesus fucking Christ, cover your eyes!" Ed hissed at me and covered my eyes with his fingers. "And don't listen either!" he hissed and tried to completely wrap my head and ears with his arms. I struggled with him as he tried to wrap my head in his arms and I spilled some of my coke in his lap which caused him to release me for a second.

But soon something was happening on the screen that he thought I shouldn't see and he pulled my face into his shirt and commanded me to not look at the screen.

"Jesus criminy! What are you doing to Baby Hunni?" Allen whispered.

"Shhhhhhhh!" several people hushed us.

"Fuck off!" Ed hollered to them.

Ed still had my face smooshed to his shirt and I was having trouble breathing through the cloth that smelled like sweat and cigarettes.

"Ed, you're hurting my face," I whimpered.

He relented a little but kept his hand firmly on the back of my head.

"We should have never brought Baby Hunni," I heard Jeffrey say.

I sat like that, with my face mashed against Ed's chest and was too scared to drink my Coke for fear of pouring it down his lap again. I did poke sno caps one by one in my mouth with my one free hand. I didn't care that I couldn't see the movie. It was boring anyway. But then my mind got to wondering about the naked lady getting in that man's tub.

"Ed?" I whispered into his t-shirt.

"What?"

"Why do men like women's breasts?"

"WHAT?"

"Do you know that word? Breasts? Why do men like them?"

"WHAT?" he asked loudly. He pushed my face back a little in order to get a good look at me. My left cheek was sweaty from being pressed against him so long.

I took the opportunity to cram a whole handful of sno caps in my mouth at once and to slurp as much Coke as I could while my face was free.

"What did you say?" Ed asked as he leaned his forehead on mine. I could see the movie screen reflected in his silvery eyes.

"Why Ed? Do you know?" I asked with a mouthful of chocolate.

"Jesus Christ. You're a handful, kid. Where do you get this shit?" I could see his eyebrows furrowing down over his eyes in the semi-darkness. He looked confused.

"They don't, do they?" I asked. Petra was way wrong. Just wait till I told her she was way wrong about the whole thing.

Ed didn't answer. He shook a bunch of my sno caps out and crammed them in his own mouth and then slurped down a bunch of my Coke and stared at me.

"Maybe you're not a full man yet so you don't know yet." I reached up and patted him on the shoulder to let him know it was ok and that I wasn't too disappointed.

He sat and stared at me for a minute with his mouth hanging open. I took the opportunity to slug down more Coke and eat more candies. Ed licked his lips in deep thought and furrowed his brows and whispered in my ear.

"Baby Hunnicutt, I am all man already and I know why I like women's breasts."

Oh good I thought, a straight answer. I listened hard.

"But. But. You are just seven years old and a kid! A strange little kid, but a kid! We've plum warped your mind," he whispered and pulled my face into his chest as more violent mayhem erupted on the screen behind me.

I sat with my face pressed into Ed's shirt the rest of the movie while he stroked my hair some of the time and covered my ears some of the time. I was happy he thought I was a year older than I was and I was still pretty sure Petra was wrong. The twins and Ed didn't drag me to another R rated movie ever again and I didn't want to discuss breasts with Ed ever again.

Here I was with Petra, in her room, five years later as she squashed her socks into more breast-like shapes.

"Grandpa is asleep! Let's sneak over there!"

I rolled my eyes but I did it while Petra had her back to me.

When Petra and I snuck out of her house to walk over to my Aunt Clem's, I was still thinking of the time I'd asked Ed about breasts in the theatre and I was smiling like crazy as I sat next to him on the porch.

"What's so funny, Blondie-Locks?" Ed asked me as he strummed his guitar.

"Nothin'," I answered and clamped my hand over my mouth to keep from laughing. I looked back at Allen to see that he had put down his chess book and was watching Ed and me.

"What in the hell has your alien friend done now? Oh Jesus, you gotta be joking," Ed mumbled as he watched Petra pivot her way over on her braces in that swinging way she had of walking these days.

"Jesus, Baby, why do you hang out with her?" Ed asked me.

"Who else is there?" I shrugged.

"Why don't you ever have that curly headed kid over? The one that always wears sandals everywhere?" Ed asked me as he furrowed his brows at me over his guitar.

"He lives way out in the country," I shrugged again. "How's he supposed to get here?"

"Hell, I don't know. If he was that into you, he'd find a way."

I looked down at my own sandaled feet on the step next to Ed's big hiking boots in order to hide the flush in my face and to hide the hurt that was there as well.

Ed stopped strumming and reached over and gently pulled one of my skinny braids that I'd put in at Petra's. "It must just be too far for him to come on his bike, Blondie-Locks," Ed said in my ear as he walked his fingers down my braid, "cuz how could he not be into you?" he asked and gave my braid a good, hard yank.

"You jerk!" I sat up and clobbered him in the arm.

"Huh! Ahuh!" he guffawed. We both looked up and saw Petra had made it across the street and was now posing and simpering in the yard, trying to get Ed to notice her. Ed laughed again a loud one and then refused to look at her and her ridiculous sock stuffed chest, but instead kept strumming his guitar and pulling all sorts of faces at me to try to get me to laugh. He would open his huge pale eyes at me as wide as they would go and then let his lids droop and grin at me. Then he would furrow his heavy, pointy brows down low and then raise them high. I still didn't laugh. I held out for my favorite which he did next which was to push his big lips at me and make his pouty, sulky face with his eyes looking sleepy and his feelings looking hurt. That one always made me laugh because it was such an exaggeration of how he looked naturally.

Petra scowled at me from where she stood in the yard with her hand on her hip and her socks jutting out of her shirt.

"Petra, men like sex, not socks," Ed snorted and laughed.

"I don't know what you're talking about," she sneered.

"I'm sure you don't," he said and looked at me and winked.

"Petra, I think I see your grandfather looking out the window at you," Allen called down to her from the porch and she hightailed it back home as fast as her braces would let her go.

Poor Petra, I thought as I watched her go. What she wouldn't do to trade places with me. Both of us without our moms. Mine dead and taken away and hers working in a honky tonk and Petra taken away. Me sent to live with cousins who were pretty fun and her sent to live with controlling grandparents.

I was lost in thought for a second about it all and gave a quick prayer of thanks that Daddy had given me to Aunt Clem and the twins to raise and not to Uncle Fritz and his five children way out in the country.

"Penny for your thoughts, Blondie-Locks." Ed strummed the guitar and smiled at me under heavy lidded eyes and pushed out his lips at me. But I didn't tell him what I was thinking, even if he knew how to work me with his faces.

***

I wasn't the only one Ed tried to manipulate with his pouting and his playing up of his intense eyes. If he gave me the right look he could get me to laugh and sometimes if he gave me just the right look he could get me to tell him things I didn't want to divulge. He was sneaky like that. But his faces did other things to much older girls. He was very aware of his looks and very confident of them and used them to elicit what he wanted from as many women as possible. The fall I was eleven I learned that a young man could be extremely charming and flirtatious and could go through women like water through a sieve and not marry or even love a single one of them.

I watched Ed bat his long eyelashes and point the intense beam of his pale blue eyes on clean-cut girls from good homes and talk them into accompanying him out to the deserted Model T out behind his mom's garden where he would try everything under the sun with them. That fall I would hide out in the sunflowers in the late afternoon with Jimmy Collins who had followed me out there, while Ed coaxed a girl into his "T-Bucket" that was an old Model T up on cinder blocks and surrounded by apple trees, and make her giggle and shriek.

We'd hear her slap him a few times and we'd hear Ed persist and plead and then it'd get quiet for a long time. My eyes would grow round with wonder as the sun set on us in the sunflower stalks and soon there'd be my own slap on Jimmy Collins' face as he tried to reach up my sundress.

I would point my rigid finger at Jimmy in warning that I was not above knocking the snot out of him, nor was I too scared to go interrupt Ed and have him knock the tar out of him too.

Sometimes Ed would hear my slap and hear Jimmy's cry of indignant pain from the sunflowers and we would hear Ed call out, "Who's there? I heard a slap! Must be the ghost of girlfriends past." And then we'd hear the girl squeal and shriek and the T-Bucket squeak on its springs.

I went out to the T-Bucket myself late one day while I waited at Mrs. Small's for it to be time to walk back to Aunt Clem's. I knew Ed wasn't out there for I had scoped it out. And I knew I wouldn't be followed by Jimmy because he had detention afterschool for pinching me on the rear in front of Miss. Waverly, the librarian, while I was waiting to check out "Pride and Prejudice". I also knew from experience that after detention Jimmy would not be allowed out of his house by his mother.

I climbed up in the rusted old car and propped my feet up on the steering wheel and stared at my sandals. Fall was here and I still only had the sandals Daddy had bought me at the beginning of the summer. My feet were crammed in them in knobby wooly socks and my toes over-ran the ends.

I had on a used pair of bellbottom jeans that were passed on to me by one of my girl cousins who had probably gotten them from one of her sisters. I also had on a used and nubby red turtleneck sweater and Jeffrey's old Levi jacket that had been his when he was my age, and was two sizes too large. I hadn't seen Daddy in three weeks. He'd been working lots of overtime and even though I was right next door at Mrs. Small's most of the week, I never saw him.

I was sitting out in the old T-Bucket, feeling sorry for myself and thinking how unfair my life was, clear from when my Mama died, all the way on to how all my clothes were hand-me-downs, except for my underpants, and on to my problem of how I liked Kai but how we never got to be together after school or on the weekends because he lived outside of town.

Being in love was hard. But I had decided that was what I felt for Kai. I loved him. We held hands everywhere we went at school. The teachers stopped trying to stop us long ago, way back in second grade. I liked to look at our two hands linked together; his so brown all year long and mine fair with little pink nails.

"Baby, come sit with me," Kai called to me earlier that day in the library. He was on a huge bean bag, reading "A Boy and His Horse," waiting for me to check out my book, when Jimmy ran past and pinched my hind end right in front of the old maid librarian.

I ignored Jimmy and his pinch. He'd been doing things like that to me constantly since kindergarten; pulling my hair, picking me plum up off the ground, chasing me around nonstop, looking up my dress when I didn't know it and all sorts of creepy stuff. Kai was good at keeping him away if he and I were together. Soon as Kai would venture away, Jimmy and his hands would materialize. I stopped telling Allen and Jeffrey years ago. There were only so many times they could rough him up. Ed was ready to just kill him altogether and be done with it and some days I gave it serious thought.

I pulled out my copy of "Pride and Prejudice" as I sat in the T-Bucket behind Mrs. Small's garden and tried to stop moping and stop feeling sorry for myself, and I tried to get interested in Miss Elizabeth Bennett and all her sisters but I had no better luck than when I tried to read while sitting in the bean bag earlier in the day with Kai. I had sat nestled next to Kai and his long, slender legs in his olive green pants, and relaxed against him in his soft flannel shirt and inhaled his sandalwood soap and couldn't stop watching him read his book.

"Baby," he smiled at me and blinked his melty brown eyes at me. "Baby," he smiled as I reached over and twirled one of his big brown curls.

"Yes, Kai?" I smiled.

"Baby, we're supposed to be using this time for reading." His eyes followed my fingers where they twirled their way around and down a curl.

"I'll read it at home when no one's around and when I'm bored. Right now, I don't want to," I trailed off and snuggled deeper into the beanbag.

Kai's cheeks blushed clear down to the dimples in the corner of his cupid's bow lips and he went back to reading and I went back to watching him.

The rest of our class checked out their books and took bean bags for silent reading time, but no one else shared one except Kai and me.

Petra had a hard time getting in and out of a beanbag so they let her sit at a table. Jimmy Collins was made to sit out in the hall on the floor. I could see him from where Kai and I were and he was watching our every move. I walked my fingers up Kai's plaid shirt, a nifty trick I'd seen a girl do to Ed in the T-Bucket one evening, and I looked up to see Jimmy scowling.

"Kai," I whispered, "come home from school with me some afternoon. Mrs. Small won't care." I had told Mrs. Small all about Kai nearly every afternoon as we sat at her table and played cards and drank hot tea. She said he sounded delightful and hoped to meet him soon.

"I can't, Baby," he said as he marked his page and set his book on his legs. "How would I get home?"

"If I get you a ride, would you?"

"Sure, Baby. Of course. But who would do that for you?" He smiled at me like I was being silly. I thought I knew two people who would do that for me, at least once, if it was important to me and if one weren't working and if the other one weren't chasing women.

I sat deep in thought in the old Model T, reliving the day at school and watching the sun slide lower over the dead sunflowers and wondering if Jeffrey would come to walk me to Aunt Clem's so I wouldn't have to walk it alone when I heard crunchy footsteps coming through the leaves of the apple trees. My heart skipped a beat and my eyes darted to see if it was Jimmy and if I needed to beat a retreat before he trapped me in the cockpit of the car.

But it was only Ed, who was nearly twice the size of Jimmy and whose fuzzed up tangles at the crown of his head caught the last rays of the day's sunlight. He loped on slow, long legs over to the Model T and climbed in, his long hair swinging over the front of his shoulders as he sat next to me.

"Baby Blondie-Locks, I turn my back on you for two days and you go and grow up and you're parking already!" he exclaimed as he sat back all the way in the seat and stretched out his long legs in his faded, high water jeans. He took a pack of cigarettes out of the front pocket of his plaid wool coat and lit up with a click of his zippo. I watched him as he smoked in silence with his face tilted towards the sky and his eyes shut. His long lashes lay in dark fans on his cheeks.

"Penny for your thoughts, Baby Blondie?" he asked without opening his eyes. He looked tired. He puckered his big lips as he took a drag on his cigarette and still kept his eyes closed.

"I dunno," I said in a small voice. I licked my lips and wondered why people smoked.

His eyes opened with a flash of silver blue and instantly found my own darker ones and held them. Ed smiled out of one side of his lips and gave me his best wistful look.

"Boy troubles?" he asked as he tilted his forehead down at me.

"How did you know?" I felt a flush grow hot on my cheeks and was glad it was coming on dusk and hoping Ed didn't see.

"No one comes out to the T-Bucket less they got the opposite sex on their minds, if you know what I mean." At that he grinned huge and pooched out his lips and rolled his pale blue eyes at me and made me gasp and cover my mouth with my hand. He made me feel like I was out here thinking about things that I should not be thinking about. He ran his hand through the side of his hair and mussed it about and winked at me. I didn't know what to say.

"Spill it, Baby." He leaned back in the squeaky seat and closed his eyes, ready to listen. His hair hung past the front pocket of his wool jacket which lay open and unbuttoned over a brown t-shirt that had red fuzzy letters on it. I couldn't see it all or read what it said.

"Well," I started slowly, and leaned back on my side of the seat and propped my sandaled feet up on the steering wheel and looked up at the sky at the first couple of stars that'd come out, "you know Kai," I trailed off.

"Yes, your true love, besides me of course, that you've been all wrapped around since your first day of school when I scared the dots off Miss Polkadot," Ed said and cracked open his eyes a hair just as I turned towards him. His eyes were like the shine of a flashlight under a crack on the bottom of a door.

"Yes, Kai and I go back years."

"And you're only twelve and you're more monogamous than I've ever been," Ed leaned forward and put his smoke out in the ashtray.

I didn't understand what he said, which was nothing new between Ed and I, and I corrected him, "Ed, I'm only eleven."

"Oh."

"Well anyway," I said and I almost told Ed I loved Kai, but I changed my mind and said, "Kai said he'll come home with me some afternoon if I'll get a ride home for him back out to his house."

"Don't that sound familiar," Ed trailed off and rubbed his lips with his thumb and forefinger and then looked right at me from where he lay back on the seat. "Just any ride?" Ed asked with his big eyebrows furrowed down for a second before the right one shot up on its own.

"No, I couldn't send Kai off in a car with just anyone."

"Of course not. With me and Allen?"

I smiled huge at Ed as my heart leapt and as I lunged across the seat at him without thinking and wrapped my arms around his neck and hugged his head.

"Would you really Ed? Would you really?" I squeezed his head and all that wild hair and kissed him on his part just like Jeffrey and Allen were always doing to me.

"Oh Ed! I love you! Thank you!"

"That's what all the women tell me in the T-Bucket, Baby Blondie-Locks," he smirked as I gave his head another squeeze.

"Oh Ed, I can't wait to tell Kai!" I pushed back from him a ways but I still held on to his shoulders. "I can't wait for Mrs. Small to meet him! I can't wait to bring him out here to see the T-Bucket!"

"Whoa! Whoaaa! Slow the hell down there Fasty-Pants! You're not bringing a boy out to the T-Bucket! For one thing, it's where I bring my action. And for another reason, they'll be none of that going on for, well for, never, Baby Hunnicutt, you got that? NEVER." He rapped his knuckles on my head, but not hard, as I gave his big messy head another squeeze and another kiss to boot.

I sighed and said, "I can't wait till tomorrow." I looked around at the apple trees and dry sunflower heads that were picked clean and heard footsteps coming through the stalks.

"Baby Hunni? Is that you back there?" We heard Jeffrey call from deep in the sunflowers.

"Jesus Christ!" Ed hissed and unwrapped my arms from around his head and pushed me away. He assumed his stretched out position of lying back in the seat with his face tilted back and up towards the sky and his eyes shut and his face slack.

"Baby? What're you doing out here with Ed?"

I didn't know how to answer. Ed made me feel like we'd been caught doing something bad wrong.

"Baby came out here to chew my ear 'bout how she needs new shoes and all her clothes are out of style," Ed sighed like I was a big pain in his behind and took out a smoke. After he lit it, he said without opening his eyes, "Tammy broke off our date so I thought I'd come out here alone and crank up the Model T on my own if you get my drift. But no, Baby Blondie-Locks followed me out here and I haven't had a moment's peace." He cracked his eyes open at Jeffrey.

"Baby," Jeffrey held out his hands, "get out, get out of that, that car. We gotta get you home, get you in the tub," he mumbled as he pulled me through the sunflower stalks.

"BYE ED!" I called over my shoulder. "See you tomorrow! I'll tell Allen!"

"Tell Allen what?" Jeffrey asked as he walked me home. But I was in another world, thinking about my Kai, and didn't hear him.

**

It was when Kai came home with me the next Friday that I became certain I was in love with him. Since neither Ed nor Allen had to work that Friday it was decided we would have Kai over that day after school and also have him join us for dinner. It was Jeffrey's idea that we have a fall bonfire and roast weenies out back by the alley. It was Aunt Clem's idea that we invite my Daddy and Mrs. Small and Petra and the Posts.

Mr. Post agreed to let Petra come since Aunt Clem and my Daddy would be there but as for him and the Mrs. Post, they would pass.

I was excited all day long that Kai was finally going to get to come home with me. We picked up his guitar case in the music room where he'd kept it all day and began our walk home hand in hand. Kai and I smiled at each other as we strolled below the yellow oak trees to Aunt Clem's. Petra who couldn't walk that far was always picked up by Mr. Post and usually on Fridays I rode home with them instead of walking to Mrs. Small's. But this afternoon both twins and Ed would be at our place waiting for Kai and me, so I didn't have to ride with the Post's.

We could see Ed sitting on the porch a half a block away from the house and we could hear him strumming his guitar. When Ed saw us coming he stopped strumming and shaded his eyes in the afternoon sun with his pick hand and whistled a loud clear wolf whistle.

"I'll be damned if it ain't Baby Blondie-Locks with her little hippie boyfriend!" he called as his way of saying hello to Kai and me. I looked at Kai to see how he was reacting to Ed. He'd not been around Ed a whole lot and I didn't want him to be frightened or uneasy. Ed had a way about him that sometimes put people at unease. But Kai squeezed my hand and smiled at me with his big soft brown eyes as we walked up to the porch.

Ed took in Kai, in his worn brown pants and his thick socks and handmade sandals his parents had gotten from one of the Shakespearian actors from their theatre. Ed looked from Kai to me and stuck out his big lips and then looked back at Kai and read his Knickerbocker Beer shirt and sized up his guitar case and cracked a sideways smile at us both.

"Baby Blondie didn't mention that you play the guitar, boy," Ed said and shot his intense pale eyes at me. "What else did you leave out, Baby Blondie? Anything else you're keeping back just for yourself?" he asked as his eyes roamed over my face. He tilted his head down at me and arched his brow just a bit.

I flushed red and embarrassed because Ed made me feel like I was hiding something I shouldn't be. Kai squeezed my hand and then let go of it as he set down his guitar case and took it out.

"Play a couple of songs?" Kai asked Ed as he put the strap over his head and sat down on the step below him.

"Sure. Why not?"

Kai surprised Ed by starting right in on the new Pink Floyd song, *Breathe*.

"Breathe, breathe in the air, don't be afraid to care," Kai sang after he played the intro. He stopped singing and kept strumming. "You know this one?" he asked Ed and tilted his curly head sideways. He strummed some more and waited for Ed to close his mouth and begin playing.

Ed looked at me and asked, "Where the heck you get this one?" And he laughed, "Huh! Ahuh!" and tossed his hair over his shoulders.

I couldn't stop smiling. Kai just kept strumming and playing. He sang the last verse of the song and nodded his head to get Ed to join him but he wouldn't.

"Don't sit down, it's time to dig another one," he sang and nodded his head to get Ed to join him but he didn't.

"You like that?" Kai asked me and began strumming a little something he'd written on his own. "What next? You pick," he said to Ed. "I'll back you up."

Ed grinned and looked shy as he scratched at the dimple on his chin and gazed down at his own big boots and began picking quietly. He looked up and flashed his eyes on mine and then said to Kai, "But I don't sing."

Ed kept picking and Kai began strumming quietly along with him and goosebumps stood out on my arms as they played together.

"Know this one?" Ed asked him.

Kai nodded and began to sing in his light voice, the beautiful and enchanted words to Don Maclean's *Vincent*. He smiled at me over his guitar from where he sat on the step below Ed. I crossed my legs and sat right down on the grass Indian style and gazed at my two favorite people in the world as they played the guitar together.

"Damn, Baby Blondie," Ed said as he pulled out his smokes. "Want one?" he offered the pack out to Kai who frowned.

"Uhh, no thanks. I'm only eleven."

"Only eleven? Jesus, how long you been playing guitar?"

"Oh I don't know. Before kindergarten I had a teeny little one. My parents run a theatre of sorts out in the country, you know." He shrugged and said, "I play all sorts of instruments but guitar is the most normal."

"Huh. Whaddaya know?"

I looked over the tops of both of their heads at Allen who sat behind them on the porch on a kitchen chair cutting up strawberries into a big bowl. He'd sat there the whole time and not said a word, with a cigarette dangling out of his mouth and his blonde curls hanging in wisps out from his ponytail.

They worked on Pink Floyd's *Fearless* together which neither one knew completely, after Ed had his smoke.

"It's open G," Kai instructed Ed.

"Oh I see, I see," Ed corrected his tuning and started back in. Kai knew all the words and sang as they tried to figure out the chords.

That night I sat between Kai and Petra as the sun sank and felt a happy fullness that had nothing to do with the three hotdogs I had eaten at the encouragement of Jeffrey, Allen, Ed, and Kai who were on a mission to see who could eat the most. Ed was still roasting them and chomping them down long after the twins had quit.

"Come on boy! Keep up with me!" He egged Kai on, as he pulled two more dogs off his roasting fork. "I'm just getting warmed up!" he ate his two dogs, one in each hand, at the same time.

I looked past Kai to watch Ed eat and saw that at some time in the evening he'd kicked his hiking boots off and peeled off his socks and now sat there with his huge feet sticking out of his too-small jeans. His ankles looked large and knobby and his feet were hairy. He'll have his shirt off next whether it's autumn or not, I thought to myself and began to laugh.

"What? What?" Ed asked and pooched out his lips and made the hurt face as he pulled his shirt up to reveal his now distended stomach, which sent me into fits of giggles because I thought for sure he was going to take off his shirt.

"Goddamn!" he hollered and smacked his round belly. "I think I'm finally full!"

I looked over at Petra to see that she was staring at Ed with her black little eyes and licking her lips.

"If you're done, let's play some more," Kai said to him in his light voice.

When Kai and Ed were tuning up and warming up on their guitars, the twins snuck out a big bag of BBQ chips and shared them between themselves when Ed wasn't looking. Jeffrey looked at me over the fire and put his finger to his lips and opened his eyes wide to me and smiled. He was trying to grow a mustache and it was just starting to come in but it looked like it was going to be auburn and not blonde like the rest of his hair. I smiled at him and Allen as they shared their chips.

Kai leaned over and had a hushed conversation with Ed behind his hand and it pleased me that he wasn't afraid of him and that he felt enough camaraderie to conspire with Ed already.

"You do the pickin'," I heard him say, "it goes like this," Kai demonstrated on his own guitar. "Your fingers are longer, and I'll do the strumming and sing it, ok?"

"Ok, ok, is this the progression?" Ed asked as he flung his long hair back over his shoulder and concentrated on his fingers with his eyebrows knitted down.

"That's it, can you remember it?"

"Got it."

They began playing a quiet song Kai knew but Ed had never heard.

"Where's this from?" Ed asked.

"A movie soundtrack they did a few years ago. My parents have the album. The Song is called *Green is the Colour*"

Ed began picking the melody of a light, quiet, lilting song and Kai came in strumming and nodding his head in time and singing, "Heavy hung the canopy of blue/shade my eyes and I can see you/white is the light that shines through the dress that you wore..." Kai sang as pure as an angel and looked right at me.

My face burned with heat and I was thankful for the dark so that no one could see how embarrassed I was. I looked around at everyone around the fire to see them all watching me and smiling at me. Even my Daddy with his flat top and his flannel shirt buttoned up all the way smiled at me.

When Daddy first came over I was afraid that he was going to be unfriendly or brusque with Kai but he only looked uncomfortable with Kai's unusual name and didn't even say anything about him needing to cut his hair.

After Kai and Ed played several songs and after Kai finally gave up trying to get Ed to sing, the twins brought out marshmallows and we all watched with wonder while Ed and Kai both roasted four at a time and ate them all at once too.

They both had sticky, white mustaches and both were having giggle fits over things none of us were privy to. Ed got up and almost tripped over Allen's lawn chair with his long legs as he went to get his guitar and almost fell in the fire.

"Shit mother eff!" he yelled in his way of correcting his swear.

"ED!" Mrs. Small, Aunt Clem, and the twins all yelled at once. I heard my Daddy clear his throat from where he sat between Aunt Clem and Mrs. Small but he didn't say anything.

"Huh! Ahuh!" Ed guffawed as he found his seat and sat down with his guitar next to Kai who was also howling at the incident and acting more rowdy than I'd ever seen him. As a matter of fact, Kai was cooking more marshmallows.

Ed began strumming the song Kai had taught him earlier and sang a snippet from it, "Green is the colour of her kind/quickness of the eye deceives the mind/many is the bond between the hopeful and the damned…" he sang and looked up with his silvery eyes past Kai and right at me. "I'll be singing that for days now, Baby Blondie," he smiled and blinked a few times and stopped strumming to pull a strand of hair out his eyes. "It's a beautiful song, isn't it?"

Kai turned and smiled at me and said, "Yes, it is," and I saw the firelight dance on his liquid brown eyes and that was when I knew I loved him.

Not too much later Jeffrey, Allen, and Ed took Kai home in Aunt Clem's big, green car, but Daddy wouldn't let me go too.

"It's late Baby and you don't need out driving around hell and back with a car full of boys," he said as he shot a hard look at the back of Ed's head as he gathered up his socks and shoes.

Daddy shook Kai's hand and said it was nice to meet him and then he waited till they all drove off before leaving himself and taking Mrs. Small with him. Aunt Clem walked Petra home and I sat down in Kai's chair next to the embers that were still glowing in the fire ring. For once I felt like Petra and wished to be grown up already. I felt like I couldn't wait a minute to be an adult. I wanted to marry Kai right then and there in front of God and the entire world and tell everyone this was the one I would love forever.

CHAPTER EIGHT

As had become tradition, the twins walked me over to my Daddy's the Wednesday night before Thanksgiving. The memories of my Mama in that house were fading fast from lack of me never being in there anymore. I didn't know whether I should be relieved the painful memories were vanishing from my mind or if I should feel guilty for not trying to hold onto them harder. For now it was just painful to think I was so seldom invited back to my own home. It was painful that Daddy had never offered me any of Mama's things to remember her by and I didn't even have a picture of her. The twins walked me over with a feeling of duty on their part and mine.

"This is ridiculous," Allen grumbled as he flicked his cigarette butt across the street. His hair was a curly blonde halo against the street light when I looked up at him. He was growing a beard and it had come in thick and blonde whereas Jeffrey's mustache and goatee were russet red.

Allen had his thick locks secured in a pony-tail with curly wisps flying about and springing loose while Jeffrey had gotten his hair cut above his ears and had parted it on the side. His shorn blonde curls made him look even taller than he was and somehow made his neck look exposed and vulnerable. He now looked years younger than his shorter, stouter twin. I looked over at Jeffrey to see him stroking his goatee and deep in thought. Both boys had on Navy surplus pea coats they had bought second hand from the gun show that had camped outside town a couple of weeks ago.

"I'm not wearing any Army shit till they draft my sorry ass and force me!" Ed had said at the time.

Now standing in front of Ed's house, Allen turned to me and complained, "I don't see why you can't just have Thanksgiving with us, Baby Hunni. For cryin' out loud, you live with us!"

"Kai wants me to come out to his place for a bit tomorrow, too. Maybe I can get one of the cousins to take me out there," I mused.

"What the hell? Baby? We're your cousins! If anyone sneaks you out of town to your boyfriend it'll be us, not those squares!" Allen growled as he pointed his finger at me. The three of us didn't move from in front of Ed's. I didn't want to go to my Daddy's. I looked to see Ed in his front yard throwing the football as hard as he could straight up in the air and catching it with a grunt and a puff of vapor as he breathed out in the cold evening.

"What's cookin' kiddoes?" he asked as he trotted over to us, his long hair flipping around to the front of his jacket. He'd washed it for the holiday and it was actually shiny from cleanliness instead of from grease.

"Sneakin' Baby out of her Daddy's tomorrow and piloting her away to her lover's out in the country," Jeffrey said as he lit a smoke and grinned.

"You in?" Allen asked Ed with hawk-like fierceness.

Ed looked me up and down and wrinkled his wide forehead at me for a second.

"Fuck yeh, count me in. We need the ladder or the big ass net?" he asked with mock seriousness.

"You guys!" I smacked Allen on his arm. "You don't have to sneak me out. I'm not a captive for cryin' out loud. And he's not my lover!" I blushed and smacked Jeffrey on his arm.

"Yeh, she's only twelve," Ed curled his lips up on one corner, "she can't take a lover till she's thirteen. Huh! Ahuh!" he rolled his big lips back over his teeth and brayed out at me and then reached over and pinched me hard on the cheek. I smacked his hand but ended up hurting my finger on his knuckles.

"Oww!" I howled and rubbed my cheek where he pinched me and sucked on the soft underside of my ring finger. "You broke my finger with your big boney old hand!"

"Baby's eleven, you wet rag, not twelve," Allen corrected Ed and ignored my injuries. "Get it right, cottonhead," he said and took a swing at Ed.

"Give me a smoke and tell me the plan for springing this chicken from the coop. Will there be any sweet Hunnicutt cousins I can score while we're over there?" Ed wrinkled his nose and sniffed back snot and took a cigarette from Jeffrey.

We still stood on the walk in front of Ed's house. I wasn't eager to go to my Daddy's. It was much more repressive than Aunt Clem's and I just didn't feel welcome in my old home anymore. I wanted to go back to Aunt Clem's which was my home now. I wanted to spend Thanksgiving at Mrs. Small's with her and Ed and the twins. I was also looking forward to going to Kai's and hadn't planned out how I was going to get Daddy to let me go. Aunt Clem would let me go in a heartbeat and probably have the twins take me out there.

"So Baby, here's the plan. Ed will cause a diversion of the loud and rude kind around two when they're all watching football and we'll squirrel you out of there. They'll toss Ed out on his ear and we'll be off to your hippie boyfriend's. Sound good?" Allen asked.

"Kai's not a hippie," I said and tossed my hair over my shoulder. I felt cranky and was tired of being under everyone else's control.

"Huh! Ahuh! That's funny, Baby," Ed laughed and grabbed me in a head lock and began dutch rubbing my scalp without warning.

"ED!" I hollered as I tried to break away. "You're hurting me and you're messing up my hair!"

He had me stretched up on my tip toes with my head tucked up under his armpit as he ran his knuckles over the top of my head.

"My hair!" I hollered and tried to protect my scalp. I felt him pop open my barrette and take it out. He mussed my hair up more and then he let me go and I nearly fell.

"Seriously, Ed," I heard Allen say but I couldn't see him because all my hair covered my face. "Seriously, Ed, Baby is getting too big for you to manhandle. She's gonna whup your ass a good one someday!" Allen jeered and I heard them scuffle as I tried to re-part my hair on the side.

"Give me my barrette back you big, hairy, jerk!" I advanced on Ed with my fists clenched and my teeth bared. He held it up high above me and made me jump for it and then shoved it in the front pocket of his pants. "Huh! Ahuh huh huh!" he laughed and backed away.

"Don't make me come take it! You already have 100's of my barrettes, Ed Small!"

"Ed Small, you're in trouble now, boy!" Allen laughed.

Now I was beyond mad because I was going to show up at my Daddy's all red faced and wild haired and he was going to lecture me and threaten to cut my hair and go on and on.

I moved closer to Ed with my hands contorted into claws. He was dancing around in his tight jeans and his red and green plaid wool coat with his clean hair flying around. His eyes were silver in the streetlight and he was pooching his big lips at me and taunting me to come take my barrette.

I ran at him with a wild shriek with my teeth bared and my long blond hair flying out behind me.

"What's she gonna do, Allen? She's scarin' me! Little Baby Blondie Hell-Cat!" Ed shrieked and tried to duck away from me as I reached out and grabbed his sleeve and pushed it up with one hand and yanked a handful of short armhair out by the roots with the other hand.

"Ahh! Jesus! Shit mother fuck!" he hollered and backed away from me, rubbing his wrist. "Here," he worked his fingers in his front pocket and pulled out my barrette, "here, come get it!" he hollered and threw it as hard as he could into the dark yard just as I reached for it.

"You fuck! Ed Small!" was all I could yell, I was so furious. I spat in the grass at his feet.

"Such language from such an angelic child," Ed smirked at me and then he reached out with his big hand and mussed my hair up again and shoved my head back roughly.

I turned on my heel frustrated and upset and clomped off to my Daddy's with my teeth clenched and my hair a mess.

"Oh no," Allen said darkly.

"Ed Small," Jeffrey clapped Ed on the back, "you are in one shit heap of trouble, boy."

"What?" I heard him ask just as I reached my Daddy's walkway.

"She's off to tell her Daddy. You better run boy!"

When Daddy answered the door I stood there not looking at his face, with my hair wild and tears in my eyes. My cheek hurt and my finger hurt and most of all my pride was stung.

"Baby! What the heck happened?"

I clenched my jaw and didn't answer. He opened the screen and instead of going in, I stepped back on the porch. He came out on the porch and stroked my wild hair and touched me on the cheek where Ed had pinched me.

"What happened?"

My eyes slitted and turned toward Ed's yard. I was mad and I was hurt and I wanted my Daddy to get involved. We could see the twins and Ed still standing in Ed's yard.

"Oh fuck." We heard Ed say in the dark clear from our yard.

Daddy grabbed my arm and strode over there in his steel toed work shoes, with his finger already out and pointing like a loaded gun.

"Who did this to Baby? Who?" he demanded.

"I did." Ed stepped forward without hesitation and stared at my Daddy with his icy blue eyes. He had more grit in him than I ever figured, speaking up to my Daddy.

"I did," Ed repeated. "I played too rough with Baby-Blondie and I hurt her and I'm sorry." Ed had his hands in his pockets of his plaid wool coat and he looked right at my Daddy without flinching. I focused on the dimple in Ed's chin and thought about how good it would feel to sock him right there but his big bony face would probably break my hand.

"You. Of course it was you. You. Keep. Your. Mitts. Off. My. Baby," my Daddy shook his finger on each word as he commanded Ed through his tight thin lips. "If you so much as make one mark on her ever again, so help me God, I'll get you down and shave that head and have you shipped off to Nam before you know what hit you. Got it, boy?"

I saw Ed's nostrils flare and his muscles twitch in his jaw. He didn't answer except to narrow his eyes and glare right at my Daddy.

"And where were you two while this was going on?" Daddy asked the twins. "You're supposed to be protecting her."

"We do. We have. Every day for nearly four years. Where've you been?" Allen asked through his clenched teeth and reached over and took my hand and pulled me away. "She won't be over tomorrow, *Uncle* Fitz. She'll be at the Small's with us if you want to come over for pie in the afternoon and have a visit." And with that Allen gathered me in front of him and wrapped his arm around my shoulders. Ed was still glaring at my daddy. I was worried something bad was going to happen; that Daddy was going to punch Ed or worse; that Daddy was going to take me away from Aunt Clementine forever.

We all stood there silent, waiting, for my Daddy to object or explode. Allen stroked my wild hair back down to its normal state and Jeffrey came and stood next to me. Ed still had his cold eyes locked on my Daddy's flinty ones.

"So, will you come over for some coffee and pie tomorrow afternoon, Uncle Fitz?" Jeffrey asked pleasantly.

Daddy looked long at me as I stood with Allen's arm around me from behind.

"That what you want, Baby?"

No, it wasn't what I wanted. What I wanted was for my Mama to never have died. What I wanted was for Daddy to slap Ed for roughing me up and taking advantage of me. I wanted him to get on Allen for not rescuing me from Ed. But I also wanted to spend Thanksgiving with Aunt Clem and the twins and Mrs. Small and even with Ed too, so long as he didn't play so rough.

It was like Ed read my mind for just as I was mulling it all over of what I wanted, he reached over and touched my cheek with the pad of his thumb right where he'd pinched me.

"I really am sorry Baby," Ed said squinting his right eye at me and his mouth twisted up on that side, "you forgive me?"

"I dunno," I whispered and turned away from him as Allen pulled me closer.

"Baby?" my Daddy asked. "What do you want?"

I was taken aback by that because he'd never before asked me that about anything. I knew I needed to take this chance to answer truthfully because who knew when he'd ask how I felt about anything ever again.

"I want to go to Mrs. Small's. And I want you to come over for pie. Or have all of us over to your place for pie." I looked at him and took in how slack his face looked, how scraped clean his cheeks were from his shaving them so close every day. I looked up at his blonde flat-top and how exact it was cut and shaped without one hair out of place.

"Ok Daddy?"

"Ok Baby. If it's what you want. I'll miss you tomorrow."

"I miss you now, Daddy."

With that Allen pulled me away and we went into Ed's and all sat down in the living-room. We were all stunned and quiet.

"Where's your mom?" Allen asked.

"Bingo. Church," Ed answered as he flopped next to me on the couch. Allen sat on my other side and Jeffrey sat on the floor. We watched tv for a while but I didn't pay attention. I was busy thinking and trying to figure out what was missing from my life when I seemed to have so much. I was brought out of my reverie by Caesar the great black and grey tabby cat jumping up on my lap and curling up on me.

"Whoaa, Devil Cat has roosted on Baby Hell-Cat," Ed said as he struggled to pull something out of the front pocket of his tight jeans. I refused to look at him or pay attention to him as he gently pulled my hair to the side and fastened my barrette back in.

"I didn't really toss it Baby Blondie-Locks."

I looked up at him as he looked down at me.

"I faked it," he murmured as his eyebrow shot up and he grinned at me.

Without looking away from his eyes, I reached down and yanked out a couple of his arm hairs and grinned back at him as he howled out in pain.

***

"Baby Blondie Hunnicutt! You little handful from hell!" Ed yelled at me as he wiped the slush ball out of his eyes. He spent several tries to get all of it out of his eyes and all of his wet hair off his lashes.

"If you ever spent time at your own home you wouldn't have to put up with me!" I taunted and lobbed another loose slush ball at his head. This one hit him in the neck and slid down in his shirt and his eyes popped open. He looked a little crazy with ice hanging off his lashes and slush sliding down his long hair.

"Quick! Grab the soap! Ed's taking a bath!" Allen jeered as he ran past and Ed and pounded him in the chest with a rock hard ice ball.

It was Christmas Eve and we were making the most of the snow before it melted. The tv was predicting record warm temperatures for Christmas and at the last minute we were sad to see it melt.

"Bing Crosby will be crying his eyes out all day tomorrow if this melts," Jeffrey joked later as he made hot cocoa for us at the stove. He had his pet mouse in his pajama shirt pocket and it was sniffing and twitching its nose at the good chocolatey smell.

It was nearly midnight and we were starting a new tradition of celebrating Christmas at midnight with Aunt Clem and of course Ed couldn't be left out. I would be going to my Daddy's first thing in the morning to celebrate with him and then we were going out to Aunt Frances' for the huge Christmas dinner.

I knew the twins just wanted to keep me up late so they could speculate on how I would take my crankiness out on everyone around me at the Hunnicutt Christmas.

"Jeffrey! Make this kid some coffee!" Allen teased and slapped me lightly on the back where I sat with my head on the kitchen table.

"And let's teach her to smoke!" Ed grinned as he lit a cigarette and kicked back on the rear legs of his chair.

"I must be out of my mind to let you kids talk me into this," Aunt Clem complained as she padded through the kitchen in her robe and slippers with her platinum hair done up in pin curls.

"Ed, we should have had your mother over."

"Mrs. Rawlins it's much too late for Mom. Don't worry about her."

"Almost midnight!" Allen cried and pointed at the clock.

Jeffrey put on the big Christmas hot pad and poured cocoa in everyone's mugs as Allen counted down, "10, 9, 8, 7…"

"Merry Christmas!" we all yelled and I got hugged and kissed by everyone.

"Baby Hunni, you make Christmas fun," Aunt Clem gave me an extra hug. "It's not Christmas without little kids around.

"Aww she ain't that little anymore and she don't even believe in Santa anymore," Allen complained.

"That's cuz Jeffrey ruined it last year when he couldn't keep quiet and woke her up," Ed smirked and smacked Jeffrey as he walked back with the empty sauce pot.

Christmas was a little different ever since I caught them all wrapping my presents and watching tv the last year and discovered there wasn't a Santa. It took away the magic and the mystery.

"Awww hell, don't be sad," Ed sighed and winked at me and then looked around the table, "she still believes in Jesus! Huh! Ahuh!"

"Don't blaspheme!" Aunt Clem whacked him.

We had our cocoa and then exchanged gifts in the living room in front of the tree the boys had gotten from Kai's parents' land. It had been a magical night going out there to pick it out. His parents invited me out to pick out a tree off their property so of course the twins and Ed had taken me one night when neither Ed nor Allen had to work. As the twins and Ed ran through the forest in the snow, arguing over trees, Kai had pulled me aside.

"Baby, come here a minute," he called to me as he pulled me behind a fat pine tree. "I have something for you. Your Christmas present early," he sounded out of breath. I looked in his big brown eyes and saw flecks of gold in them and saw that they danced with excitement. A smile played on his small red mouth and his big brown curls blew on the wind around his collar.

"Baby," he said barely above a whisper as he pulled me towards him by my mittened hand and then he pulled my mitten completely off and stuck it in his coat pocket. He pulled a small white box from his other pocket. My eyes opened up all the way when I saw that tiny little white box and I had to cover my mouth to keep from crying out. I didn't want Ed and the twins to ruin this moment.

"Baby," Kai said again as his warm hand held my bare hand, "I have something special for you," and he pulled me closer and kissed me on the mouth. It was just a quick kiss on the lips but it was my first. When Kai backed away my eyes were still closed and I still felt the burn of his lips on mine.

"Here Baby, Merry Christmas," he said in his light, mellow voice.

I swallowed hard, and as the snowflakes accumulated in my hair and on my eyelashes I opened it. Nestled in the green silk in the small box was a tiny, gold ring with a circle on the band with a tiny, but real four leaf clover captured under a protective crystal of some sort, like a watch face, to keep the clover safe forever.

"Do you like it?" he asked.

"Ohh Kai, I love it!" I breathed out. I slid it out of its little nest in the box and put it on the ring finger of my left hand.

"It's perfect!" I gushed.

"You'll always have the luck of the Irish now, wherever you go," he smiled at me.

I threw my arms around Kai in his corduroy coat and kissed him on his lips. I was so happy and loved him so much, I didn't know what to say. I felt him run his hands through my hair that ran down my back as we held the kiss longer this time.

"Whoa! Whoa, whoa, whoa! Whoa there Little Miss Fasty-Pants!" we heard Ed holler as he came trotting around the tree we were behind. "Allen! Jeffrey! Better get over here!" Ed called behind him. He had a hacksaw in his hands and he waved it at Kai and grinned. "Whaddaya think you're doing with my own true love-child there, boy?" he asked Kai and laughed his big laugh up at the sky.

It had been a great night picking out the tree and getting my first kiss and my second kiss for that matter, not to mention the little gold clover ring melted my heart.

Ed took the mickey out of me all the way back into town about me being a worldy woman and working my wiles on Kai to get him to buy me trinkets.

Now here we were in Aunt Clem's living room, in front of the fat pine Kai had kissed me behind and Aunt Clem had decorated with little red and white striped elves all over it.

"Creepy little fucks," Ed said to me out of the side of his mouth as he flicked one with his big forefinger, knocking it completely off the branch. "Oww!" he howled, "they're solid wood!"

When presents were passed out the twins and Ed presented me with a small box that was a little bigger than the one Kai had given me. They were all three grinning at me. Jeffrey's face was completely scarlet as he smiled and said, "Open it Baby, open it, and see if you like it!"

I did. It was a small gold necklace with three hearts on a chain. One big heart and two small ones.

"Look closer, Baby," Allen told me. I looked up to see Aunt Clem had tears in her eyes and was dabbing at them with a tissue she pulled from her sleeve. I looked closer back at the hearts to see the big one had "Baby" engraved on it.

"Turn it over," Ed grinned and opened his eyes wide at me as he slurped his cocoa and had a mustache of it above his big lips.

On the back it said, "Ed".

"What?" I asked and I turned the other two hearts over and one said "Jeffrey" and the other said, "Allen".

"I wanted them to put 'Baby Blondie-Locks Fasty-Pants Hell-Cat' on a heart for you but they wouldn't. Of course. Never let me have any fun," Ed pouted and winked at me. He had several days of beard growth on his chin but I could still see his dimple and I reached out and flicked him in it.

***

The New Year brought with it many new changes; none of them I liked. The last day of Christmas vacation found us all in the living room of Aunt Clem's watching some teenager show called American Bandstand. Petra was always telling me I was so lucky to live with the twins who were like overgrown teenagers. Jeffrey still didn't work while Allen still worked at Cloyd's where he'd worked since he was fourteen. Ed had gotten fired at Christmastime because he refused to work New Year's Eve.

Petra thought I was lucky to be exposed to all the grown-up adventures of the boys but she was way wrong because I was never exposed to anything. Case in point: we were watching a bunch of slick looking people gyrate around a big dance floor on American Bandstand with the camera swooping in on them at the unlikeliest angles and Ed had his face pretty much plastered right to the screen with his butt sticking out in the air for the world to have to look at.

"I don't think any of them womens got any under-britches on!" he exclaimed as a girl twirled around.

"Ed, for crying out loud, not in front of Baby. She's just a kid."

If I had a nickel every time the twins or even Ed said, "Not in front of Baby, she's just a kid," I'd be a millionaire and I could move out on my own.

Ed turned his head around to look at me. "What?" he asked and pulled his hair out of his eyes. "What'd I do?" he asked as I snarled at him.

"All you ever do is look at women. Don't you ever stop?"

"That's the problem. All I do is look these days! If I don't end this dry spell my hair's gonna fall plum out of my head," he despaired to me and pulled a hurt face.

"And take root on your hand!" Allen cracked and kicked Ed in his butt.

"Not in front of Baby, guys. She's just a kid!" Jeffrey shot a look at me to see if I understood what they were talking about.

I was fed up with all three of them. Christmas break cooped up in the little house with the three of them was too much. I went and lay face-down on my bed.

They got even rowdier in the living-room after I left. They were probably glad I was gone so they could say all the nasty things they held back on when I was around. But then it got quiet. I heard the front door open and close. And then there was complete silence.

I tiptoed out to see what happened and found the three of them standing in a circle in front of the tv where teenagers were still dancing while Dick Clark spun disco records. Ed had his mouth wide open and was gaping from one twin to the other with his hair in his eyes. Jeffrey looked like he was going to faint dead away. Allen turned around to face me with a look of such seriousness I thought someone must have died.

"What?" I whispered. "What happened?"

"Shit mother fuck," Ed hissed. "They're not taking me." And he started for the door. "I ain't goin', I tell ya," he said as he flew out the door.

"Come back and let us know if you got yours!" Allen called out after him.

"What? What?" I began to panic. "What's wrong?" My voice wavered in time to my speeding heart.

Allen waved a white piece of paper he had in his hand at me. "We got drafted. Jeffrey and me. We gotta report to the draft in thirty days," he swallowed hard, "We're going to Vietnam."

Jeffrey's eyes were wide open and fixed in one spot as he sat down on the edge of the couch.

"No," was all he said as one tear leaked out of his eye.

I looked back at Allen, waiting to hear his plan of how he would fix it.

"Allen?" I asked him as he just stood there with his arms hanging limp by his side. "Allen? You can't go, I won't let them take you."

I ran to him and wrapped my arms around him. He held me on his lap the rest of the afternoon as if I were six again and as I cried for hours. Ed came back and Jeffrey and he sat on the couch and chain smoked and none of us talked. Ed hadn't gotten a draft letter but he looked like he was heading for the gallows all the same.

"Just a matter of days till I get mine. Probably tomorrow. At least we can all three ship out together," Ed said as he wiped at the corners of his eyes.

I cried every day, for at least part of the day, for the next two weeks. I cried at school when Jimmy Collins groped my back looking for a bra strap to snap and he got detention for five nights.

I cried when I went to Mrs. Small's after school and watched Ed wait on the mailman for the draft letter that never came. I ached inside so much so that I begged Aunt Clem to let me stay home the second Friday in January.

"You should let me stay home the rest of the month because I may never get to see the twins again," I pleaded with her before she went to work.

"Jeffrey, Allen, take care of Baby and for cryin' out loud, make Ed behave and leave her alone. And do what you can to cheer that child up. She didn't cry this much when her Mama passed."

"Yes Ma, we will Ma," the twins answered.

"Be double sure Ed doesn't do anything to upset her," I heard Aunt Clem say one more time before she left. "Something's plum wrong with our little Baby," she said and I heard the door shut.

I lay in my bed in a ball and I ached throughout my sides. I felt a great pain yawning inside me. I had a headache and felt crabbier than I'd ever felt in my life. It felt like my life was crumbling apart.

"Baby," I heard the door creak open and Jeffrey come in. "Baby, can I make you tea or fill the tub for you?" He came and sat down on the rag rug next to my bed. "Baby, Allen and I will be ok. The war is nearly over and by the time they get all Allen's hair shaved off and get us trained up, the dang war will be over and we'll be back home. I promise." He stroked my hair and sighed.

I gave what he said some thought and sat up.

"Nice hot bath?" he asked and smiled.

I just nodded but said, "I can do it."

But after going to the toilet I was hollering for him to come in there and then I hollered, "Don't come in! I don't have pants on! Something's wrong! Something's happened!"

I knew what it was for Petra had told me all about it a couple of months earlier.

"In like two years we'll get our periods and we'll have to keep it a secret from the boys because once they know, it makes them go crazy." She told me as she showed me the boxes of feminine products she had stashed in her closet.

"Why'd you buy these if it's not for years?"

"I want to be ready. And I'll probably get mine earlier because I'm much more mature. You probably won't get yours till you're thirteen or even fourteen."

"I'm bigger than you."

"I can't help being small. It's my muscular dystrophy. See my hands?" And she held her olive toned hand next to my fair one and her hands were quite a bit larger than mine and so was her face. Maybe she was right. I hoped she was because I never wanted my period, ever. Especially if it brought with it all the unpleasantness Petra warned me of.

"You'll grow boobs overnight! And they'll ache and hurt if anything at all touches them," she warned as she cracked her Dentyne at me.

"What would touch them?" I asked in a panic.

"Everything does, Baby. They stick right out and everyone bumps them and boys grab them and your clothes rub them."

I looked at her horrified.

"And when you get your period you have to wear one of these." She showed me a big white pad that looked like a giant bandage for a head-wound. "AND you have to carry these around at school and put fresh ones on as the old ones fill up with blood."

"WHAT?" I asked and felt the thick pad between my fingers. "How am I supposed to walk around with that between my legs?"

"AND after you get your period you'll have to watch what you do with Kai because THEN you can make a baby!" Petra's eyes were swirling with madness.

"This is nuts," I told her and I left and went back to Aunt Clem's.

"Don't worry, Baby, you won't get yours forever! You're too immature!" she called out to me as I ran across the road to Aunt Clem's.

But Petra was way wrong for here I stood in the bathroom with an ache in my side and blood running down my legs.

"What do I do, Jeffrey?" I called through the door as I wadded up toilet paper to stop the blood from dripping on the white tile.

"I don't know Baby! What's happening in there?" He sounded as scared and panicked as I felt. He turned the knob this way and that but I had locked it.

"Don't come in!" I shrieked.

"Tell me what's going on in there, Baby!"

"I'm bleeding!"

"Jesus Christ! Baby, open this door!" I heard Allen as he pounded on the door.

"Allen," Jeffrey said to him, "I think we need Ma. I think it's a woman thing."

"Baby," Allen said slowly.

"What?"

"Did you get hurt?"

"No."

"Do you know what's happening?"

"Sort of," I said and had trouble putting much volume in my answer.

"I'm going to get Ma on the phone. You get in the tub and take a bath and try to relax till I get her. Ok?"

"Ok."

I did just that but the twins weren't able to get Aunt Clem on the phone at the denture lab.

"Get Mrs. Small," I heard Jeffrey tell Allen.

"We're getting Mrs. Small," Jeffrey called to me through the door and I was glad because the bathwater was getting cold. I got out and put a dry wash cloth between my legs, wrapped my hair up in the one pink towel we had, and wrapped my body up in the Scooby Doo towel and went and sat on my bed.

But it wasn't Mrs. Small that came over.

It was Ed.

"What's he doing here?" I hollered, with mounting hysteria at the sight of Ed in his "I Heart My eddy Bear" shirt that he'd ripped the T off of. Ed with his long hair that hadn't been touched by a brush in days. Ed in his tight faded jeans and his big clunky boots. Ed who looked at women constantly and chased women constantly was the last person I wanted over here during my personal catastrophe. He just stared at me with his mouth in a pout and his eyes looking confused as I pulled the towel around me tighter.

"Ed knows women," Allen stated and shrugged. "He's the only one we could get to come help who knows women."

"But I'm not a woman!" I howled and wanted to die. I pulled my pink towel down off my head and covered my face with it and peeked out at him.

"Here," was all Ed said as he handed me a powder blue box and when I didn't reach for it, he just set it on the bed next to me. "You're a woman now, kiddo," he said with his face grim and backed out of the room and shut the door.

The doctor told Aunt Clem it was the stress of the boys being drafted that sent me into early puberty. That word itself scared the hair off my head, as Ed would say. It was like being at the top of a long slide you couldn't see the bottom of and being given a big ol' shove at the top when you weren't ready.

"Let's keep this between us, Baby. No need for your Daddy to worry, ok?" Aunt Clem said to me when we came home from the doctor's.

And I agreed with her.

***

When the twins got called for the draft we found out Jeffrey was E4. The Army physical turned up that he had the same heart defect as my Mama and he was told to not do anything strenuous. He was also told by the Army doc to not smoke anymore but he still did.

At the end of January, we said goodbye to Allen at the train as he went off to boot camp with his gold curls clipped off short. Jeffrey, Aunt Clem, and I cried and were inconsolable. Ed stared off into space with his watery, pale eyes and his lips drawn down and his hair a wild mess and didn't talk to any of us. He had to pry me off Allen's neck where I clung for dear life, crying into Allen's collar and touching his shorn head, because Jeffrey didn't have the heart to pry me away from my Allen. Ed had to carry me, wrapped around *his* neck because I couldn't walk away from Allen on the platform.

Daddy came with us to the train station too and couldn't have been prouder of Allen if he'd been his own son. Daddy hugged Allen twice and shook his hand several times too.

"I'm so proud of you today," Daddy told him. Allen just looked serious and tight-lipped. He already looked like a soldier and not like my Allen, my protector.

"I love you, Allen!" I called to him as Ed carried me off, and my face crumpled in sobs and I wrapped my fingers in Ed's hair and cried in great gasps into his wool coat. I looked up to see Jeffrey hug his brother goodbye even longer than Aunt Clementine did and then Ed turned the corner and crossed the street and left the train station with me in his arms. He carried me all the way home, to Aunt Clem's by side streets. I guess he didn't want to be in a car with them right then. I was much too big to be carried like that, but I let him. That day I let him.

We had said our goodbyes and it was harder for me than saying goodbye to my own Mama. I had known Allen longer than I had gotten to live with her and part of me felt guilty for having gotten to know Allen better than I knew my own Mama, though I couldn't explain why that was my fault.

We said a prayer that God would keep our Allen safe in Vietnam. I am sure that Mrs. Small said a prayer of thanks that her Ed didn't get called.

CHAPTER NINE

I think Jeffrey would have had a complete nervous breakdown after Allen went "in country" if it weren't for Ed. The rest of that winter and the spring too, Ed came over on a regular basis and got Jeffrey out of bed and spent time with him. Whether it was just sitting on the couch talking or taking him fishing or taking him out for beers after they turned 21, Ed did what he could to make sure Jeffrey didn't just fall apart.

I was glad when summer came and I was more glad that Ed showed up everyday like clockwork at noon to wake Jeffrey and make him get dressed. It was Ed that rounded us up to go out to the Rush /La Rue pool just like old times and it was Ed who drove us out there. Jeffrey, for some odd reason could not bring himself to drive out of town. As a matter of fact, I could have counted on one hand the number of times I had seen Jeffrey drive at all since I'd moved in with Aunt Clem when I was six.

It was Ed that drove us out there to the pool in Mrs. Small's black '69 Cutlass that was so fast I had to belt myself in the backseat to keep from being tossed around by Ed's wild driving. He cranked the Pink Floyd and blasted our way down the county black top to the pool pretty much every day.

I loved going out to the pool with the boys though Allen's absence was constantly obvious. None of us talked about him or reminisced about him though reminders of him and the things we had done together were everywhere. We didn't want to talk about him like he was already dead. We knew he was ok for he wrote home every week to tell us that he worked in the mess tent as a cook and that he hadn't seen any fighting. He wrote home to ask for paperbacks and Aunt Clem and Jeffrey packed up several boxes to send while he was over there. Ed always threw in a few magazines of naked women too. I always put in bags of hard candy from Cloyd's. Mr. Cloyd never charged me for them because he knew they were going to Allen.

Going to the pool everyday with Ed and Jeffrey got me away from the influence of Petra who was still filling my head with tidbits of things I didn't want to know about yet. It also gave me a chance to hang out with Kai, something I didn't get enough of during school time.

Kai's house and his parents land and their Prairie Shakespeare Theatre which was the open air theatre that held plays and musical festivals was just a few miles from the pool. He biked down the black top nearly every day that summer to meet up with me at the pool. He wasn't like Jimmy Collins who was always trying to grab me now that my body had started to change. Kai was still sweet and quiet and funny and was never grabby, even when he kissed me, which he did more often these days.

Jeffrey gradually came out of his sad trance. I think it was Jimmy Collins who brought him out of it. I can only recall my cousin Jeffrey getting rough with a person one time in my life and that was with Jimmy at the pool the summer I was eleven, the summer Allen was in Vietnam. Jimmy grabbed the tie to my bikini as I walked past him with Kai. I was eating an ice cream cone and carrying a coke as Kai and I walked back to our seats at the pool. Jimmy reached out and pulled the tie to my top till it came undone. I dropped my Coke to keep my top from falling off.

 Jeffrey saw it happen and grabbed little Jimmy Collins, snot nosed son of a bitch and not so harmless toss pot toe rag and slammed his forehead into the metal pole of the big umbrella hard enough to make it reverberate with a resonating CLANG.

 The other thing that helped bring Jeffrey out his sad state was when Ed, bless his heart, introduced Jeffrey to Lisa. Lisa with her jet black, kinky hair that was as long as mine, looked like an Egyptian queen as she sat next to Jeffrey and got a tan. You can bet that Jeffrey was gentlemen enough to not pull loose the tie on her bikini, though I am betting Ed pulled on enough at the pool that summer alone to make up for it. Ed walked a thin line that summer between being playful and getting arrested by the cops.

 Jeffrey got married at the end of the summer of 1973 to Lisa out at Rush State Park. Daddy drove Aunt Clementine and me out there in the truck while Ed and Jeffrey followed in Ed's mom's Cutlass with Mrs. Small. Lisa came out with her family and Kai rode his bike there in his pressed cargo pants and tie-dyed shirt and sandals.

As our little motorcade passed the entrance to Dragon Park I turned in my seat to stare at it and saw the stone dragon in the middle and I remembered the day Allen brought us out there, the day it was too cold to swim, the day that Ed hit me in the face with the see-saw and knocked me plum out. I turned all the way around in my seat in the cab of the truck to look back at Ed and Jeffrey and wondered if they were thinking the same thing.

Jeffrey and Lisa got married near the lake under a copse of flowering trees and Ed and I both stood up with Jeffrey. Ed was his best man and me as a stand-in for Allen who was in Vietnam.

Jeffrey helped me comb my long straight hair that morning for old times' sake and parted it for me, for probably the last time, on the side and secured it with a barrette. Lisa had made me a crown of wild flowers and Jeffrey pinned it in my hair just before the ceremony. It went well with my green calico sundress.

Jeffrey had grown a big bushy mustache and equally large muttonchops for the event and looked very sweet and handsome. Ed's clean hair hung in his eyes and blew all around his head and over his mouth throughout the entire ceremony.

He turned around and leaned down to me once in the middle of the prayers and mouthed as he pulled his hair out of his mouth, "Shit mother fuck" with his big lips enunciating the words silently and made me laugh.

Jeffrey and Lisa were happy and I was happy for them. But Ed wasn't and he hitchhiked out of town without telling any of us that night after the small wedding reception back at Aunt Clem's.

CHAPTER TEN

February 1974

One afternoon at Mrs. Small's, six months after Ed disappeared from town, she asked me to do her a huge favor.

"Baby," she asked me as she looked at me with her red, teary eyes, "I really need you to do me a huge favor."

Mrs. Small was still heartbroken that Ed was still gone and that he'd only bothered to call home three times since he'd left. The first time he called was twelve days after he took off on the night of Jeffrey's wedding. We were all sick with worry that he'd gone and gotten killed and that we'd never know what happened to him. We had no idea that he'd just up and run off.

Mrs. Small was ecstatic when he called one evening out of the blue to tell her he was alive and well, if not a little hungry, and that he was sixteen hours away in Breckenridge, Colorado, learning to ski. He was working odd jobs here and there in return for a couch to sleep on and a meal or two and lift tickets so he could ski. We were all left bewildered. I couldn't recollect Ed ever skiing even. Mrs. Small told me he never had even talked of skiing and she was at a loss to where it came from. She begged him to come home but he wouldn't.

Since that first call in September, Ed had only called two more times. Once at Christmas to wish his mother Merry Christmas and to ask about Allen who was now for real 'in country' in that he was now an infantryman with a company and was out of the safety of the mess hall. If Ed asked about me, Mrs. Small didn't mention it.

Now here it was February and Mrs. Small told me Ed called for the third time in six months, just the night before, and asked her to mail him more clothes. I was mad that he never once called me or sent me a message by way of Mrs. Small.

"Don't do it, Mrs. Small. Make him go without. It's what he deserves for leaving us without saying goodbye."

Mrs. Small sobbed and honked her large red nose into a silk hankie she pulled out of her bra.

"Baby Hunnicutt, that's what I need help with," she sobbed.

"What?"

"I haven't been in Ed's room since he left."

"You didn't even go in there when he first disappeared to see if he'd packed a bag and ran off or not?"

"The police did."

The police. Ed would love to know the cheese had gone through his room. I would have loved to tell him. Heck, I'd give my hair just to see him and to sock him one. Jeffrey married and moved out and Allen off in Vietnam and Ed goes and runs away and leaves me alone. I could have moved into Mrs. Small's for how much time I was having to spend there now that it was just me and Aunt Clem living in the little white bungalow.

"What do you want me to do?" I asked Mrs. Small.

"Would you mind cleaning Ed's room out for me?"

"Sure, I guess." It sounded scary and it sounded icky to be honest but I didn't say that. It only sounded slightly more fun than sitting on the couch with Caesar, re-reading <u>Pride and Prejudice</u>.

"Would you mind gathering up his laundry for me to wash so I can send him some clothes?"

"Laundry?" I asked, not sure I had heard right. I fidgeted with the hearts on my gold chain and I fingered the large one in the middle; the one that said "Baby" on one side and "Ed" on the other.

"Yes, laundry, dear."

"I suppose." I couldn't imagine picking up Ed's six month old dirty laundry but I saw how much pain Mrs. Small was in and I agreed to do it.

I'd always wanted to see Ed's room but I didn't want to see it this way. I stood outside his room with my hand on the doorknob and I closed my eyes and rested my forehead on his KEEP OUT sign. This was where Ed was when he wasn't with us at Aunt Clem's. This was where Ed came when he came home, when he slept. I couldn't picture him at work at The La Pierre in his pressed white shirt and black silk vest, clearing tables in his tight jeans with his wild long hair. I didn't want to remember him and all his women out in the T-Bucket. But I did remember all the times he roughed me up, the times he picked me up against my will and tossed me about, and the times he sat in our recliner with his dirty feet propped up eating cereal and watching The Flintstones at our house, and the times he put me back together after I'd had a scrape or two at school at the hands of the boys. Half of me remembered Ed as a saint and half of me remembered him as the Devil.

    Here was yet another house where someone I loved was gone and had left behind a slew of their things. And it was right next door where the most important person in my life had gone and died and left behind a house of dusty memories I wasn't allowed to visit. I pondered the idea that I would spend my entire life meeting people, loving people and losing people. With that thought a shudder ran through me clear to my heart and I shook it off as Caesar rubbed against my calf and I opened the door to Ed's room.

    It was dark and dust motes danced in downward swirls in the strip of sunlight that fell across the room from the edge of the curtain. Caesar jumped up on the end of Ed's huge, rumpled bed and curled up. Curiously, the low bed rippled and undulated under the cat. I pushed down on it and it gave way. A waterbed. How spoiled. How Ed. It was covered in a brown and red plaid flannel duvet that was handmade by Mrs. Small. She had tied it like a quilt with red yarn. His down pillows were squashed and flattened in their middles from the last time he'd slept there; the morning of Jeffrey's wedding.

I stepped over the stacks of books and magazines and piles of laundry to make my way to the head of the bed and I picked up a heavy pillow and lowered my face to it slowly with my eyes closed and breathed in.

"Breathe, breathe in the air, don't be afraid to care," I sang as I took in the musky, smoky, dusty scent of Ed's hair. I remembered hugging him at the train station over a year ago when we said goodbye to Allen and I dropped the pillow back on the bed. It made slow waves and Caesar lifted his head and meowed at me once.

I looked around at all that was Ed, from his jeans turned inside out all over the floor, to the holey socks and the sweaty t-shirts balled up here and there to the Pink Floyd posters on the walls and wondered how he could have just up and left without warning, without taking anything with him, without saying goodbye.

"Baby dear," Mrs. Small stuck her head in the door. "Oh my, what a mess. Poor Ed."

Poor Ed? I was the one left to clean up after him.

Mrs. Small twitched her head and said, "Here are two garbage bags. One for garbage and one for the clothes we'll wash and send to him, ok?"

"Ok."

I began chucking all his clothes in one bag. Worn jeans, stiff socks, sweaty t-shirts and ick, his under-drawers. Ed would flip his wig if he knew I was in here picking up his undies. I must have really loved Mrs. Small a lot to do this. I worked my way over to his desk and sat down. I looked back at Caesar, he was asleep, and I looked back at the door, it was closed, and I opened the drawer to his desk.

It was full of pencils and guitar picks, lighters and of all things a Goody hairbrush full of long hairs and under that a color picture of the Sycamore Shopping Center Santa Claus with me in my winter coat on his lap. I looked to be about six and I had a huge pout on my face. My hair was in big curls almost down to my waist and parted on the side and held back with a red barrette. I didn't remember having the picture taken. I turned it over to see if there was a date but stuck to the back of my photo was another one; this one also of the Sycamore Santa, but it was black and white and it wasn't of me. There were two little boys about seven and four years old. The boys had identical pouty lips like little rose buds. The smaller one had large dark eyes and the older one had heavy lidded eyes so pale that even in black and white you could tell they were icy blue. I flipped it over and in small cursive writing it said, "Ed and Dale". I dug in the top drawer more to see if I could find more photos but all I found were three well worn magazines of naked women.

The next drawer produced incense, more lighters, old Kleenex with God knows what balled up in them, a flashlight and several paperbacks of space adventures.

When I opened the last drawer, the bottom drawer, I gasped and sat down on the floor. It was full of about fifty or more, colored, plastic barrettes. Every barrette he'd ever pulled out of my hair for the past five years and shoved in his pants pockets were in that drawer. From plastic barrettes shaped like fruits and vegetables on to ones shaped like bows and cats and flowers, they were all in there. Allen kept bringing me more home from Cloyd's and Ed kept taking them out.

I looked at the bag of dirty laundry I'd just picked up and wondered. I was brave and pulled out his dirty jeans and digging through them I found three more barrettes. Two of them were the new tortoise shelled ones I'd gotten from the Montgomery Wards last summer. I looked at them in the palm of my hand and didn't know what to do with them. I ran my hand through all the colored plastic ones and thought of how Ed would pop open my barrette before I even knew what he was doing and how he would walk his fingers through my hair and re-part it to the middle with the side of his thumb. He would always struggle to get it to part in the middle and afterwards it'd be a little wild and fly about and he'd tuck it behind both my ears and tell me now I looked like his own true love-child. I dropped the tortoise shell barrettes in with the colored ones and I wanted to bag them all up and mail them to him, I was so furious.

Instead I yanked the big heart charm off my necklace and I yelled for Mrs. Small.

"What is it dear? What's the matter?" she asked from the door.

"I want to send Ed a letter." I didn't look at her as I said it. I knew my face was red with anger and I couldn't help it.

"Of course dear. I'll give you an envelope with a stamp and his PO box."

"Thanks, Mrs. Small."

"That's kind of you dear."

I only smiled at her in response to let her think I was being kind.

I took my heart charm, the one that said "Baby" on one side and "Ed" on the other and wrapped it in a picture of a naked woman that I ripped out of one of his magazines and stuffed it in the envelope. I wrote on the back of the envelope, "You're a big hairy jerk. Signed, your love child, Baby Fasty-Pants".

Let him make of that what he wanted. I didn't know what I meant by it but I hoped it worried Ed. I hoped it hurt his feelings. I would have to drop it in the post myself because I couldn't let Mrs. Small see that.

Walking out to the kitchen with the plastic bag of clothes for Mrs. Small to wash I spied an old 8x10 of Ed from when he was sixteen. I stopped with the bag over my shoulder to examine it. His face was less defined then and fuller but he had the same broad thick lips and the same dimples in his chin and in his cheek as he still had. His startling pale eyes were half-lidded by his long lashes and he smirked on one side of his mouth like the smart-aleck he had been back then. I ran my finger over the glass over his sunstreaked mess of hair and remembered that first summer of going to the pool with Ed and the twins and I missed those good times.

"Mrs. Small?" I called as I set the laundry down in the hall.

"In the potty, dear, out in a moment," she called.

I snatched the photo, frame and all and shoved it between my notebooks in my book bag without even thinking about it twice.

"I'm all done, Mrs. Small!" I called. "I'll take the laundry downstairs!"

"Ok dear," she called from the bathroom.

***

"Mrs. Small," I asked her a couple of days later as we sat at her table watching it sleet, "who is Dale?"

Mrs. Small's blotchy face paled as she swallowed her tea.

"Did Ed tell you about Dale, dear?"

"No. I found a picture in his room."

"Oh." She licked the orange lipstick off her lips and thought for a minute.

"Dale was Ed's baby brother," she said and looked at me with a small wistful smile.

"What happened to him?"

"Little Dale and Mr. Small were in a car wreck, Baby," she said in measured tones as if trying to balance all the words on the table.

"Oh."

"Mr. Small was supposed to take both boys for ice cream. But. Ed was naughty." She shook her head slowly at the memory of it, "He was naughty and Mr. Small said he had to stay home and only Dale could go." She stated it like it was something she had memorized and pulled out for such occasions when people asked her about it. Her lips turned down as a sadness came over her face and then it left without a trace. I could see where her mouth had once been full like Ed's but years of pressing her lips together in a worried line had flattened them out.

"I knew it was Dale who was the naughty one, not Ed. But I didn't say anything. It was Dale who drew on the kitchen trim with marker, not Eddy," she said as she examined her hands. "But it was Eddy who took the blame so his brother could go get ice cream." She shrugged and pressed her lips together. "He blamed himself, you know. He blamed himself and he promised he'd never leave me after they were gone."

"You still have him, Mrs. Small. He's just in Colorado. Go out and get him back." I took her hand in mine.

"I can't," she whispered and covered her mouth with her other hand. "He won't listen to me."

That night I went to bed and I prayed that God would keep Allen safe and bring him home soon, just like I prayed every night. Then I took out Ed's picture that I'd swiped and I stuck it under my pillow and as I looked over at the twin's empty bunks I prayed God would keep Ed safe and bring him home too.

***

A small package came for me just two weeks later, no return address. It was addressed to "Baby Blondie-Locks My Own True Lost Love Child". It had so many layers of tape on the back I had to have Aunt Clementine cut it open for me.

We were going to watch Gone with the Wind and eat dinner in front of the tv. Kai and Jeffrey and Lisa were all over that Saturday in the late afternoon when the postman rang the bell.

"Did you get it open Aunt Clem?"
I hadn't heard from Ed since he disappeared back in August. He must have gotten my angry note and my secret surprise inside and I could not wait to see what sort of rotten thing he'd sent back to me. I bet I made him mad. Or maybe I made Ed feel guilty and maybe he sent me a gift.

I looked at Kai before I opened it and felt guilty to see him watching me so intently and chewing his bottom lip.

"It's from Ed!" I tried to explain but no words came out. "He's like, he's like a third twin to me!"

"Open it Baby," Jeffrey said as he put his arm around Lisa.

Inside the box was a tiny note with lyrics from the Pink Floyd song, *Echoes*, that said "No one sings me lullabies and no one makes me close my eyes, so I throw the windows wide, and call to you across the skies."

Below the little note, nestled down in some cotton balls was my broken heart charm but now it was attached to a short leather cord.

"Oh, it's a choker," Lisa said in her rich, smooth voice as she looked at it. "Those are in style now; and it's engraved too." Jeffrey pulled her away and quietly explained it to her. I hadn't told anyone about mailing that charm out to Ed. But Jeffrey knew. He always knew.

"Will you wear it, Baby?" Kai asked me.
I looked down at the tiny gold clover ring that Kai had given me nearly two years ago.

"You should wear it. Here, let me," Kai said and he put it around my neck, over the top of the gold necklace that still had Allen and Jeffrey's hearts on it.

I held the charm all during the movie as I sat next to Kai in the dark and I thought of how Ed's fingers had recently touched it too.

Shirley Johnson

PART II

CHAPTER ELEVEN

I didn't see Ed again till the summer of '78 which was also the summer I turned sixteen. He rolled into town unannounced and strolled into Aunt Clem's backyard in the middle of my birthday, just as everyone was singing to me in my new strapless dress.

Petra had strong-armed me into trying on the strapless yellow sundress the week before. She said I had a woman's body and it was time to put it out there. She also said I'd never have the guts to wear it in front of anyone. She smirked at me in front of the racks of dresses in the Juniors Department of the Montgomery Wards and pretty much dared me to try it on.

Daddy had given me money to buy a new outfit for the party, but I had no idea what to get so I brought Petra on the bus downtown with me to help me pick something out. My body had changed the past year and my old dresses were too childish but I hadn't had the nerve to ask Daddy for money for a new one.

"That," Petra exclaimed as she pointed to the pale strapless dress, "can be your new outfit for your birthday!"

I looked at her like she had lost her last marble as she leaned on her walker and flipped through the rack to find my size. Petra's muscular dystrophy had progressed as she grew and she now needed a walker to get around. She had been right when she said when we were eleven that she was supposed to be taller than me. Finally her body kicked into high gear and she out grew me by a half a foot. But all that height didn't help her muscle problems, so now she had the walker. She didn't let it slow her down with the boys. She leaned on it like a prop of some sort and simpered at the boys like nothing was out of the ordinary.

"Here's your size," she said as she held the tiny little dress out to me. "I'll try one on too," she cracked her gum and picked out a black one for herself.

"No fair, yours has straps!"

"My body's funny looking, and I have trouble walking. I need more coverage and support. You have no reason to not expose yours more." She led the way to the dressing room with her walker.

I felt like I was looking at a stranger standing in front of the three-way mirror in the dressing room. Petra banged in with her walker, wearing her black strappy dress to see how I was doing.

"Ohh so sexy! Kai is going to flip," she cracked her gum and made me spin around "Look at your boobs! You even have cleavage!" she shrieked out loud in the dressing room for everyone to hear.

"Shut up, Petra!" I hissed. Every inch of my body flushed with embarrassment. "I can't wear this. How can I wear this? One false move and I lose the whole she-bang," I revolved around. "This is one of those dresses that you can't even dance in!"

"It's not for doing the fox-trot, silly! It's for parties, and picnics and slow dancing and making out in"

I was used to wearing my old dresses that had lots of cloth and covered my entire chest and tied in the back and had straps that kept it all up. I wasn't used to having to keep track of what I put in a sundress, because I never had anything before. Now I had something to put in it and I had to make sure it stayed in it and the dress stayed up.

I was used to my calico sundresses my older cousins passed on to me from the Hunnicutt side of the family. They all had such tight bodices that I didn't even need to wear a bra ever and with the straps I didn't need to worry about it falling down. I felt like even though I didn't have a lot, what I did have was just sticking out there for the world to see in this strapless, yellow dress.

"You're just used to being crammed into your dresses that hold you smashed in tight. Loosen up. And besides, you don't have the underarm zipper zipped. " It was like Petra read my mind.

Once she zipped that little zipper I did feel better and more secure but still I pulled my long blond hair over either shoulder and covered myself with it.

"Now, I feel better," I smiled.

"Now, you look topless."

"I do not."

"You look like you're wearing just a skirt and no top at all. Jimmy Collins would spasm right out of this earth if he saw you like that."

I looked in the mirror and saw myself standing there, only 5'3 and fair skinned with a pale yellow flowing skirt on and with my chest completely covered by my white blonde hair. Next to me was little Petra with her dark hair cut in a trendy flip and her short bangs framing her dark eyes.

I thought of Jimmy and hoped he didn't show up at my birthday party at Aunt Clem's.

"You cannot tell Jimmy about my party!" I pointed my finger at Petra again.

"Does this mean you'll get it?"

She talked me into getting one. I could always chicken out and just wear one of my older sundresses. Who would really care?

The day of my sixteenth birthday we hit record high temps of 98 degrees. Kai and Petra were the only friends I invited to Aunt Clem's for my party. I hoped that Jimmy Collins didn't show up. It'd be just like Petra to let him know about it and encourage him to gate crash.

Of course Daddy came and Mr. and Mrs. Post too. Allen, who had come home after getting his leg shot up in his first year in Nam, was sitting in a lawn chair off from everyone, drinking cold beers.

Jeffrey was at the grill with my Daddy, and Lisa was helping Aunt Clem bring out chips and potato salad and food for the lunch. Kai in his shorts and button down shirt was damp with sweat clear to his curls. He turned on the hose and wet his head to try to get some relief. He had already given me my present before everyone else arrived. He'd braided me a dark brown leather bracelet and I loved it.

"Oh Kai, I love it!" I gushed as he fastened it on my wrist. "Thank you!" And without thinking I kissed him on the mouth right in front of my Daddy and the twins.

"You're welcome, Baby," he said and smiled and grabbed me and kissed me back harder and wrapped his arms around my waist and pulled me into him. As he kissed me deeper and ran his hands up and down my back I heard my dad clear his throat.

"Kai," I broke away from him and tugged my strapless dress up a little. "Watch the dress, please."

"I am Baby, I am," he said and grinned at me.

I looked around to make sure Daddy didn't hear.

Petra, Kai and I spent the time before lunch playing lawn darts while the others set up the picnic table and cooked the food. Petra kept trying to get me to do the hula-hoop in front of Kai but I wouldn't in my new dress even if I knew the secret side zipper was zipped up secure.

"I think it's time for the unveiling of the cake!" Petra announced to everyone and gave me a pointed look. The adults were all humoring our self-centered foray into our teenage years and all sat down on lawn chairs to indulge us.

"Ta-da!" she cheered as Jeffrey brought out a large, fluffy yellow cake layered with whipped cream and strawberries and everyone began to sing but I was left speechless for there on the other side of the gate was Ed, shirtless and bronzed, in worn out jeans with his hair longer an dirtier than I'd ever seen and with a full beard and a glint in his wild, pale blue eyes.

"Sweet mother of mercy, I have been away too long!" he cried out and for a moment his eyes grew wide as they lit on mine.

"Jesus Christ! How long have I been away?" he asked as he came in the gate.

I looked down at his big, bare feet as he walked across the grass towards me. His eyes took me in slowly from head to toe and back up again and I felt the urge to run inside and hide under the bed.

I felt angry at Petra for making buy this ridiculous dress that was obviously meant for some girl much older than me. I felt ridiculous and childish in it in front of everyone. Who was I trying to fool? Why did I let her talk me into this? I flicked a glance at my Daddy, certain that if Ed didn't stop staring at me, this reunion would end as abruptly as it began, at the hands of my protective father.

Everyone froze for a second except for Jeffrey and Allen who came right over and clapped Ed on the back and shook his hand.

"Bro, it's good to see you," I heard Ed say to Allen.

"You too."

Lisa and Aunt Clem were frozen in the act of putting plates on the picnic table and Kai just stood by the hose dripping water out of his curls where he had sprayed his head again. I glanced over at my Daddy as I stood there feeling much too exposed amongst way too many males and saw him glaring at Ed with a spatula in his hand. Mr. and Mrs. Post had their mouths wide open and Petra was roving her eyes all over Ed from his long tangles and naked bronzed stomach down to his tan toes in the grass.

After Allen and Jeffrey welcomed Ed back with many hugs and pats on the back they backed away from him and he came towards me with his arms out wide. I eyed all his long hair and his full beard that framed his big pouty red mouth and tried to recall what he had looked like the last time I saw him. Out of habit I reached up and felt the gold heart on the leather cord that I still wore on top of the gold chain with the twins' hearts.

When he left town on the night of Jeffrey's wedding without telling anyone and took up residence in Breckenridge we considered sending someone out there to bring him back. But Allen was in Vietnam at the time and we had no one else to send out except Mrs. Small. She said it would do no good and that he needed to get it out of his system.

    I had slept with Ed's picture under my pillow every night for four years. I prayed for his safety every night and for his return. But mostly I prayed to hear from him, and every so often I did but it was nothing to be counted on. He sent me his "I Heart My eddy Bear" t-shirt and I was ashamed to think of it now but I had slept in it every night since I got it. He sent me little notes from time to time which were just cryptic messages in the form of Pink Floyd lyrics. I sent him a kitty-cat barrette, one that I pilfered out of his desk drawer and I actually admitted to him in the little note that I missed him and I wanted him to come back and I signed it Baby Hunni Hell-Cat. After that it was a long time before I received anything from him. He simply said, "How I wish you were here," in his next note. But he never let me know how he was or what he was doing or if he missed me. He never even asked how I was and in my mind he didn't care. I was just some little kid he'd helped take care of for a couple of years. I figured he'd never come back.

    Allen came home from Nam just after being in country a little over one year, with a shot-up leg that needed several surgeries and would always be shorter than the other one. He wrote to Ed and tried to persuade him to come home, to no avail.

After a year of healing up, Allen took a greyhound out to Ed but came home a month later without him. He didn't tell us much about Ed except that he was skiing a lot and thinking of going to college in Boulder.

Now here was Ed, tall as life and as dirty as he ever could be when we spent that first summer together when I was six. He grinned down at me with his white teeth and focused his icy blue eyes on mine. I looked up at the blazing crown of his greasy, sun streaked hair and just wanted to hit him.

"You jerk!" I growled and socked him in his bare stomach.

"Now, Baby Hunni," he smiled and enveloped my fist in his hand, "is that anyway to welcome me home? What am I to think with a welcome like that?" He pooched out his lips in that old familiar pout which was now surrounded by a full beard and then smiled at me again. His teeth were blinding bright against his tanned face. He was darker than he'd ever been even when we spent every day at the pool. He looked like a mountain man.

"My own, true, love-child not happy to see me?" He gave me his hurt feelings face, the one that used to send me off laughing and I remembered playing all those games with him on the porch where he would try to make me laugh. My face turned red because I instantly felt like I was six. I chewed my lips and looked down at his feet which were close to mine and I felt him tug my small leather barrette out of the side of my hair.

"Tsk, tsk, still wearing these stupid things," he whispered

and I watched him shove it in his front pocket. I wondered if he'd put it in his desk drawer. I looked back up at him as he tucked my hair behind my ear and I smiled a small smile at him.

"Remember when I busted you in the chin with that see-saw?" he whispered close to my face as he stared at me with his fierce wolf eyes. He ran his thumb over my bottom lip and cradled my chin in his fingers. My eyes grew huge at his touch and I shuddered from head to toe.

"You sure were a strange kid," he whispered as his eyes roamed from one of my eyes to the other and still he held my chin and quick as a wink he leaned down and wrapped his long brown arm around my waist and picked me plum up off the ground and pulled me tight into his body.

I hugged him tight around his neck. It was like the return of my long lost mother. Except Ed was not my mother. He smelled strong of sweat and cigarettes and his hair looked dusty and shiny all at the same time. He pulled me tighter into him and I buried my face in his hair and cried into it. I let out a shuddering gasp and let loose the tears onto his neck.

"Ed," my Daddy said from the grill.

"Ed, put Baby Hunni down now. For cryin' out loud, she hasn't even seen you in years and here you are squeezing the tar out of her." My Aunt Clem railed Ed and pulled at his arms. She was tiny next to him. I squeezed Ed tighter as Aunt Clem tried to get him to let me go. He'd just got home and I wasn't ready to let him go so soon.

"She's my own true love-child," Ed said to Aunt Clem and then sighed and whispered to just me, "Shit mother fuck, why'd I stay away so long?" and kissed me on top of the head.

At that, Ed sat me down on the grass. I was dizzy from the emotion of it all and had to hold onto his arm for a minute to make the world stand still.

"Baby? Are you ok?"

"Who's this?" Ed asked.

"This is Kai," Petra answered. "Remember him?"

"No. Why don't you refresh my memory?" Ed asked me.

"He's my boyfriend," I answered with my eyes closed.

"Boyfriend? So you meant what you said, Baby Blondie Fasty-Pants?" Ed grinned.

"Shut up," I hissed and hit him in the arm.

"Just like old times, Baby's beating me up and playing too rough. She'll have me crying before it's all said and done. Huh! Ahuh!" he laughed and it was like being in a time warp.

"You're just in time for some cake, Ed. Let me get you a slice," Petra pulled on Ed's arm with her hand.

"Wait! Baby needs to make her wish!" Jeffrey called as he lit the candles.

"Can't believe you're seventeen, Baby," Ed said as he broke from Petra and put his arm around my waist and pulled me away from Kai.

"Sixteen, Ed," Allen corrected him as he limped with us towards the cake.

"You never could keep track," I said, looking up at the bright sky towards his face.

"Hell, it's all the same," he smirked down at me. "Blow 'em out, make a wish!"

I couldn't take my eyes off Ed. It was like seeing a ghost. My prayers had finally been answered. There was only one thing left to wish for and with that thought I took a huge breath and blew.

***

The Monday after my party found me curled up on my quilt after Aunt Clem went off to work. I had acted like I was fine while she was there so she wouldn't worry and make me go to Mrs. Small's. I wanted to stay home alone, though technically I wasn't alone; Allen was up in his room in the attic where he'd relocated after returning from Vietnam. That was where he spent most of his time now.

It was the first day of my cycle and the cramps were always so bad I would spend the day on my bed, curled up, waiting for them to pass. Sometimes I listened to records with the big headphones. Sometimes I hurt too much to do that. Growing up was a pain.

That was where Ed found me when he let himself in without knocking.

"Baby Blondie? You all right?" he asked as he sat down on the rag rug. I still couldn't believe he was here and I had to beat down the panic in my mind that he could be leaving at any time to go back to Colorado.

"Baby Blondie?"

I was curled up on my side in my denim skirt and the Dark Side of the Moon shirt Jeffrey and Lisa gave me for my birthday. I had my knees pulled up to my chest and my back to Ed. I felt him stroke my hair from the crown all the way down my back.

"You okay?"

"I'll be fine," I said, looking at the wall. "Allen's up in the attic."

"Is he?" he asked and kept stroking my hair. It was making me sleepy.

"Did I stay away too long, Baby?" he whispered.

"Yes." I had my eyes closed and wanted to relax.

"You mad at me?"

"Not anymore." I sighed. I didn't want to waste what time I had with Ed being mad and fighting with him.

"But?" he asked.

"I will be if you take off again."

He was silent for a while but he kept stroking my hair.

"You be careful Baby, with your hippie boyfriend," he said out of nowhere. I rolled over and faced him, and curled back up in a ball with my knees pulled up between me and Ed.

"Why?"

"You're not a child anymore, that's why."

"What am I?"

"Well, Baby Blondie," he reached out to my hair and his fingers searched the strands of hair over my temple.

"I don't have one in today," I reached up and pulled his hand out of my hair and held on to his fingertips as I lay my hand back on the bed. His eyebrows were furrowed almost to a frown as he looked at my face.

"You're a woman now, Baby Blondie. Be careful with whatshisname."

"You're wrong."

Ed pooched his lips out at me and shook his head back and forth. Several strands of hair fell in his face and got hung up on his eyelashes. I let go of his fingertips and pulled the strands away and tucked them behind his ear and grinned at him.

"I'm telling you, Blondie, you're not a little girl anymore, you're a woman now and," he said as he took hold of my wrist as I tucked his hair behind his ear and then he held my fingertips in his hand.

"You haven't been around in years," I interrupted him. "You don't know Kai like I know him. I've known him since kindergarten. And I'm not a woman, not like you're thinking." I blushed to think about how Ed was thinking and I hurried and said, "and Kai's not like that. He's not that kind of boy."

"He's exactly that kind of boy. We're all the same," Ed licked his big lips and then he stuck out his chin and scratched thoughtfully at the dimple under his beard. I pulled my knees up tight to my chest as the pain rolled through my sides as Ed continued, "He looks at you like a woman. He sees you as a woman." Ed nodded at me and sucked on the inside of his cheek and opened his eyes wide at me. I didn't comment.

"You think because you've known each other since you were small that he still looks at you like you're small? That he still sees you as the six year old you were when you first met?"

It was uncanny how Ed could sum up how I felt about Kai and about himself as well. I still felt six around Ed. As soon as I saw him yesterday I felt like a little girl. When I looked at Kai, a lot of the times, I still felt the same about him as I did when we were six.

"Trust me, Blondie-Locks, he does not look at you like you're six. He looks at you like a starving man looks at a hot meal. Like a man looks at a good-lookin' woman, because that is what you've become. I know that look. Trust me. Be careful. I saw how he was with you at your party. How he held on to you tight. How his eyes followed your every move. How that dress of yours made him plum crazy."

I flushed red and felt hot in the face and told Ed, "I'm not even a woman yet."

"You are. I wanted to smack that look right off his face."

"A woman is more than that."

"A woman is just that to a teenage boy."

"A woman is someone in control of her life. Which is not me. Everyone else is in control of my life. Everyone else makes my decisions."

"Just don't let hippie boy be in control. Don't let him make the decisions. That's all I'm asking."

"You're one to talk," I said and reached out and pulled his beard and then rolled back over to try to sleep.

But Ed didn't leave. He just sat there on the rag rug and ran his hands down my long hair.

"You didn't even ask why I came back, Baby." He'd been quiet so long and I'd just laid there, concentrating on getting through each cramp, and letting him stroke my hair, that I'd drifted off into a light doze.

"Huh?"

"You never asked what I came back for."

"I never knew why you left in the first place, Ed."

"I left, to go grow up."

"What's that mean? Couldn't you have said, 'Goodbye, I'm gonna go grow up now,'? Did you have to just leave in the middle of the night with just the clothes on your back? Did you have to go away for so long and never call?"

"I did. If I would have stuck around to say goodbye I would have never left."

I wanted to tell him he should have never left to begin with, but I had a huge ache in my throat and couldn't talk at all.

"Allen was off in Nam being a soldier and I had been so worried about getting drafted and then never did. Jeffrey married and playing grown-up and me still chasin' skirts at the pool for cryin' out loud. I had to go grow up."

"Did you? Grow up? You look the same. Except you're hairier." I turned around and smirked at him. At least he had a shirt on today, if not shoes and socks.

"I think I grew up some." He shrugged and pulled his hair out of his eyes.

"Didn't you miss me at all out there?" I went right to the heart of what mattered to me. "Didn't you ever wonder how I was? Didn't you know I was here, worried about you and heartbroken?"

"Heartbroken?"

"You're the third twin to me. You raised me."

"So you agree, you are a woman now?" He smiled and cocked an eyebrow at me. But I stayed serious. He was avoiding the questions.

"I missed you Ed. I was mad at you. I would still be mad at you but I don't want to waste what time I have with you while you're here." I let a tear creep out and slide down my cheek.

"Well I'll be here all summer at least." He reached out and dabbed my tear with his thumb and cleared his throat and looked away. "Mom's got cancer. That's why I came home. She needs me." And he gave me his sad look, but this time it was for real.

After Ed planted that little seed in my head about Kai, I couldn't wait to see him again to test and see how he looked at me. Only problem was, in the summer I never got to see Kai unless I could find a ride out there. I did remember from the party that Kai did spend much of it with his hands on me; on my back, wrapped around my waist, pulling me onto his lap on the lawn chair and holding me close. I had to tell him several times to watch his hands and watch out for my strapless dress and he always assured me he was.

Did that mean he was sorry and would pay better attention or did that mean he knew exactly what he was doing?

CHAPTER TWELVE

"What is Mrs. Small's diagnosis?" Aunt Clem asked me at the dinner table as she served meat loaf to Allen and I.

"Colon cancer," I answered as I put my napkin on my lap.

"Did Ed tell you what stage she's in?"

"No. I didn't ask. He's taking her to an appointment this week over in Rush and then they're going to operate soon after that I guess."

"Why didn't you tell me Ed was here yesterday?" Allen asked. His blonde curls had grown out just past his ears and he had grown a big mustache like Jeffrey's.

"I told Ed where you were. But. He just talked to me and we caught up, I guess."

Allen gave me a dark look and cut open his baked potato while he stared at me. I had to look away. I couldn't see what I'd done wrong.

When Ed showed up the next morning and walked on in after Aunt Clem left for work, I told him immediately, "Allen is up in his attic, go on up." Then I filled my bowl with Frosted Flakes and sat down at the table to read <u>Out of Africa</u>. But Ed didn't go upstairs to Allen's hideaway.

"Whaddaya doing this morning, Blondie-Locks?"

"Not much. This is it," I held up my paperback.

He ran his hands through his hair. It was a wild mess. Then he sat down at the table and helped himself to a huge bowl of cereal and several spoons of sugar from the bowl.

Ed sat and ate Frosted Flakes with me but he didn't talk at all so I just read my book and listened to him crunch.

"Go with me tomorrow," he said with a rasp.

"What?"

He cleared his throat, "Go with me tomorrow. Will ya?"

"Where?"

"To take Mom to her appointment over in Rush." He rested his elbows on the table and pressed his palms into his eye sockets.

I chewed my lip. "I don't know if I can."

"You booked up with social engagements?" he asked from where his head was still lowered and his eyes still covered.

"No, but I don't know if Aunt Clem will let me leave town with you."

"Why wouldn't she?" he flashed his clear eyes up at me. His eyebrows were heavier than when he left town four years earlier. He looked like an older wolf now.

"I don't get to do anything anymore, Ed, now that I'm not with the twins."

"I thought I was the 3rd twin."

"You are to me. But to Aunt Clem you're Ed who split town without telling his own mom goodbye."

"Hmmph."

Ed visited Allen for a few hours up in the attic. When he came down he found me out in the back yard in cut-offs and my bikini top.

"Jesus, Baby," he said as he came out in the sunny yard, shading his eyes. He sat in a lawn chair next to me and lit a smoke. "What the hell happened to Allen in Nam?"

"Why?" I asked and saved my place in my book and put it down.

"He's fucked up, pardon my French."

I didn't say anything.

We didn't expect Allen to just jump right back into working at Cloyd's like everything was normal when he returned. But we weren't prepared for the Allen that came home either.

"Work your magic on him, Baby Blondie," Ed squinted and sat back in his chair and tilted his face towards the sun. "Work your magic on him and bring him 'round," Ed repeated with his eyes shut as he stripped his shirt off, stretched his long torso out and kicked back in the chair in just his jeans and finished his smoke.

Without realizing what I was doing I let my eyes roam over his chest and his stomach and wanted to reach out and touch the smooth, brown skin next to his belly button. I realized my hand was reaching out and I felt horrible for looking at Ed like that.

"Baby? You listening to me?" Ed asked me.

I had my eyes squeezed shut and I had turned my face away from him.

"What?" I asked not looking at him.

"What's wrong with you?"

I didn't answer. I didn't know what was wrong with me. I was a bad person that was what was wrong with me.

"Work your magic on him. You know, like you used to when you were a kid."

"What does that mean?" I chanced a glance at him and was relieved to find I found him to just be normal, shirtless, Ed with filthy hair; nothing out of the ordinary.

"Wrap him around your finger like you had all three of us wrapped when you were a kid. "

"I had you guys wrapped?"

"You know you did. You worked us, Blondie." He sighed and squinted over at me and shook his head like I was pathetic.

"I don't recall that. I never got my way with you guys." I scratched my head and sat forward to let a little air to my sweaty back. I pulled all my hair around to my front and sat that way a minute and then held it all above my head. But absolutely no breeze was moving and my back was just as hot as ever so I tossed all my hair back behind me again.

"See? That! Right there!" Ed pointed at me.

"What?" I asked as I still felt hot and sweaty under my hair and pulled it all out to the side again and twisted it in a side tail and held it up a while but I had nothing to hold in place so I shook it loose.

"You got attitude of the hair-shaker kind!"

"What?" I asked and flung it back behind me and resigned to having a hot back.

"You got attitude of the hair-shaker kind," he said and grinned and looked at me under his heavy lids.

"Are you even speaking English?"

He rubbed his chin and pooched out his lips and said, "Some little girls grow up to be paper-shakers, but our Baby Blondie has always been a hair shaker."

"What's a paper shaker?"

Ed's eyes flashed open all the way and I felt their intensity more than the sun directly over our heads.

"Paper-shaker, you know, pom pom girl."

"Eww."

"Eww? Five hundred boys at La Rue High would beg to differ."

"Is that what boys like? Paper-shakers?"

"Not what hippie boys like," he said and grinned with a wicked curve in his lips.

"Ugh." I let my head lie back down and shaded my eyes. I wondered if Ed knew my parents had always referred to him as a hippie.

"Bring him out of it, Baby. For cryin' out loud if anyone can do it, you can. My God, Blondie, now that you're all grown up your big ol' eyes are enough to make me do anything you wanted," he said and leaned back in the lawn chair and peered over at me and winked and made me blush.

I was glad we were off the pom pom girl subject but I wasn't comfortable talking about my eyes making Ed do things either. It made me squirmy and I wanted to get back to talking about Allen.

"He doesn't like me at all anymore," I said to Ed. I remembered how heartbroken I was when Allen got drafted and how much I worried while he was gone. I was so happy when he came back home but he never really acted happy to see me. I looked over at Ed to see he was trying to get comfortable in his chair and not really paying attention to me.

"Where's the other lounge chair?" he asked.

"This is it," I said and patted my lounger where I was stretched out in my strapless bikini top and cut-off jeans.

"This is fucking uncomfortable," he growled at me with his cigarette hanging off his bottom lip.

"Your pants look uncomfortable," I said, looking at how tight his jeans were.

"What're you saying there, Baby?" he smirked at me and batted his eye lashes. "You think I'd be more comfortable with them off?" he asked and grinned.

"Ed!" I felt like running inside. There were no twins around to tell Ed to watch his mouth, that I was just a kid. I was on my own now, so I said it, "Ed! I'm just a kid!"

"You're the one makin' comments about my pants, what am I to think? And besides, you're not just a kid. You done went and grew up while I was away, in case you haven't noticed it yourself. I know your hippie boyfriend has noticed." He tilted his head back and smiled up at the sun. His beard grew clear down his jaw to his throat.

I didn't say anything and just lay there on the lounger watching Ed as he smiled up at the sun with his already tanned face and I wondered how I looked to him since he'd come back.

"You gotta learn to watch what you say around men," Ed warned me as he opened his eyes a crack and looked over at me. I saw all the muscles in his stomach tighten as he sat up a little. "I know what you meant. But other men would choose to take it wrong. Other men would think you were checking out their package. You're not gonna be safe out there in the world, Baby. You're gonna get eaten alive."

"I've been safe till now, till you came home."

"You just been let loose from the sheep pen. You're out with the wolves now, without the twins to watch out for you.

And you've grown into a pretty good lookin' sheep. You need a great big shaggy sheep dog to watch out for you."

"Good thing you're back in town, then." I smirked at him but he was looking up at the sun.

He glanced at me from where his head was still tilted back. "Ain't that the fuckin' truth."

***

"How often do you see your little boyfriend?" Ed asked me as he stretched out in the orange plastic waiting room chair at Rush Hospital the next morning. It was only 7:30 and Mrs. Small just got called for her turn to see the doctor.

The ride over had been a quiet one. I'd sat in the cupped black leather seat in the back, belted in, because I remembered how fast and wild Ed drove his mom's Cutlass. I wasn't awake enough to talk and besides I didn't have anything to say.

"I might need a few tests today, so it might be a long day, dear," Mrs. Small worried about my being too young to spend a day in the hospital. Now I was worried about being grilled all day by Ed in the hospital.

I looked over at him to see that he had on fresh jeans that didn't look like they'd spent the night on the floor, inside out, and a clean t-shirt that said, "When You're in Breckenridge, you're high", and blue and white striped sneakers without socks.

"How often, Baby. It's not a hard question."

"Not much." I shrugged.

"He still live way out?"

"Yes."

"With his hippie folks?"

"Of course."

"And all those theatre people in and out of there?"

"Yes."

"Hmmph."

"What's that mean?" I didn't like how he sounded.

"Nothing. But if I were he and you'd been wrapped around me for the past who knows how many years, I'd find a way to get my hippie ass into town to see you, that's all."

I remembered how years before Ed had let it slip that Kai must not be that into me or he'd find a way to get in to see me.

"Nothing could keep me away, if I wanted to really see you Baby. He's a fool to not be into you, to not want to be with you every minute of every day. He's a fool to not figure it out. Maybe he's got something out there to keep him occupied."

The thing was, when Kai was around me, he was totally into me. But over the summer I couldn't get a ride out to him or the pool and so we didn't get to see each other. Maybe Ed was right.

"Hey," Ed reached over and touched my bottom lip with his thumb. "Gonna trip on that," he said and pushed on my lip. "Hey, Blondie-Locks," he came close to my face and squinted at my eyes and smiled for just a second. "Hey, I didn't mean to upset you."

I bit my bottom lip and tried to look through Ed. He wouldn't move his face away. I chewed my lips and tried to turn away but he guided my face back to his. "Baby?" His eyes looked back and forth between mine. I focused on his chin and I frowned because I didn't want to cry.

"Baby," Ed said in a whisper and rubbed his thumb high on my cheek, "maybe it's time to date someone else."

I looked at him in his pale eyes and then he said, "I think it's time to move on from that guy, whatshisname." And with that Ed reached down to my left hand and took off my gold clover ring just like he had every right to take it off and he shoved it in his front pocket.

"Hey," I complained and reached for it but it was already gone. "If your pants weren't so tight," I hissed at him under my breath.

"What's that?" he asked out loud. Several elderly people stared at us. "What'd you say about my tight pants, Baby Blondie?" He grinned at me as I burned scarlet with embarrassment. I was determined to show him I wasn't a scared six year old, that I was sixteen now and could stand up to him, so I called his bluff.

"I said, Ed Small, if you're pants weren't so tight, and if I was certain you hadn't worn those jeans for a week solid without bathing, I'd stick my hand in there and take my ring back."

Now the old people were really staring.

"Go for it, little Baby Blondie. Stick your hand in the wolf's pocket." He grinned out of one half of his mouth and winked at me and leaned way back in his chair with his legs stretched out far in front of him and his arms behind his head.

I gritted my teeth and growled at him and stared him in his eyes and looked down at his tight, worn jeans and grabbed his upper thigh as hard as I could with one hand, to try to hold him still and dove into his pocket with my other hand. Ed nearly sunfished right out of that orange plastic chair. He grabbed my wrists and popped out of the seat in a twisty, arching spasm. I grabbed at the cloth of the inside of his pocket and would not let go.

"My ring," I hissed as I dug for it.

"My God Woman! Take your hand out of my pants!" he hissed at me. His hair crackled on end in wild disarray as he leaned his forehead towards mine and stared directly into my eyes.

"No," I said and I made a wild attempt to search his pocket with my trapped fingers and caused him to sunfish around some more.

"Baby, Jesus fucking hell! You win! You win!" He sounded like he was almost choking. "I'll give it back! Take your hand out for the sake of what's holy!"

By now we were both standing and both sweaty and breathing hard and red in the face. I let Ed pull my hand out of his pocket and I eased my grip on his thigh. He pulled the small gold ring out with his two fingers, held it to his big lips, kissed it as he looked me in the eyes and then dropped it down the front of his pants.

"Now, it's safe," he said and looked satisfied. All the old people looked scandalized.

I didn't talk to Ed for fifteen minutes. I sat there with my arms crossed over my chest and my legs crossed in my sundress. That is till Ed slapped my calf with a stinging smack without warning and knocked my leg off my knee.

I still didn't talk to him and I didn't acknowledge the red handprint he left on my leg.

"I'm feeling mighty comfortable," he spread his legs wide and leaned over to me and said in my ear, "I'm feeling real good."

"You are a sick, sick man."

"You want the ring back?" He smiled, wild eyed at me and kissed his lips at me in the air, making me blush. But I wouldn't let him bait me.

"You want it Baby Blondie-Locks?"

"You should be ashamed of yourself." I looked at him as he pouted and looked hurt.

"What? What?" he asked with all his hair in his eyes.

"Acting like this with me, while your mom is seriously ill." I threw my hair over my shoulder and shook it out for emphasis.

"That's why I had you come, Baby. To keep my mind off it and to entertain me," he said and opened his eyes wide and grinned at me with all his big white teeth.

***

The next afternoon Ed sauntered up just as I was getting a drink out of the hose in the front yard. It was upwards of 90 degrees and I'd been out on the front porch most of the morning reading the end of <u>Out of Africa.</u> I'd just read the part where Denys is killed and I was very upset and soaked in sweat and I needed to cool off and take a break from reading.

Lisa had dropped Jeffrey off to hang out with Allen and they were up in Allen's attic still. How they stood the heat up there, I don't know. The house was absolutely sweltering.

"Baby Locks? That you?" Ed called to me as his bare feet whispered in the dry grass. "You taken to showering outside these days?"

"Ed," was all I said as I finished my drink and sprayed off my hot feet and arms and turned off the spigot.

"You still mad at me, Baby Blondie?"

"No." I wasn't mad but I was a little embarrassed for having a public scuffle with Ed at the hospital the day before which involved me putting my hand in his pocket.

"Good!" he hollered and grabbed me in a head lock while I was still bent over, turning off the water.

"Sheesh! Ed! Let go!" I hollered as he led me around the yard by my head, grinding his knuckles into my scalp like he used to do when I was a kid.

"Shit mother eff, I missed you, Blondie-Locks, my own true love-child! It's just so good to be able to come over here every day! Who's been takin' care of you and who's been roughin' you up since I been gone?" he asked. "Who told you, you could go and grow up and become so pretty while I was away?" He squeezed my head in his arm on each word.

"Ed, you're squeezin' my brain!" I screeched and pulled at his arms.

He spun me around and let me go and I fell in a lump on my butt in the grass. I looked up at him through my mussed hair and asked, "You always have to be so rough?"

"Awww, sorry, Blondie. Don't know my own strength." He grinned down at me and gave me a hand up and I dusted off the back of my dress. "Here, Baby Blondie, let me help," he said and I felt him run his fingers through my hair and zip the edge of his thumb down the middle of my head as he parted my hair. I looked up at him as he looked down at me and tucked my hair behind my ears. I felt his pale eyes bore into mine and I had to look away.

"What the hell you wearin' anyhoo?" He took me by the shoulders and held me away from himself. As he looked me up and down I concentrated on staring at his big, tanned feet.

I had on one of several homemade sundresses from Aunt Frieda. She sent me new ones, made just for me, whereas Aunt Frances made new ones for her daughters and then sent them to me when they grew out of them. This one was made out of several red and blue bandanas and had a jagged hemline. I thought it would be something cool to wear in a few weeks for the 4th of July party out at Rush Lake.

"I look at you and I just want to blow my nose all over you!" Ed said and came at me bent over with his hands reaching out for my hem.

"Get away!" I shrieked and smacked at his hands.

"Huh! Ahuh!" he chortled and sighed and gave up chasing me. "Fuck," he sighed and sat on the step and lit a smoke and ran his hands through his hair. I sat down on the step next to him, glad that he was done playing rough with me.

"Fuck," he said again and wiped at the corners of his eyes. "I missed you guys so much. Why'd I stay gone so long?" he asked as he shook his head and inhaled on his cigarette.

I scooted closer to him and tried to see his face but it was hidden by all his hair and his beard as he looked down the road away from me. I leaned in closer but I could only see his turned down mouth and his t-shirt that said "I go down fast in Breckenridge". He flashed his cool blue eyes at me without warning and I caught my breath. When I was smaller I would have jumped back but experience taught me to hold my ground. There was no reason to jump back from Ed, and no use either. If he wanted to manhandle me and play rough with me, he would, whether I jumped back or not. Fighting him just made me frustrated, and it made him laugh.

His eyes looked from one of mine to the other and back for a few seconds and I waited for him to say something smart or to pull my hair or do something 'Ed-like' that would annoy me.

"I need something to eat, Baby Blondie. Ahuh!" he laughed and smiled as his mood went from reflective and sad, to goofy and hungry in a blink with a flash of his white teeth and a pop of his dimples.

"Go in and help yourself. Cereal's out on the table still. Go up and see Allen and Jeffrey while you're in there," I said as I picked up my paperback.

"Sick of me already, Blondie?" he asked and reached over and pinched me on the arm. I smacked at his hand but was too slow.

"Don't hurt my feelings and make me cry, Baby Blondie. I'll need that dress to boo-hoo into," he gave me his best sad and pitiful face with his eyes turned down and his bottom lip out and reached for my dress when he thought I was distracted by his sad face.

"Ed! Don't make me call for Allen!" I shrieked as he gave my hem a yank. I was worried he'd rip it and I'd never get to wear it again.

"Do you think he'd even care? Do you think he'd even come down?" Ed ran his hands though his tangled hair and took a last inhale on his smoke before putting it out in the coffee can.

"Oh look, Petra's coming over," I said and pointed.

"Gotta go!" Ed called to me and slammed the screen door behind him as he went in the house.

"Baby," Petra called as she came across the street with her walker, "Kai has been trying to get a hold of you but you're not answering your phone! He's been calling all morning!"

"Oh?" I should have heard the phone through the window but must have been too wrapped up in Denys dying in my book this morning. I was upset. I wanted Karen and Denys' romance to last till they were old and I was distraught when he was killed. Denys was perfect. I wanted a free spirited man who would take me up in a plane over Africa and make my soul soar.

"What does Kai need? Is he ok? Should I call him?" I ran out to Petra to help her get her walker over the curb. She had on white clamdiggers and a tight red top tied high on her ribs.

"Shoo! I'm fine! I'll manage!" she smacked my hands away when I tried to help. Petra's nails were filed and long and shiny red.

"Petra! Let me help!" I begged.

"I'm not helpless." She bared her little teeth at me.

I tossed my hair over my shoulder in frustration at her.

"What are you waiting for? Go call Kai! But don't talk about anything juicy till I get there!"

"I'll wait," I said. It could take Petra a while to get up the stairs.

"No! Go!"

I ran up the stairs and into the house to find Ed scratching at the rear of his jeans and then putting his hand in the box of Frosted Flakes.

"ED! That's so gross!"

"What? What?" He turned around to face me as he shoved dry cereal in his mouth.

"OH! Ed! You're buying us a new box!"

"Oh that reminds me, Baby," he said with his mouth full of crunchy cereal, "I need you to help me at the grocery store." He picked up our carton of milk and chugged right out of it.

"OH! Ed!" I reached for the carton but knew I could never get it away from him and I just let my hand drop to my side. "That's just wrong, Ed! You're not at your own home!"

"What?" he asked and I saw he had a big milk mustache on his real mustache above his big lips.

"Ed," I frowned at him.

"What? What do you want, Blondie? What do you want?"

I thought for a second. I thought about Ed telling me I could get him to do anything I wanted. "Ed? Will you come out here and help Petra?"

"What?" He looked at me with his eyes squeezed together and his mouth wide open like I was crazy.

"Please, Ed, come help Petra get up the stairs," I waved him to come to me.

"You must be fucking joking," he rolled his frosty eyes at me and shoved more cereal in his mouth.

"Please, pretty please?" I walked over close to him and batted my eyes at him and then I smiled up at him; the kind of thing he'd done to me when I was small when he was trying to persuade me without force to do something I didn't want to do.

"Oh my God. Baby Blondie-Locks, put away the face. For cryin' out loud. How many boys have you worked over with that face? Where'd you even learn such a face? What have you been doin' while I been away?" he asked as he advanced on me, wagging his finger at me.

"Please?" I asked again and took a hold of his large hand in my small one and ran the back of his fingers across my cheek and looked up at him.

"Oh. My. God. Those eyes. Those eyes will be the death of me." He stared at me a second and took his hand away from me and stared at it like he'd never seen it before and strode out the door on his long legs.

I heard Petra say, "Oh Ed, oh Ed, you're so strong," and I ran to the door just in time to hold it open for Ed as he carried her in. She had her skinny arms wrapped around his neck and was gazing up at him. Ed's eyes were blazing and fierce and his lips were pushed out in a scowling pout as he looked at me.

He set her in the big chair and marched over to me, his hair swinging into his face as he glared down at me. "Baby," he said, trying to work up a tough glare, "Fuck," he giggled and then straightened his face again, "Baby," he tried again to intimidate me, but smiled down at me through all his hair, "Baby Blondie," he repeated, as he pulled his hair out of his face with his fingers, "you owe me a huge, huge, favor," he said with a giant smile.

"Thanks, Ed," I said sweetly and batted my eyes at him again and tried to look coy and then ran over to Petra with the phone stretched out on the cord.

"Oh!" I said to her, "I'll call him now and see what he wants!"

"Shit mother fuck," Ed hissed, "I did that so you could call your hippie boyfriend with her in here?" Ed asked with his hand in the cereal box again. "He'll be the one gettin' all my favors," he

I Heart Ed Small

said with his mouth full of Frosted Flakes and stomped up to Allen's attic.

CHAPTER THIRTEEN

"Peaseblossom," I told Jeffrey as he sat between Lisa and Allen on the couch.

"Gesunheidt, Blondie. Good thing you're wearing the hankie dress," Ed said and pointed at my bandana dress. He was propped up in the recliner with his big bare feet up and eating BBQ chips right out of the bag.

Lisa had come back to get Jeffrey just as I got off the phone with Kai and just as Mr. Post had stormed over, purple faced and furious, and brought Petra home. We were lucky he hadn't seen Ed carry her up the stairs or he probably would have called the cops. Petra's eyes were still starstruck, from her close encounter with Ed, when she left. At least she was able to hear my call to Kai.

"What's a Peas-Bottom?" Jeffrey asked with interest as he stroked his goatee. Ed snorted and laughed.

"Pease*blossom*," I corrected Jeffrey. "She's a fairy in one of Shakespeare's plays. Midsummer Night's Dream. Kai has asked me to play her. His folks said I'd be perfect."

I didn't know anything about Shakespeare except the plays were hard to understand. Kai had assured me I would only have four very short lines and that I was made for the role.

"How are you gonna get out there, Baby Blondie?" Ed wanted to know.

"I'm not sure. Kai's folks said we'd figure it out and get me there and back for all the rehearsals," I trailed off and looked longingly at Allen, wishing I was brave enough to ask him to give me a ride out there, but he wasn't even following our conversation. He was staring off out the front window.

"Scooch over," I tapped Jeffrey on the leg and had him scoot over closer to Lisa and I squeezed on the couch between the twins.

I loved my Allen and I missed him even though he'd been back over two years. Even when he wasn't up in his attic, even when he was down here with us, he still wasn't present. He was unconnected from all of us but mostly from me.

I squeezed in next to him and lay my face against the sleeve of his soft green t-shirt. It was one of his Army t-shirts with a blue and white star on the chest. I felt him stiffen a little and then I heard him sigh.

"Allen," was all I said. This was the closest I'd been to Allen since he moved back in. Of course he'd hugged us all when he got off the train, but he hadn't touched me or let me near him since he'd been back and I missed him. I had been scared to try to touch him for two years. Sometimes he was not only stand-offish with me but he was even hostile towards me and he was very critical about everything I did. Sometimes I was glad he didn't talk to me at all because he never said anything nice. I figured with Ed and Jeffrey right there I'd be safe to try to get close to him.

"Allen," I said barely above a whisper and took his thick fingers in my hand and gave them a small squeeze. I held his hand in my lap and rested my head on his arm. I missed my protector. I missed the twin that always had a plan for us whether it was something fun for us to do or a way to get one of us out of trouble. Allen was our leader and my guardian, my knight errant.

I heard him sigh as if he were listening to all my secret thoughts, as if they weighed too heavy on his heart, as if I were asking too much of him. He sighed and untwined my fingers from his and stood up and went back up to his attic without saying goodbye.

All I could do was blink at his back as he walked away, and feel the emptiness in my hand as it lay in my lap where he'd let it drop. I couldn't look at Jeffrey and Lisa. I didn't want to see Jeffrey's big blue eyes crinkle at me with his sad smile. Allen allowed Jeffrey to come up every day into his room if he wanted and they talked or did who knows what up there for hours. I wasn't allowed in at all, ever. Even Ed was welcomed into his attic, but not me.

"Awwww, Peas-bottom, let's go outside, let's have a smoke, let's go for a walk," Ed said as he folded up the recliner and came over and took my empty hand and pulled me up.

Ed walked me down the block to Cloyd's in his bare feet and bought me a bottle of Dr. Pepper and himself a pack of smokes. Mr. Cloyd never crabbed at Ed about his bare feet in the store. Ed just couldn't keep on shoes. It was a wonder he had on a shirt, it was hot out after all. We stood there on the corner of Cloyd's and watched the traffic and I drank my pop and Ed smoked as we leaned against the pop machine.

"Don't give up on Allen, Baby. If anyone can bring him around, it'll be you." Ed put his arm around me and gave me a squeeze as he smoked. "If anyone can work him, it's you, Blondie-Locks," Ed said with the cigarette between his lips. "He's still wrapped around you, Baby-Locks. He loves you more than you know," Ed said and flicked his smoke into traffic and leaned down and kissed the top of my head.

**

Between Lisa, Ed, Aunt Clem and Kai's parents we figured out a way to get me to and from rehearsals out at the Prairie Shakespeare Theatre. Rehearsals usually ran from two to six or seven every night and even though my part was small, only four lines, I had to be there for all of it.

I had never met so many interesting people in all my life. I felt absolutely wrong for the part after I met them all for they could all sing or dance ballet and they could all move so beautifully and speak so eloquently and so loudly.

"Kai," I pleaded the first day there, "why did your parents want me? All these people are real actors." I clung to Kai's hands and pleaded with him to change his parents' minds.

"The Peaseblossom with this company broke her arm falling off the stage up in Hyde Park and a replacement couldn't be found, Baby. But you're perfect for it. Don't sweat it. Mom and Dad have been wondering for a long time when they'd have the chance to get you in their theatre."

"Kai, I don't know. Everyone's a lot older than me." I rested my forehead on his worn chambray shirt and could smell all the grasses and wildflowers where his mother had hung it out to dry.

"Oh Baby, I know you'll steal everyone's hearts up there," he whispered to me as he stroked my hair.

I looked up at his big brown eyes and his sunburnt face and he kissed me with his sweet Cupid's bow lips and I nearly melted into the prairie.

"Baby? Is this our Peaseblossom?" The director, a woman with long, straight, blonde hair like mine glided over in a long, gauzy skirt. She had her arms out wide and a clipboard in one of her hands. "Oh, Kai," the director sighed, "she's beautiful."

Kai held me out as if he were showing me off.

"Hi, Baby. I'm Nancy. Call me Nan. I'm your director. You ever act before?"

I was too shy to answer and I clung to Kai's hand.

"Baby?" she asked.

"No Ma'am, I've never acted before," I answered and looked down at my feet.

"Oh Baby, do I look that old?" she asked and ran her fingers through all her long blonde hair.

"No! Definitely not!" I tried to repair my mistake.

"Oh my goodness!" A man with a red afro and horn-rimmed glasses, who was also carrying a clipboard, sauntered up to us. "Peaseblossom?" he asked Nan, his eyebrows going up and huge grin breaking out on his face as he nodded his head up and down.

"Yes," Nan answered him and smiled at him.

"Perfect," he said and looked me up and down. "Something in white. Virginal with little green blossoms, just a few, here and here," he touched me lightly all over my body with his finger. "Only four lines but they'll all fall in love with her, Nan." He whipped out a measuring tape and measured me in places I'd never been touched by a man before.

I blushed to the roots of my hair and looked to Kai for help. He kissed me on the cheek and wished me luck.

"Come on Baby, we'll pair you with Bill and Ryan, also known as Nick Bottom and Cobweb. Bill has a large role so he is in the actual rehearsal quite a bit. And Ryan, who is also a fairy like you, is our Cobweb. Bill has been doing theatre since about your age, Baby," Nan told me as she took me towards the stage.

I looked back to see Kai pulling his little wooden flute out of his shirt pocket and walking off in the prairie flowers.

"So, he's very relaxed and knows the most," Nan continued telling me about Bill. "He'll help you find your feet," she said as she led me up the stairs to the back of the stage. "Ahh here he is. Bill?" she called to a man about Ed's age. He was wearing only old denim overalls and was very muscular and had olive colored skin. His hair was just below his ears and cut in feathery layers. He had a short goatee and thin mustache and large, liquid brown eyes.

"Bill, here's our Peaseblossom. It's her first time, so take her under your wing and introduce her around. Especially to Ryan. I want you two to take care of our little Baby," Nan told him and she strode off in her long skirt.

"Virgin eh?" Bill looked me up and down and held out his hand for me to shake. I had just stopped blushing from being measured all over and flamed red anew at Bill's assessment of me.

"Ohhh!" he exclaimed and jumped back from me. "I didn't mean it that way. I meant it's your first time on the stage," he said and smiled. He had a friendly face and his eyes seemed to dance on my face.

"I've never acted in anything," I explained and wrung my hands.

"Well, we're glad you're here. I'll show you the ropes while I can. Then I'll hand you over to Ryan who's a fairy like you," he winked at me and it made me wish Ed were here. I'd never been amongst so many outgoing strangers as the theatre troupe.

"Is that really your name?" A group of girls in their twenties called to me from down in the grassy audience. I glanced down at them and wondered how they already knew my name.

Bill ignored them and said, "Here's Ryan, Cobweb in the show. Cobweb, this is Baby, our new Peaseblossom. Take care of her for Nan. It's time for me to work on my blocking. 'Bye Baby," Bill called and blew me a kiss as he skipped off to the front of the stage.

"Do you know those girls?" Ryan asked me. He looked about nineteen and had all his hair shorn short except for his bangs which were past his chin. He was not much taller than me and very slender with a goatee like Bill's.

"No, I don't know them," I answered Ryan and looked down in the grassy audience where the group of beautiful girls with elaborate long curly hair-dos and heavy eye make-up were cat calling up to me and making fun of my name.

"Is that really your name?" Ryan asked me.

"Yes, I've always been called Baby."

"Just Baby?"

"Yes," I answered and thought of all the different names Ed called me. "Just Baby," I smiled at Ryan.

"Well, now you're Peaseblossom and I'm Cobweb. Let's call each other that, shall we?" he asked and bowed low to me with a wide sweep of his slender arm.

"Ok," I answered and smiled as he held out his hand for me to take.

"Let's get a lemonade!" he suggested and pulled me away from the sight of the girls still catcalling up to me.

And that was how I spent my first day at rehearsals. I met several people through Cobweb and Bill who was playing Nick Bottom, the man whose head is transformed into a Donkey. Some people were friendly, some were too busy to care about meeting me, and some were rude to me but Ryan quickly pulled me away from them.

When Ed found me that evening the theater troupe was done rehearsing and were letting loose a little in the grass behind the stage. Several men were playing bongos and two were juggling oranges and rings. The girls with the heavy eye-makeup and elaborate long curls were trying to hula hoop but not having much luck. I was sitting on Kai's lap with his arms around my bare stomach. I had gotten hot during the day and Cobweb had showed me a trick the dancers in theatre did; which was to roll my shirt up ending in a hidden little ball of a knot high up on my ribs. Kai seemed to enjoy wrapping his arms around me and putting his hands on my stomach and had been holding me a while when the cat-calling girls made their way over to us with their hoops.

"Let's see if Baby can do this better," one of the girls called out to me as she emphasized my name and made her friends all laugh. She had what Aunt Clem would have called 'bottle blonde' hair that was cut in long layers and curled back into large feathers. She sauntered towards me on slow, long legs and said, "Let's see if Baby is any better at this than us." She sneered to her friends as they walked through the circle of actors who were all sitting in the grass, relaxing, and came towards me.

I squeezed Kai's forearm as they came closer.

"You leave Baby alone," it was Bill who was sitting with several older men from the show. "She's a virgin, so back off," he called to the girls.

Several people stopped talking and the bongo players stopped tapping out their little rhythms to listen to what was happening.

"We're just having some fun, Bill," the leader of the girls, a girl with long tangerine colored hair done up in layers of large curls flashed her dark eyes at Bill as she and her friends spread out in front of me with their hula hoops. They all had on tight shorts and their legs were shapely and long.

"Little old to be playing with toys, aren't you?" Cobweb called to them from where he sat sharing a skinny cigarette with several of the musicians of the troupe.

"Then it should be perfect for a Baby," a girl with feathery, yellow-gold curls said with her lips twisted in a cruel snarl.

"Baby," the one with the tangerine hair held the hoop out to me where I sat in Kai's lap, "why don't you show us how to do it?"

"You don't have to," Kai whispered in my ear and clutched me tighter around the waist.

"I don't mind." I got up slow and rolled my shirt tight around my ribs and tightened the hidden knot like Cobweb had showed me earlier in the day to make sure it wouldn't fall down. I pulled up my loose old bellbottom jeans and stepped out of my sandals into the cool soft grass and pulled the hoop to my waist. I stood still and looked down at Kai with my mouth serious. He smiled up at me and I tossed my hair over my shoulders and began to hula hoop with just the smallest movement of my hips. Kai's lips split in to a wonderful smile and I could see his cheeks flush in the twilight of the prairie and I began to hula faster as I let out a small laugh.

I could hula hoop all day without even thinking about it at Aunt Clem's. I did it all the time in the yard to the delight of Petra. It was the only thing I did that really pleased her. I'd been trying to teach her how since kindergarten but she just couldn't do it. She loved to watch me go and I could even do two at a time. It was a little kid's toy just like those girls said. One I'd had since I was a kid which wasn't too long ago for me.

I was hula hooping along fine until several people began cheering and whistling and the guys started up their bongo playing at a beat to match my hips and then I almost faltered but I just laughed at how easily they were entertained and kept going for a little while more. That is until Ed walked into the circle and then I let it drop to my feet. Everyone stopped watching me to look at Ed.

"Jesus Criminy, Baby Blondie-Locks Hunnicutt. What in the name of Pete are you doing?" Ed stood there in his jeans that were faded at the knees and were too tight and too short. He was barefoot and shirtless and looked like a wild man. He stood there with his long dirty hair that was in a sunstreaked, windblown mess and stared at me with his lips pushed out and his eyebrows drawn down. "Sweet Jesus, Baby," he said to me as the fading sunlight hit his silvery wolf's eyes. I tried to focus on the dimple on his chin that I knew was under all that beard. I couldn't look at his eyes; he looked so fierce, he frightened me.

"Just hula-hooping, Ed, tha's all," I said and stepped out of the hoop.

"Jesus," he repeated and looked around at every single person in the field. The jugglers let their oranges drop and the bongos were silent. The hula hooping girls with the beautiful curls and the dark make-up were devouring Ed with their eyes as they asked each other who he was.

"Get over here Baby-Locks." He held his arm out to me and then snapped his fingers and pointed to a spot on the ground right next to him. "Time to get your behind home," he said and pronounced it bee-hind.

I was frozen to where I was at. He waited for me and when he saw that I wasn't going to come to him, he tilted his forehead down and scowled and came charging at me with long strides. He got to me fast and before I knew what he was doing, he reached up under my t-shirt, making me shriek, and he yanked it back down over my stomach and picked me plum off the ground and threw me over his shoulder and carried me off the field while the theatre troupe watched. We heard them applaud as we got half-way across the field, back to Mrs. Small's black Cutlass, where Ed finally set me down.

"Good God Blondie-Locks. You're in the theatre one day and you're entertaining them all with the hootchie kootchie dance with your shirt up to here!" Ed took me by my arm, his fingers barely holding me, and guided me into the front seat of the car. "Jesus Lord. I was starving and thinking we'd hit up the Dairy Freeze but I think you done scared the hunger right out of me," he said as he shut the door and strode around to the driver's side.

Nothing could put Ed off food. Not even me dancing the hootchie kootchie, as he called it, in front of the whole theatre troupe. He did take me to the Dairy Freeze and even parked where I'd always wanted to park, where the waitresses roller-skated out to your slot with your food on a tray that they hung on the car.

Ed finished his fries and mine plus two cheeseburgers and a shake and was eyeing my cheeseburger that I'd hardly touched.

"Blondie, you gotta eat," Ed said to me as he sucked down the last of his vanilla coke. "Come on Blondie, don't be like that. You're no bigger than a minute as it is, you need to eat."

I hadn't spoken to him since we'd left Kai's. Since he'd carried me out of the field.

"Be glad I don't tell your Daddy about you being in that play."

I looked at Ed. His eyebrows were tilted as if he felt sorry for me and his lips were shiny with French fry grease. He wasn't expecting me to get mad at him for threatening me with my Daddy. He was expecting me to beg him not to tell on me. I could tell by his sympathetic eyebrows and the pucker of his mouth that he was just waiting for me to plead with him. He definitely wasn't expecting me to reach over and pinch him hard on the underneath side of his arm near his armpit.

"Fuck Blondie! Shit!" He rubbed his arm and I felt wicked and happy and smiled at him and batted my eyelashes. "Fuck, Blondie, you look at me with those big eyes as innocent as can be and then pinch the shit out of my arm," he croaked and shook his hair out of his eyes. "What the fuck," he breathed out and lit a smoke and kicked back in the seat. "I oughta tell your Daddy about that and about the whole theatre thing too," he said and rubbed his arm some more as he held his smoke between his lips.

A slow grin spread across my own mouth and I tossed my hair. "And I should tell my Daddy all the things you do to me and all the curses you say around me every minute of the day. And how fast you drive, and how much you smoke and how you talk about things in front of me you shouldn't AND how you made me put my hands in your pants the other day!"

"Wait, wait, wait! Wait one fucking minute there, Baby Blondie," he waved his hands at me and grinned so huge he almost dropped his cigarette. "Hold the phone there Fasty-Pants. I never had you put your hands anywhere in my pants, little Missus."

"Which brings me to, where is my ring, Ed Small?" I poked my finger at him but didn't want to actually poke him because he still didn't have on a shirt.

"Huh! Ahuh!" he laughed and chucked his coke cup at the garbage can outside the window but missed. "Shit mother fuck," he cursed under his breath and ran his fingers through the part of his hair but didn't get out to pick up the cup.

"Ed, where is my ring? Is it still in your dirty undies somewhere on your floor or did you put it in with the rest of your collection of stuff you've stole from me over the years?" I asked, my eyes widening at him in the dark car.

"Huh! Ahuh!" he barked out a laugh at me. "Huh! Ahuh!" he doubled over and began giggling in his seat. I looked at the part in his hair as he leaned over and saw that it went this way and that in a zig zag from the front to the back of his head.

I reached out and touched his part with the tips of my fingers as he was bent double still laughing. He didn't even feel me trace it with my fingers from the front of his head to the back where it ended in a mussed up mess.

"Oh Blondie, oh Baby," he howled as he tried to get control of himself, "I never wear underdrawers, didn't you know? Huh! Ahuh!" he laughed still bent over and smacked at his knee and then quick as a cat he grabbed me by the wrist where my fingers were still stretched out above his hair and he sat up smiling with his dimples caved in on his cheeks and his pale blue eyes glowing by the dash lights.

"Ahhh," he sighed as he calmed down and still he hung on to my wrist and he tugged on my arm and brought me closer to him. Now only a small smile played on his mouth and his eye lids hung heavy and he almost looked sleepy when he looked at me.

"Ed?" The hairs on the back of my arms stood up as if on alert and I didn't understand why.

"What?" he looked at me from under his heavy lashes. My cheeks burned for being caught at touching his hair and I tugged my hand but he only tightened his hold on my wrist. "I reckon you want your ring back now that you'll be out with your little hippie boyfriend every day, huh?"

"Yeh."

"I guess he found a way to bring you to him, huh?"

"Uh huh."

Ed slid his hand from my wrist to my palm.

"Guess he wants to see you pretty badly to move mountains like that," Ed inclined his head at me, "to uh, get you cast in a big play like that, huh, Blondie?"

"Yeh."

"Guess I won't be seeing you too much this summer after all, before I go back to Colorado," he said and pooched his lips out and gave my hand back. My heart sped up fast and I felt a panic at the thought of losing Ed again.

"You could pick me up every night?"

Ed tilted his head down and looked up at me through his eyelashes. I thought of my Mama and how my life had turned in ways she would have never let me go. She would never have let me spend time with Ed. She would never have let me sit in a dark car eating junk food and spar with him. She would never have relied on him to take me to and from places, to get me out of scrapes, to entertain me and tease me. She would never have let me get to know Ed at all.

"Do you depend on me or do I depend on you, Baby Blondie?" he asked me as he pouted with his full lips and then smiled wistfully at me.

"I don't know," I whispered but I thought it was probably a little of both.

"I guess I'd better get out there when I can, when I'm not taking care of Mom, and make sure you're keeping your top on!" he said and he reached out and put his palm on my forehead and gave me a small shove backwards and grabbed what was left of my cheeseburger and shoved it in his mouth.

"You're one to talk!" I yelled and reached out and pinched him hard on his naked side.

CHAPTER FOURTEEN

"Over hill, over dale, Thorough bush, thorough brier, Over park, over pale, Thorough flood, thorough fire, I do wander everywhere," I practiced singing on the front porch a week later as I waited for Lisa to arrive to give me a ride out to Kai's. She brought Jeffrey to see Allen most every morning and then she would give me a ride out to Kai's. Ed came and picked me up every night and he usually arrived early and sat in the grass with Kai and watched us finish rehearsals as the twilight came quietly down onto the prairie flowers.

It turned out I had many more lines than just four. The other fairies in the play were all young men and then there was me, a young girl who blushed and looked down every time the actor playing Puck talked to me off-stage. Nan, the director, saw this on my second day at rehearsals and decided to make my fairy the one that would sing and interact with Puck onstage.

Puck was played by an energetic man named Chris, who at age twenty-four still had the body of a fifteen year old boy. He was small and muscular and had tufted golden hair that stuck out all over his head and he had eyes the color of Mountain Dew bottles. He smiled devilishly at me and didn't understand my need for personal space. He loved to run his fingers down through all my hair as he danced around me. And he loved to swoop in for kisses on my cheeks just to watch my face burn. He never stopped smiling, he always had a wicked sunburn and he could not stay away from me after I met him on the second day.

"You are just a child!" he exclaimed when we were first introduced. "Just a child! Playing a fairy!" he cried as he leapt all around me, barefoot in his cut-off jean shorts and white t-shirt. "Oh I love her, Nan!" he declared as he ran his hands through all my hair and bounced in and gave me a kiss on my cheek. He smelled of Juicy Fruit just like a child. I looked down off the stage at Kai who was sitting in the grass playing his flute and he just smiled up at me and waved his hand as the breeze caught his curls. Chris continued to leap around me in a dizzying circle, singing out, "Oh we will have wicked fun with this one! Peaseblossom and Puck, good and evil will surely- *meet!*" he grinned at me and then said, "The audience won't know which love story they love!"

It was then that I found out I had to sing a song to Puck, the fairy sprite who frightened all the maidens in the village, who played tricks on everyone in the play, and in real life as Chris. Part of my song was to ask him if he were not Puck, the causer of all sorts of wicked mischief and in every rehearsal when he answered, "Thou speak'st aright, I am that merry wanderer of the night," he never failed to raise a flush from my chest clear up to my cheeks.

Nan loved this affect he had on me and demanded that he not be around me off-stage during rehearsals until we met face to face on stage so that I wouldn't become dulled to his affect and stop my blushing. But he answered and played his eyes on me a little different every time, and he imbibed his reply with new innuendo each time so that I was never prepared and always produced a scarlet flame of embarrassment when he answered my line.

When Lisa dropped me off at rehearsal that afternoon I was greeted by Tony with the red afro, who was in charge of costumes.

"There you are, Baby, our Peaseblossom," he crooned to me. The entire troupe seemed to delight in the fact that I was ten years younger than them all. I didn't quite understand their fascination. I'd been running around with the twins and Ed for years and they were around ten years older than me and never made a fuss about it.

"We're going to fit you today, little Pease, and you're to do your rehearsal in costume. No make-up today, just costume. Come with me!" he grabbed my hand and led me far behind the stage where there were many large white tents. Some were living quarters for the troupe and some were dressing rooms and prop rooms.

"But I'm nearly naked," I cried to Tony ten minutes later and tried to cover myself as he tucked and pulled on the costume he'd given me to wear. It consisted of a light peach camisole top that hugged me tight and ended two inches shy of my belly-button. Then it had very thick, pale pink, footless tights that had several holes and rips all over them. They felt comfortable and made me feel like leaping about, which was good because I was supposed to be a playful fairy and we had to do somersaults and frolic about in the play. On top of the tights I was to wear a pair of stretchy peach colored high-cut briefs that were not unlike a pair of panties except made out of a little tougher material. I felt absolutely unclothed yet I did feel transformed and as mischievous as a fairy.

"Wait! There's more! Your wings!" Tony said as he draped a strip of pure white silk over my head and my shoulder and across my chest. The part that went down my back was long and jagged and hung down nearly to the ground like a limp wing. "And your other wing, my little Pease," Tony breathed and put the other sash of silk that crossed my other shoulder and over my chest and also hung low in the back.

"Oh the time, the time, what's the time?" Tony asked himself and pulled a watch out of his pants. "Yes! Let's do your hair! I don't do the hair, but today I can do your hair. Sit down, mind the wings!"

He directed me to a stool in front of a make-up table and began to brush out my long pale blonde hair.

"So beautiful Baby," he oohed as he ran his hands down it. "I'll just weave a few of these little green blossoms here and here," he whispered, his fingers light and fast as butterflies in my hair as he worked in a few green silk buds with white blossoms.

"Ok go! But don't run. And don't be late. You're up soon for lines and wait for me. I can't wait till Puck sees you."

When Chris, as Puck, answered my line with his, "Thou speak'st aright, I am that merry wanderer of the night!" his eyes were like to jump out of his head and his usually mischievous grin turned into a devouring leer as he danced and pranced around me in a tight circle and reached out and ran his fingers over my stomach and around to my back. I was not allowed to break out of character and swat his hands away from me like I wanted to. But I couldn't help blushing from my toes up to the roots of my hair and that is what Nan counted on me to do. I didn't even think the audience would be able to see it but she was sure they would.

"Excellent! Excellent Puck! Make her blush every time! The audience will die!" Nan clapped her hands from where she sat in the director chair and encouraged Chris to improvise his action with me differently every time to catch me off my guard.

I looked over at the girls who'd had me hula hoop my first night to see them rolling their eyes at me. One even mimed vomiting onto the stage. But I couldn't look at them long for Chris that naughty Puck, continued his mad prance around me, swooping in with his sunburnt face and green eyes, chanting at me little rhymes I was scared to follow or comprehend.

Fortunately every evening when it was time for Ed to come get me, Chris had run out of energy and interest in me and would leave me alone. Kai and Ed both would walk me through the field past the white tents behind the stage, through the pine tree forest and back over to Kai's where Ed had parked the car.

The night after my first costume rehearsal both Ed and Kai were waiting for me in the lush grass in front of the stage.

"Sweet God, Baby Blondie, you looked stark naked up there on the stage under all those lights. You gonna tell your Daddy about this play? He'll drop dead if he sees his Baby up there stark nekkid," Ed's eyes opened all the way up as he said this to me.

"I'll tell him soon, I think. I'm fully clothed and covered so it's ok. He won't mind." I had grown used to my outfit and hated to have to take it off and leave it at the theatre. I felt like Peaseblossom in it and not like my plain old self.

"If you say so," Ed said and looked me up one side and down the other as the sun slid lower and lower through the pink clouds. I looked over to Kai to find that his eyes were roaming all over my peach and white costume as well but he didn't say anything.

"What are these?" Ed asked and reached out and took one of the strips of silk from my wings that draped over my shoulder and lay across my chest in his hands. He ran the silk through his fingers and looked at it like it confused him. "What are these supposed to be?" he asked as he looked around me at the wings lying down behind me.

"Watch it," Kai warned Ed and took his hand off the silken wings.

Ed let him remove his hand from the strip of cloth but his eyebrow shot up as he looked down at Kai. I saw a flicker in his silver eyes as they reflected the sun and I watched him as he pushed his lips out in a meditative scowl.

"Don't rip Baby's costume," Kai told Ed and took a step forward.

"Seriously, boy?" Ed asked him as he rubbed his hand over his beard. I heard it scrape back and forth across his palm. "Seriously?" Ed repeated and tilted his head further down to Kai. Ed stood there with his bare feet in the grass in his shirt that said, "I like to be on top at Pike's Peak" and scratched at his head and eyed Kai and reached over to me again. He ran the back of his fingers up my bare arm to my shoulder and made me shudder and he took a hold of the thin strip of silk that hung across my chest and rubbed it again between his thumb and fingers while he fixed Kai with his icy blue eyes.

"If I wanted to rip it, a young cuss such as yourself wouldn't have much to say about it," Ed breathed out and it made me swallow hard. I wanted to say something to defend Kai but was so shocked at how angry and how possessive Ed was I was at a total loss.

Kai stared Ed right in the eyes back and as his face flushed in the dusk he reached over and took my hand and pulled me away from Ed. "I'll take Baby to the dressing room so she can change."

"You do that. I'll be right behind you."

Both Kai and Ed waited for me outside of the dressing room as I changed out of my Peaseblossom costume and back into my denim skirt and the old yellow Kawasaki shirt I had on from when Jeffrey was a kid. I heard Kai tell Ed he couldn't smoke while I was changing.

"What?" I heard Ed ask and heard the click of his Zippo. "What? Can't smoke? Are you for real?"

"It might burn down the prairie," Kai told him in his light voice.

"What?" Ed asked again. That was his way, to ask 'what' over and over and wear you down till he got his way. Ed didn't ever take no for an answer if it was something he wanted to do. For one thing, he usually never asked if it was ok in the first place. He just did as he pleased.

When I came out they were both facing each other with their arms folded over their chests and scowling at each other. Ed had his cigarette hanging off his bottom lip.

"Hey, Blondie," he grinned at me out of one side of his mouth and winked at me.

I went over to Kai and put my arm around his waist.

"Oh. I see," Ed said as he pulled his hair off his face. "Oh, I see," he said and inhaled on his smoke. "Um hmm, I'm good for driving you around and buying you dinner and taking you here and there but curly boy is the favored one," Ed laughed and reached over and socked Kai playfully.

Kai wasn't in a playful mood and scowled at Ed and pulled me away and began to walk me through the pines.

"Ok. Ok, I see," Ed said from where he still stood by the dressing room tent. I turned around and pulled against Kai's arm which was holding me tight to his side, and I saw Ed still standing there smoking in the dusk.

"Baby," Kai said to me and pulled me further into the forest and behind some trees, "maybe my parents can give you a ride home from now on so he doesn't have to come out."

I took both of Kai's hands and faced him. "I thought you liked Ed," I said, and looked into his big brown eyes.

"He just doesn't fit in out here. He's not nice," Kai said and put his hand under my chin and leaned in to kiss me. "You have to decide Baby, do you want him here or me," he whispered and kissed me and pulled me close to him. He kissed me again and it was harder than he ever had before. His lips enveloped mine and he filled my mouth with his tongue and when I tried to move back just a little he gripped me by the back of my hair so I couldn't get away. My hand flew up to his to try to untwine his grip on a hank of hair close to my scalp but he wouldn't let go.

With my arm stretched up to the back of my head, his other hand found the hem of my t-shirt and crawled up my ribs and brushed against my breast and I whimpered and shoved at his chest one-handed just as Ed strode by on his long legs. Ed didn't see us there and as he passed he flicked his glowing cigarette butt off into forest and kept walking. Kai released my breast and let go of my hair to run after it and I took off after Ed feeling very shaken.

"Come on Blondie Locks," Ed said without slowing down and without looking at me, "Don't make me carry you out of here again."

I scrubbed at my lips with my fingers and trotted up next to him and grabbed a hold of his hand with both of mine and leaned into him as we hurried away from the pine forest.

***

"Are you a woman making your own decisions yet, Baby Blondie, or are you letting your hippie boyfriend call the shots out there at the Shakespeare Ranch?" Ed asked me after he'd ordered us four cheeseburgers, three fries, two chocolate shakes and two vanilla Cokes at the Dairy Freeze.

"What?" I asked, using a page out of Ed's book.

"You know what." He looked down at me with his eyebrows heavy over his pale eyes.

"Scoot over here, Baby-Locks," he told me.

"Why?"

He didn't say anything, he just motioned that I should scoot closer to him on the black leather seat. I complied a little. He made up for my reluctance by coming closer to me.

"Here," he said gruffly and reached out to my hair. I winced away from him but he caught me gently by the shoulders. "Shhh, Baby Blondie," he whispered into the top of my head. "Why so jumpy?" he asked and pulled me closer to him. A shudder ran through me and Ed tightened his grip for a second on my shoulders and kissed the top of my head. "What's going on, Blondie? You're like a scared housecat."

I looked straight ahead at his throat and watched his Adam's apple work up and down. "What's all this stuff in your hair? That's all I wanted to see," he trailed off. I felt his nimble fingers climb here and there through my hair but I didn't feel them retrieve anything. "Ahhh," he sighed, "little blossoms. Nice," and that was all he said and I felt him retrieve one blossom from the top of my head. "I'll just take one," he whispered as he held it up before our eyes and kissed it and put it in his front pocket.

I was thoughtful as I chewed my cheeseburger after the waitress had hung all the food on Ed's window.

"You should hang it on her window, she's the one who eats most of it," he called out to the waitress as he stuck his head out the window and watched her skate away. "Jesus," he whistled and passed me a shake and a cheeseburger. "Huh!" he laughed and took the lid off his shake and began dipping his fries in it. "Fries?" he asked me with his mouth full and handed me the little bag and I did the same as him; took the lid off my shake and began dipping my fries in it.

"My own love-child," Ed said as he watched me eat. I took a vanilla coke from him and sucked a bunch of it down and produced a huge belch that almost made Ed choke to death laughing. "Jesus! Baby Blondie! Small and mighty!"

We finished eating in silence and Ed lit a smoke when he had consumed every last bit of food, including the pickles I'd pulled off mine.

"Shit," he sighed. "Best food in town. Even better than the shit over at The La Pierre. 'Member when I worked there?" he asked and leaned back with his eyes shut and smoked. "That's when you first started getting wrapped around your little hippie man."

I didn't say anything but just sat back in the big seat of the Cutlass and watched him smoke. I smiled when I saw his stomach bulge out through his tight shirt.

"You still wrapped around little hippie man? You want your ring back for real, Blondie?" he asked and flashed his eyes open at me.

I didn't answer. I didn't know. I didn't want to think about Kai grabbing my hair and grabbing me under my shirt. "Maybe," was all I said.

"Maybe?"

"Maybe I'm not normal," I said out loud when I'd only meant to think it.

"Course you're normal. You're the most normal you could be considering who raised ya."

I chewed my bottom lip and stared at Ed.

"Why don't ya think you're normal?" Ed asked as he sat up and put out his cigarette.

I chewed the side of my lip and tried to look away from him. I was thinking of Kai grabbing me and it reminded of all the times Jimmy Collins tried to feel me up at school in the hall. It didn't feel any different from that. Wasn't I supposed to like it from someone like Kai? I just wasn't normal. I hung my head and let my hair fall in front of my face.

"Baby?" Ed reached over and with just his fingertips he pushed my hair back over my shoulder. "Baby?"

I looked up at him to see his forehead tilted down to me, his eyes cool and serious, crawling over my face.

"Baby, something's the matter," he insisted.

My eyes widened.

"Baby, tell me."

I didn't move or make a sound. I tensed.

"Baby," Ed repeated my name for like the one thousandth time and I saw his nostrils flare and his jaw tighten. "Blondie," he said between his teeth and he reached out for my head and I flinched away. "Baby!" Ed hollered and grabbed me by my shoulders and looked me in the face. "Baby-Locks," he whispered and pulled my face into his chest and wrapped his arms around my back tight. "What in the fuck is going on, Blondie-Locks?" he demanded with his chin on top of my head. I snaked my arms around his waist and pulled him closer to me and pressed my face against his old shirt.

"He did something, didn't he? I'll kill him, Baby. I'll kill him," he said and kissed the top of my head and squeezed me tighter.

"It's not like that, Ed," I said into his shirt.

"Oh, I see how it is. You haven't flinched from me since you were six, Baby Hunnicutt." Ed stroked the back of my hair and I flinched under his fingers and I shuddered as I thought of Kai gripping a hank my hair and squeezed Ed around the waist as I tried to burrow my face into his chest.

"Baby!" Ed cried out with my flinching, and he pulled me even tighter to his chest. "You're not frightened of me all of a sudden, are you?"

I shook my head back and forth, my hair rubbing into a mussed up mess against his shirt.

"What did he do?" Ed's voice was flat and cold like a flint.

I didn't answer.

"Baby. Tell me."

"No. You'll kill him," I said with my eyes squeezed shut.

"I might kill him whether you tell me or not. Tell me." He squeezed me to him with one arm while the other stroked my hair. "Tell me," Ed commanded.

"He touched me." That was all I could squeak out. I felt Ed's arm go loose and slack around my back and his hand rested and was still on my hair for a second. He cleared his throat and pulled me closer. I nestled my face into his broad chest and inhaled the familiar Ed-smell of musk, and smoke, and sweat.

"Ahem, Baby, where? Where did he touch you?" he asked with his voice breaking. The fear in his voice sent goosebumps racing across my arms. A long silence stretched out in the car between us. I didn't want to tell Ed where. It would sound foolish and childish that I was worked up over Kai reaching under my shirt and grabbing me. If I told Ed, he'd know for sure I was not a woman.

"Baby? Tell me." I felt his mouth on my hair.

"Under my shirt," I swallowed hard and breathed out a big sigh. There was another silence. I snaked my arms back around Ed and squeezed close to him.

"Did you let him?" Ed sounded tense.

"I couldn't stop him," I breathed into his chest.

"Jesus, God, Blondie. I'll kill him," Ed hissed and pulled me closer into him. "I'll kill him tonight," he said and started the car with his arm still around me and with all the food still hanging on the door.

"Ed, no!" I popped my head up. "No, Ed, the food, the tray. You can't kill Kai, he's just a kid!"

He put the car back in park and tooted the horn for the waitress.

"He's not just a kid. He's a man the same as me." I looked up at Ed. His face was dark and his eyes were half shut and dangerous.

"I won't have to kill him," he said and smiled and gently pushed me back into my half of the seat. "I won't have to kill him," Ed smiled with all his white teeth out, his eyes glittering in the neon light of the Dairy Freeze. He took a cigarette out and lit it. "Oh no," he said as he exhaled smoke out the window and turned to me and licked his lips. "I won't have to kill him. I'll let Allen do it."

CHAPTER FIFTEEN

Ed found me the next morning lying on my back on Jeffrey's old bottom bunk, listening to records on the headphones. He came right on in my room without knocking and squeezed right next to me on the bunk with his long legs pressed up against mine. "Whaddaya listening to?"

I pulled up one big headphone and said, "What?"

"What are you spinning, Baby Blondie?" He looked over at me with his eyes half closed.

"Umma Gumma," I answered and let the headphone clamp back to my ear.

Ed pulled it away a millimeter, "Live or studio side?"

"Live. The best part of the last song is coming up," I said and pressed the headphone back down.

Ed grinned at me with a wicked curl to his lips and leaned over and asked me in the ear as he pried the headphone from my head one more time, "You like it when he has his Floydgasm at the end?" He let the headphone pull tight to my ear and he propped himself up on his elbow and looked down at me grinning and batted his eyes at me.

"Shhhh," I told him and shut my eyes and listened to David Gilmour sing his heart out at the end of Saucerful of Secrets. When it was over I took the headphones off and carefully rolled over on my stomach without rolling on top of Ed.

"How are you this morning, Baby-Locks?" Ed asked and stroked my hair. He held a hank of it between his fingers and rubbed it with his thumb and then he crabbed his hand over my scalp and felt around the side of my head by my temple and popped out my barrette and pulled it out. "Huh!" he laughed under his breath as he watched my hair fall into my eyes.

"Oh, Ed." I pushed all that hair behind my ear and tried not to look at him but when I saw him rub at his eye with his palm, I chanced a glance.

"Did you tell Allen about Kai?" I asked him.

"Yup," was all he answered and then he too rolled over on his stomach and he hid his face in his arms.

"What happened? What'd he say?" I asked him from where we lay side by side on our stomachs.

Ed had been upstairs for almost an hour and I knew he was telling Allen about Kai. I knew there was nothing I could do to stop Ed from telling him. I had no clue how Allen would react. I knew Ed hoped Allen would come out of his two year stupor and wake up and want to kill Kai.

"What happened?" I asked Ed as I looked at the back of his head. His hair looked like he hadn't brushed it in weeks. It hung in thick, loopy hanks down to his shoulder blades.

"He's up there bawling," Ed said into his arms.

"He's what?" I pulled on the back of Ed's head to get him to look up at me so I could see his face and understand him better. He let me pull his head up and when he looked at me his eyes were watery and pale blue and his face was red.

"He's up there, bawling. When I told him, I tried to get him fired up about protecting you but he crumbled. He fell completely apart." Ed dropped his head back down and put his face in the pillow. I let him lay there till he chose to look up at me. "I mean, what the fuck happened to him in Nam, Baby?"

"I don't know. But now he hates me."

"He doesn't hate you. But it's something to do with you, I think."

"I wasn't in Nam. I didn't send him to Nam. How could I have anything to do with it?"

"I don't know but I think he's totally fallen apart now." Ed dropped his face back into the pillow.

"Get up," I elbowed him in his armpit. "Please, Ed, I gotta go up there." I pushed at him but he was a solid lump that wouldn't budge.

"Whaddaya think you'll accomplish up there that I didn't? He won't even let you in."

"I'm not asking for an invite, I'm just going in." That is if I could get Ed to let me out of the bunk. "Come on, Ed, move."

"No," he mumbled into the pillow.
I started poking him in the ribs and making him jerk this way and that.

"Ok, Ok, I'll get up but don't go up there," he said as he rolled off the bed. "You'll just upset him more." He stretched and popped his back and walked into the living room. "Why don't you come over to my house today? Help me get groceries and visit Mom. You haven't been over to see her in a while."

"I have rehearsals."

"Look outside, Blondie. You're not gonna have rehearsals. I bet Kai is happy,"

Ed grinned as he looked out the window.

Ed was right; it was dark out and starting to pour. I could hear thunder off in the distance.

"Baby," he said as he sat on the couch.

"What?"

"Blondie, don't take this the wrong way."

"Oh lord," I said. Ed was looking me up and down and he looked like he was cooking up something in that head of his.

"But maybe," Ed trailed off, chewing his lips, "maybe think about the fact that you're growing up and maybe talk to your friend across the street about boys, and saying no, and maybe start wearing a bra."

I crossed my arms over my chest. I had on another old shirt of Jeffrey's. This one said, "Would you like a little boy? Please take my brother" and it was from when Jeffrey was around 11. It was lime green and the fuzzy felt letters were almost worn off.

"What did you say?" I asked Ed and felt my face flame with anger and embarrassment.

"Hasn't Aunt Clem taught you anything about boys and bras and things like that, Baby Blondie?" Ed squinted his eyes and winced as he said it.

"I have a bra," I said to him and tossed my hair over my shoulder and marched off to the kitchen to get a snack. "I choose not to wear it!" I yelled as I dug in the fridge and pulled out an apple and headed back to my room. "And," I hollered at Ed as I went to my room, "I know how to say no!" I said no to Kai last night, didn't I? I asked myself. He just didn't listen.

With the apple in my mouth I took the record off the turntable and put it away and put another one on and lay down on the bunk with the headphones on. I had on old denim pedal pushers and I put my bare feet up on the bottom of Allen's old bunk.

Ed sauntered in and sat on the edge of the bed. I kept listening to my record, hoping he'd leave. I didn't need him to tell me how to grow up and I didn't need him to tell me to seek Petra out for advice about how to do it right. For one thing, she'd never tell a boy no if he tried anything with her. And secondly, she'd have me wearing a stuffed and padded bra if I listened to her and I'd rather walk around looking like 100% me than some pointy-chested alien. I wasn't doing it. Ever.

I opened my eyes and Ed was still sitting there staring at me. I took the headphones off.

"What?"

He just looked at me through his half closed eyes and he twisted his mouth in deep thought.

"You know," he finally said, "I'm gonna have to be the one to kill him after all. Before I go back to Colorado, I'm gonna have to kill him," he said and tilted his forehead down to me and let his hair fall in his eyes.

"Do you really," I started to ask but lost my voice in the middle. I cleared my throat but still couldn't speak so I reached out to him to brush the hair out of his eyes but just let my hand drop on the bed before my fingertips reached his hair.

"Do I really what, Blondie? Have to kill him?" Ed asked and pulled his hair out of his eyes and off his lips. "Yes. I do. For touching you. Yes. And I also think he hurt you, but you're not telling me." Ed cracked his knuckles and ran his hands through his hair.

"Are you really going back?" I finally croaked out.

Ed looked away from me to the door. When he turned back to me he said, "Yes, Baby. I have to go back. I got into school. Helicopter school," he smiled.

"Helicopter school?"

"Yeh. North of Denver. Going to learn to fly. Be able to fly the choppers up on the mountain. It's just a year."

"Then you'll be back home?"

"Ahhh, then I'll be back in Breckenridge, I hope."

I swallowed hard. So Ed hoped to be away from me. The tears began before I could even think of pulling it together.

"Baby," Ed reached down to my face and brushed them off my cheeks but he couldn't keep up with them. His thumbs were hot on my face.

"So," he stood up, "I have to kill him before I go back at the end of the summer. That's all." He smiled weakly at me and said, "That is unless you can draw Allen out and get him to do it." Then he went back out in to the living room.

I turned back over on my stomach and put my headphones back on but the record was over. I sat and stewed in all my depressed thoughts. I was thinking how Kai and I were probably over. I was thinking of Allen upstairs crying and falling apart. And I was thinking of Ed leaving and never seeing him again. I threw my apple core and it hit the bedroom door with a loud 'thock' and brought Ed back in smelling of cigarette.

"Penny for your thoughts, Blondie-Locks," he said as he sat on the edge of the bunk.

I rolled over on my back and rubbed at my sore eyes. "What's it matter? You're leaving soon and the next time I see you I'll be old and dead." I covered my face with both my hands and cried more.

"You'll come out and see me," he said and tried to pull my hands away from my face.

"No I won't. I can't even get out to Kai's," I said and took my hands down from my face.

"Well, I'll come back and see you. Nothing will keep me away this time. I'll find a way to get here this time."

"You didn't even call last time. You won't ever come back. You'll get married and have kids and be busy with your own family and forget all about me."

He didn't say anything. He just reached out and rubbed my eyebrow with his thumb and caressed my cheek with his fingertips and rested his palm on the bed near my face and leaned over me.

"No one will be here to watch out for me. No one will take care of me. I'll be stuck in this house forever, never getting to go anywhere. I'll be stuck here with a crazy, bawling cousin upstairs and an aunt who works all the time and a daddy three blocks away who only visits on holidays, and.."

Ed clamped his smoky hand on my mouth. "Shush. Enough, Blondie Locks. You're gonna make me pack you in my suitcase and take you with me if you don't quit."

I shut my eyes and turned away from him. I didn't feel like being humored.

"Are you on the rag or something?" Ed asked right near my ear and it made me furious. I turned back again to face him and I smacked at him hard and hurt my hand on his elbow.

"You jerk! That's what boys always say anytime a girl is in a bad mood!" I swung at him again and again trying to smack him so he would leave. But I only ended up hurting my hand on him as he blocked me with his arms.

"Baby," he laughed and took a hold of my wrists and folded them into my chest. "Baby, calm down," he grinned and lay down on the bunk next to me with his hands still holding my wrists crossed and folded into my chest and his face close to mine. He threw his long leg over both of mine to stop me from trying to harm him.

"Baby," he said and pulled my legs closer to him with his leg. I could feel his bare foot on my calf. My arms went limp because I knew there was no sense in fighting Ed; that I could never overpower him, but still he held my wrists, my arms crossed over each other over my chest. "Blondie?" he asked with his eyes looking almost sleepy and he squeezed my wrists and uncrossed them. He pushed my arms into the mattress above my head and climbed on top of me. My heart rammed against my ribs as soon as I felt his body pressing into mine. His chest brushed against my small breasts and I whimpered and tensed under him and I heard the bunk squeak with our weight.

"Blondie?" he asked, his voice almost a groan as he pushed my knees apart and nestled his body between my legs.

"Yes," I said as I squirmed a tiny bit underneath him, my arms still held down above my head by him.

"Your eyes are big as quarters and dark as midnight and yet you won't tell me to stop. I thought you knew how to say no," he said with his eyes close to mine and his hair hanging all around my face. I could smell his warm, smoky, musky scent that was distinctly Ed. He moved his bare foot up and down my calf.

"I know you're not scared of me," he whispered with his thick lips close to my mouth. "What is it? What is it you're thinking?" he asked and moved his body against mine and sent shivers through me and made me quiver.

"Um hm." I couldn't form any words and I couldn't take my eyes off his eyes. I could see all his dark lashes. I could see his big red lips up close. My breathing became short and ragged and I was aware that he was moving against me just a little bit between my legs.

"Penny for your thoughts?" he asked and tried to shake the hair out of his eyes and mine and he let go of one of my wrists and pulled his long strands off my face.

I wiggled under his weight a little and I shuddered and realized I'd been holding my breath a long time and I let it go and shuddered again.

"Baby?" he asked as he brought his face closer to mine and I leaned my head back into the pillow deeper. He was going to kiss me and I couldn't understand why he would do that. His eyes went from my eyes to my lips as he came closer and closer. My breathing became so rapid and yet I couldn't get any air. I shut my eyes.

But he didn't kiss me. He brought his mouth right by my ear. "Are you frightened, Baby?" he asked.

"I don't know," I lied. I felt a panic rising in my chest. I felt if I let him hold me down, he'd stay and not leave but if I struggled and said I was frightened, he'd get off me and go. For some reason I didn't want Ed to get off me, but yet I was scared of what was happening.

"Well I am. Are you hungry, Baby? Because I'm like a starving man." Ed nipped my earlobe and breathed into my ear and shuddered himself and rolled off me and walked out of my room.

I just lay there with my hands still flattened into the mattress where he'd held my wrists down.

"Come on, let's go get groceries and visit Mom," he said as he stuck his head back in my door. He had a cigarette hanging off his bottom lip and his face was flushed. Then he came in and pulled me up off the bed.

In a daze I helped Ed shop for groceries for him and Mrs. Small. But I was no help at all and just followed him around the store, clutching weakly at a box of Quisp. When we got to their house I saw that her garden was run over with weeds and runner beans everywhere and I felt guilty. I should have offered to help keep it up but with the excitement of the play it'd never even crossed my mind.

I helped Ed make lunch for Mrs. Small and my hands burned when he bumped mine as we both reached for the bread.

"There's those eyes again, Baby Blondie. Big as quarters and dark as Caesar's soul," he said and furrowed his brows at me and licked his lips.

That afternoon we all played Parcheesi at the kitchen table. I thought about little Dale drawing in marker on the trim of the kitchen and of Ed taking the blame so his brother could go get ice cream. I wondered what Dale would have been like. I looked at Ed with his hair in his face, pulling on his beard with his fingers, with his mouth hanging open and his pale eyes staring off into space when without warning he flashed his eyes on me. He smiled a crooked grin at me and winked over the Parcheesi board, making me start and jump in my seat.

I felt summer slipping by and with it Ed. Who knew if I'd ever see him again. When he drove me home later that afternoon it was still pouring out and he reached out and grabbed me by the hand before I got out.

"What?" I asked, a little frightened.

"Work your magic on Allen, Baby Blondie. Bring him out. Get him to slay a dragon for you. Make him feel needed. Make him feel like a man."

I looked at Ed right in his pale blue eyes and I looked at his full mouth and his full beard and his words hit home to me. Work my magic. Make him feel needed. Make him feel like a man. Then I pulled my hand away, afraid he knew what I was thinking, that with his pale eyes he could see my thoughts.

"There's not much time!" Ed called as I slammed the car door and ran to the house.

CHAPTER SIXTEEN

"Baby," Ed said my name for like the one thousandth time at the dining room table the next morning. I didn't know what to say to him this morning after everything that happened yesterday. It was still dark and still storming out and I knew that play practice would be cancelled once again and I wondered if Ed would want to spend the day with me.

I was eating my Frosted Flakes and trying to read <u>Out of Africa</u> from start to finish again because I wanted to relive their romance before Denys was killed but I couldn't concentrate on it before Ed showed up and I definitely couldn't concentrate now that he was here. I didn't know what to make of what he did to me yesterday. I couldn't even have said exactly what he did to me. And I didn't want to think about how I felt about what he did to me. I relived it all night long and tried to remember what happened in exactly the same order and I tried to recall what I did to make him climb up on me. I wondered if he was waiting for me to tell him no yesterday.

"Baby," he said again.

I swallowed hard and looked up at him through my hair that was hanging loose. "What?" I asked.

"What's that dress made out of? Allen and Jeffrey's old jeans?" he tilted his head and smiled at me.

I had on a hand-me-down sundress made out of faded denim patches. My Aunt Frances had made it for one of her daughters and it was in the box of sundresses I received last spring as a care package of hand-me-downs from the cousins. It had patch pockets on the front and it tied over the shoulders with denim strings. I liked it a lot.

"Come on Baby. Talk to me. You mad me?"

I just looked at him and shook my head.

"Please tell me what you're thinking, Blondie-Locks," he pleaded and pouted. "There's those eyes again. How those eyes could work me right over," he trailed off and sighed and picked up the cereal box.

"Are you mad about the bra comment?" he asked and looked at me around the box. "I don't care if you wear a bra. Hell. Or the rag comment? You still steaming about that? Or are you on the rag for real?" he asked.

I glared at him about that comment, but I wasn't mad at him. I was a little frightened of him; frightened of how unpredictable he was. Frightened of how I felt about him now. With Kai, I had worried I wasn't normal in how he made me feel when he touched me. With Ed, I was too scared to put into words how I felt. Scared because I didn't want him to stop.

"Huh! Made you look!"

"You jerk."

We were both quiet for a minute and we looked up at the ceiling as we heard Allen moving around up there. The steep stairs to his room were behind a door in the dining room. Before he took up residence up there we had always kept the turntable cabinet in front of that door. Now the turntable cabinet was in my room.

"You work your magic with him yet?" Ed asked me as he filled up a bowl with Frosted Flakes.

"No. How could I when I was with you all yesterday?"

"Come on what'd I do so wrong? You weren't mad at me at Mom's," he said with a mouth full of cereal. "Needs more sugar," he said as he dumped some right from the sugar bowl. "Go up there now," he said as he crunched.

"What?"

"Go up there. Tell him about Kai. Tell him you need his help," he said in between crunching bites of cereal.

"He doesn't let me in, ever."

"I didn't ask you to go in. I told you to go knock and tell him you got boy troubles."

I clamped my mouth tight and flared my nostrils at Ed.

"Little Baby Blondie Hell-Cat. You're gonna hafta draw him out. That's all."

"How do I do that?" I asked Ed.

He was leaning over his bowl, shoveling cereal into his mouth with his hair hanging in his eyes.

"What always made him pay attention to you when you were little?" he asked as he looked up at me, through all his hair.

"I dunno. You knocking me out?" I asked and meant it as a barb to stick Ed with.

"Exactly. Whenever I hurt you or picked on you or cussed around you he'd come out like a knight in armor. That's how we draw him out. If you won't tell him about Kai, I'll just kill Kai myself but in the meanwhile, we gotta draw him out and you're the bait, Blondie-Locks."

Ed looked at me with milk dribbling off his bottom lip and down his beard. A drop hung up right over the dimple in his chin. His eyes were as wild as his hair that hung past the middle of his chest. Today's shirt said, "Be Cool Ski Naked" but I couldn't see all of it for his hair.

He scratched his head and licked his lips in deep thought. "We're gonna draw him out, soon as I'm done with my cereal."

Now Ed was scaring me. I wanted to go in my room and lock the door and listen to records but the door didn't lock. He tilted the bowl up and drained it of milk and looked at me. "You done with yours?"

I looked down at mine to see the flakes soggy at the bottom of the bowl.

"Yes," I answered. I felt ready to run. Ed was cooking up something in that head of his and it looked like it involved me. I licked my lips as he stared at me like I was next to go in the cereal bowl.

"You ready to scream, Baby Hunnicutt?" he asked as his heavy eyebrows dropped in a squall line over his eyes and his mouth grew serious.

"No," I answered with a tremble. I tried to get up from the table slowly but I got my legs and dress hung up on the dining room chair and almost tripped over. "Ed," I held out one of my hands towards him as he pushed back from the table. "Ed," I said again and backed away from him. I left my chair out away from the table to block his way. "Ed, I don't think this is a good idea, whatever it is you have planned. It's not good to play with Allen's emotions with him in his fragile state," I tried to keep the waver out of my voice and tried to speak slow but the closer Ed crept towards me, the faster I talked. "Ed, I think Allen bawled all night long," I lied to try to get him to stop. I backed around the table away from him. He was almost a whole foot taller than me and his arms were much longer than mine and he was beginning to reach for me.

He was silent as a cat and his icy blue eyes and his tiny black pupils locked on mine. His heavy eyebrows hung over his eyes in deep concentration and his mouth was open a little. "Baby," he said, "I'm not gonna hurt ya, I just want you to scream and get him down here. We gotta draw him out," Ed's voice was thick and his face had a flush rising up his cheeks.

"Ed, what are you gonna do?" My voice shot up high as I began to panic. He was coming faster. We'd gone all the way around the dining room table and now he was backing me into the kitchen. There'd be no escape from the kitchen.

"Ed, I don't like this. I'm warning you. Don't make me defend myself. You won't like it." I was backed up against the kitchen sink while Ed filled up the doorway completely. His hair hung in his face and he looked at me through half closed eyes.

"Am I scaring you yet, Baby?"

"Yes," I admitted right away. I wanted to give up and say, you win, you scared me, I give up, now let's quit. But he didn't look interested in quitting any time soon.

"Good," he answered. "Now scream Baby and draw Allen out."

"No Ed. No. I won't do it."

"You will have to." His eyebrows shot up in points and he leered at me with his pale eyes through long hanks of hair that hung in his face. "I'll make you scream if I have to."

"Something must have been very bad in those Frosted Flakes!" I shrieked as he leapt at me with his hands out. I spun around and with my back to him, turned on the sink and grabbed the sprayer and shot him in the side of the face with the cold water as he grabbed my dress and wrapped his fist up in the loose part of the skirt close to my waist and pulled me into him.

"Scream! Dammit!" He commanded me and wrapped his other arm around me to the front of my chest; where his hand squeezed tight on my small breast.

"No!" I screamed. "I won't do it!" I shrieked and bucked in his arms as he squeezed me hard and I shot him full blast in the side of the head from over my shoulder.

"Ahh!" he hollered. "Shit mother!" he choked out and scrabbled for my hand that held the nozzle as I stretched my arm up as high as I could, which wasn't high at all and continued to shoot him in his head. Water gushed down my bare arm and froze my armpit and soaked my side. I tried to break away but he balled his handful of my skirt around his fist tighter and pulled me to him. He pulled the nozzle right out of my wet hand like it was nothing and began spraying me in the side of the head. The freezing cold water hurt as it jetted into my skin and it took my breath away as I bucked and slammed against him again and again, trying to escape.

I wasted no time in twisting around and smacking at his face even if I couldn't see him for all the water blasting me in the eyes. My small hand smacked against his beard and his mouth but didn't deter him as he twisted his head this way and that to avoid my slaps. He towered over me and turned me back around so I faced away from him and shoved me into the cabinets with his body pressed up behind me. The floor was flooding and both our feet were bare and we were slipping as I tried to escape and he tried to keep me pinned.

I could barely hear him as he commanded me in a rasp to scream. "Scream Baby!" he rasped to me as he shot icy water down the back of my head and I twisted hard against him and the cabinets. He rammed his knee between my thighs and pinned me harder against the cabinets and bent me over into the sink. I tried to pull free and heard the seams rip in my skirt where he had his fist balled up in the cloth. I was smacking at his chest behind me one minute and trying to hang on to his wet shirt the next as I felt my feet slide out from under me. But I was wrong, I wasn't sliding. I was being pulled away.

Ed threw the sprayer back into the sink and pulled me to him and rammed me in the stomach with his shoulder and picked me up. He slung me over his shoulder with my head hanging down behind his back and all my long hair drenched and hanging down towards the floor and his hands under my dress, gripping tight on the backs of my thighs.

"NO!" I tried to scream but water ran up my nose upside down and choked me as I looked down at his bare feet and saw he was standing in an inch of water and saw for once he didn't have on too short of pants and the bottoms of his jeans were drenched.

He carried me out into the dining room and I feared he'd drop me on my head. I struggled to not be upside down but couldn't do anything about it. I felt his grip on my thighs slip a little and I began to cough as I tried to holler as his hands slid up and gripped me by my rear-end. I felt him squeeze my butt a hard one with both his hands and panic shot through me as I heard him grunt his pleasure. I wriggled but was stuck, flung over his shoulder as he walked down the short hall to my bedroom. His bare feet made squelching sounds on the wood floor. My soaked hair swung back and forth and smacked at the back of his jeans.

"Ed!" I panted. "Ed!" But all he did was tighten his hold on my butt and I heard him groan.

He was silent and didn't ask me to scream as he entered my room.

"Ed!" I tried to yell but only whispered as I beat at his butt with my fists as I hung upside-down but was scared of falling and grabbed a handful of the tail of his drenched shirt. "Ed!" I croaked out as his hands slid down my hind-end to the back of my hips, his palms hot on my skin, his fingers gripping my thighs, and then he slid them back up to my rear again as he squeezed me hard with his huge hands on the back of my panties.

The world spun fast all around as he turned me right side up and lay me down in one piece on top of my quilt with one of his hands still gripping my butt under me. He lowered himself on top of me, his drenched hair hanging all over his face and running with water down the bridge of his nose and dripping off his full bottom lip onto my face as he pressed my body into the bed with his body. He pressed me into his hand underneath me which was still gripping my butt tightly and I felt his fingers work their way into the waistband of my panties. Panic ran rampant through my heart as I looked up in to his wild, icy eyes. Then rubbing his cold, drenched shirt against the soaked top of my dress, he pulled on the straps of my dress till they popped as his hot mouth covered mine.

"Jesus Christ forgive me," he whispered as he ran his hand up the back of my legs, under my dress and ripped off my underpants. "Sweet Baby Blondie forgive me," he whispered as he kissed my face and my neck and was all over me.

"Ed," I whispered with his long wet hair in my face. "Ed, you must stop," I breathed out as he nuzzled his beard in my neck and nibbled on my throat while he stroked the backs of my thighs and pulled my knees up and slid his hand between my legs and slipped his fingers into me.

"Ed," I started to protest and buck away from his touch, but he slanted his mouth over mine and silenced me with his full lips as he slid his fingers in and out between my legs. I clung to his wet shirt and I couldn't catch my breath.

"Baby Blondie, sweet heavens, you are sweeter than I ever imagined," Ed groaned as he slid his fingers further in me with one hand while his other hand worked the top of my cold, wet dress down past my breasts. I wriggled underneath him.

"Baby," he groaned, "Don't squirm so much" he commanded me and he pushed my dress down to my waist and kissed me hard on the mouth and squeezed my breast with his big hand as he slipped his fingers all the way inside of me with his other hand, causing me to gasp and grab him by his hair.

"Jesus God," he groaned, "you are too fucking sweet," he panted and lowered his mouth to my breast and enveloped most of it in his mouth and sucked in the same rhythm as his fingers stroked me. I pulled at his hand between my legs and tried to sit up but he pushed me back with his mouth on my breast and continued stroking me. He suckled hard and made me arch my back and press myself into his face. I entangled my fingers in all his hair clear to his scalp and hung on tight as I held him to me and hoped he never stopped.

"Sweet God, forgive me," Ed groaned and pushed my knees open wider. I heard him unzip his pants and I stiffened and pulled his hand from between my legs and clamped my knees together tight and locked my ankles one over the other.

"Sweet God, what I have done?" Ed asked as he palmed both of my breasts and squeezed them as he groaned out loud and kissed me long and slow and licked at my lips to get me to open my mouth for him. As he kissed me I thought of all the times Jimmy Collins tried to feel me up with a quick zing of a hand across my chest and I thought that he had no idea how to do it right as Ed kneaded my small breasts in his big hands and pushed my legs open with his knees.

"No, Ed, we shouldn't do that," I said and was glad he still had his jeans on as he forced my knees apart and pushed himself against me.

"No, you're right," he answered with his lips in my hair and pulled away and reached down and pulled my skirt down and tucked it tight around my knees. But he let his hand work its way under my butt and squeezed a whole handful and I heard him grunt as he pressed into me. I could feel his desire for me, pressing through his jeans and was frightened at the unfamiliarity of this part of Ed. He was nearly panting as he cupped my other breast and then he began to pull the top of my dress back up. He'd only pulled it up to the bottom of my breasts when he bent his head and suckled and nipped at my other nipple and pulled it hard into his mouth while he squeezed my other breast and made me arch and shriek at the top of my lungs.

"There it is!" he growled and sucked harder. "There's my shriek."

I couldn't stop looking at his face which was completely flushed. He licked his lips and bared his teeth at me; his eyes clouded and his pupils huge, he growled low in his throat and devoured my breasts. I squirmed against him and pulled at his hair and unlocked my legs and wrapped them around him.

"Jesus!" I cried and felt bad because I'd never blasphemed before and realized the absurdity of my worry considering what I was doing and I tried to get my legs back together again. I knew in my sixteen year old brain that down there, between my legs, was what he really wanted and was what he was fighting to keep away from; that going there would be going to a place we could not turn back from.

"Baby, Sweet Baby Blondie, how could I do this to you?" Ed asked as he dove with his face below my dress and parted my legs wide. I could no longer reach his hair so I clung with clenched fists to the quilt and shrieked with all my might again as his beard scratched and rubbed me as he lapped at me and devoured me with his mouth in places I was not familiar with myself.

Ed came out from between my legs with a gleam in his eyes and his tongue hanging out of his mouth in a pant. His lips glistened and his hair was wilder than it'd ever been. He pulled the skirt of my dress back down to my knees and tucked it in tight one more time and then he pulled the top of my dress back up over my breasts. He nuzzled his face in my hair that ran from my head like a river in all directions. He pulled the top of my dress up again as it had started to slide back down but he pinched my nipple one last time and rolled it between his thumb and finger and sent me into unknown ecstasy before he covered me completely.

He stroked my hair and held his face close to mine. I looked at his long eyelashes that hung heavy over his pale eyes and shuddered under him with my legs clamped shut.

"You okay, Baby?" he asked with a rasp as he stroked my cheek with the back of his hand.

"Um hum," I sighed and shuddered again and wrapped my arms around his neck and kissed his swollen bottom lip. I touched his hair and his beard and the dimple in his chin and realized it was something I'd always wanted to do and wondered what the hell had happened and how. Why did Kai's hand offend me but Ed's hands and mouth left me weak and unable to think or move at all? My neck and chest felt raw from his beard and his suckling and my lips felt swollen. I felt very wet and tingly between my legs and I was weak all over.

He rubbed my eyebrows with his thumbs and rolled off of me and peeled off his wet t-shirt as he walked out of my room.

***

"I won't see you for a few days," Ed said to me from where he sat on the front porch watching it drizzle when he heard me come out. He was sitting on the top step smoking a cigarette and looked up at me as I sat next to him.

"Where's your dress?" he asked as he squinted his eyes at me.

"You broke it, remember?"

After Ed left my room I'd gone to the bathroom to splash my face and brush my wet hair back into some semblance of order and put on cut-offs and my Dark Side t-shirt that were in the hamper.

"No, I mean you always wear a dress."

"Not always."

"You okay, Baby?" he asked and reached over and pulled on the frayed edges of my shorts.

"Sure," I said and swallowed. I was okay as long as I didn't have to walk because I wasn't sure I could keep my knees from knocking, I was that shook up. I was altogether a little dazed.

I looked over at Ed as he lit a cigarette off his old one and I saw that he looked as shook up as I felt. His hand trembled as he tucked his hair behind his ear and I reached out and stroked the springy hairs of his sideburn. I found it interesting that he could produce such thick, curly hair and I could not.

"Baby," he turned to me with his cigarette between his big lips, his eyes blazing pale blue. His hair was still a wild mess where I'd pulled at it and held on to it like reins. "Baby," he said, "you can't just reach out and touch me anytime you want. You have to watch it." He smiled sweetly at me and shut his eyes. His eyelashes made dark fans on his cheeks and I had to stop myself from reaching out to them with my fingertips.

"Why?"

He opened his eyes and looked at my face a long time. He looked tired and his eyelids almost closed as he gazed at me through his lashes. "Baby," he grinned, "this is something people wouldn't approve of."

"I know. I won't tell anyone. Promise."

"You'll tell 'em by how you touch me without saying a single word, Baby Blondie," he said and reached out and ran his long fingers down my hair. My eyes followed his fingers and I smiled at him.

"Jesus," he said and pulled his hand back. "What have I gotten myself into?" he asked in a whisper and scooted back away from me and took a drag on his cigarette.

I laid my head on my arms on top of my knees and watched him as he sat in deep thoughts.

"I won't be around for a few days next week," he frowned at me. "Mom's starting her therapy at the hospital. It'll be easier for me," he said sounding hoarse and he cleared his throat a few times and continued, "be easier for me to spend the night in the hospital with her. But I'll be back next Friday probably."

Today was Friday. Ed would be gone a week and he wouldn't be able to give me a ride home from Kai's for a week.

He cleared his throat and stood up. "I'll call you from the hospital, Blondie-Locks," he said and reached down to me and ran a long strand of my hair through his fingers and licked his lips as he gazed at me. "Who's gonna give you a ride home every night?"

"I don't know." It felt like Ed was leaving for Colorado when he was just going to be gone for a week.

"Who's going to make Kai keep his hands to himself?" he asked. I wondered if he thought someone should be around to make sure he kept his hands to himself. But I hadn't minded Ed's hands. What did that make me? Was I bad for liking it?

"Do what you can to get Allen out, Baby. As I always said, if anyone can, it's you. Wrap him around your finger like you've wrapped me," he said and swallowed hard and his eyes opened up wide, "though not quite like me," he reached over and tilted my chin with his fingers and kissed my forehead and held his lips there for a while before he released me.

"Bye," he stood up and he smiled down at me. "I'll call you."

"Bye," I smiled back at him and I watched him walk down the sidewalk with his t-shirt in his hands.

CHAPTER SEVENTEEN

"Baby, telephone," Aunt Clem called to me in my room where I lay on the bottom bunk reading <u>On the Road</u> by Jack Kerouac and listening to Pink Floyd on the headphones.

"Who is it?" I asked getting off the bunk, figuring it was my Daddy. I hadn't heard from him since my birthday at the beginning of the month, almost three weeks ago, when Ed returned to town.

"It's Ed, Baby, for you," Aunt Clem said as she went back to the living room to watch her Friday night programs.

It was one week since Ed had carried me over his shoulder to my bedroom. It was one week since I'd seen him. He had told me that afternoon he'd carried me off, the afternoon that he'd torn my underpants off, the afternoon he'd done things to me I'd never imagined having done to me, that he needed to take care of his mom the whole next week and wouldn't see me for a while.

Lisa and Jeffrey had helped me get to and from rehearsals all week. I missed Ed and wondered what our friendship would be like after that afternoon. That afternoon had had an effect on my acting. Now I blushed and cowed even more when Puck danced around me and delivered his lines loaded with innuendo to me. Nan, the director loved my new reactions and swore my acting was getting better.

"I wouldn't dream it possible but I think somehow our Peaseblossom has gotten even more innocent. Look at how she blushes," Chris who played Puck danced around me in the grass behind the stage. "Is it possible to get even more innocent?" he asked Cobweb and the other fairies, Moth and Mustardseed.

"I wouldn't have thought it possible but it seems that since we last had rehearsals, Baby has become even more virginal," Cobweb stated as he eyed me up and down with concern in his face.

"I must reach the bottom of this virginal mystery before the show is at its end," Chris, who never really ceased to stop being Puck, hopped around me and reached out and ran his fingers down my arm, making me flinch and blush more.

The fact that he thought I'd become more pure, in light of what all Ed had done to me made me blush even harder. The exclamation of my innocence made me flash back on all the things Ed did to me that day and flash back on how close he came to completely taking away all my innocence very quickly.

I spent many hours the past week analyzing and remembering it all. And I was worried that Ed would never talk to me again when here he was on the phone.

"Hello?" I asked into the receiver.

"Sweet Baby Blondie? What are you doing right now?"

"Talking to you?"

"Before that."

"Reading. Listening to records."

"Morc Floyd?"

"Yes."

"Hmmm... Can you come over?"

"Now?"

"Yeh."

It was seven on a Friday night.

"No. I dunno. Probably not." I looked over at Aunt Clem watching tv.

"Do you want to, Sweet Baby? Do you want to see me?"

"Sure," I said barely above a whisper, my heart up in my throat. Part of me really wanted to see Ed to make sure things were ok between us. Part of me felt wicked and wanted Ed to touch me again. Part of me was scared of things not being ok and part of me was very scared of Ed touching me again.

"Let me talk to Aunt Clem," Ed said. I handed the phone to her.

"It's Ed. He wants to talk to you," I kept my voice even and tried to look uninterested.

"Ed?"

I listened to her side of the conversation but didn't glean much and started to walk back to my room when Aunt Clem called, "Baby, you feel like going over to keep Mrs. Small company while Ed goes out?" My heart dropped. No Ed after all, but I couldn't say no to Mrs. Small.

"Sure," I said and reached for my sandals.

"She says sure. You'll come walk her over and walk her home later? Not too late. Baby looks tired, she'll fall asleep over there if you come back real late to walk her home," Aunt Clem lectured Ed.

I shot a glare at her that she didn't see. She was making me sound like I was six, like I would just fall asleep on the couch at ten PM.

"Ed's walking over to get you Baby. Go brush your hair," Aunt Clem told me as she went back to her shows.

I went to the bathroom and brushed my hair fifty strokes and brushed my teeth and looked at myself in the mirror. What did Ed see when he looked at me? A short little girl with big blue eyes and sunburnt cheeks? Did I look like my namesake? A baby? With my hair parted on the side and my barrette holding it all out of my eyes did I look like a child? Is that why he always took my barrettes out because he didn't like them?

He always had a smart comment about my sundresses too. I guess they were all mostly odd. Today I had on a new sundress I'd finally grown into made by Aunt Frances, just for me. The top was bright blue crochet with a peach lining and it tied behind my neck. The skirt of the dress was old patchwork quilt in bright blue and green octagons. It was probably the strangest dress yet. Stranger than the bandana dress, but I liked it very much because it was comfortable and bright. I knew Ed would have forty-eleven smart comments about it but if he were going out, I wouldn't have to hear them too long. He was probably even going out with a girl. With a woman. I would haul off and kick him right in front of everyone if he were. That would be pretty low of him I thought to myself as I continued to stare at myself in the mirror and saw that now my cheeks weren't the only part of me looking sunburnt. Now my neck was red and inflamed with anger at the thought of Ed going out with a real woman.

"Baby! What the hell? You done gone and died in there? Will you even be fit for company, woman?" Ed pounded on the bathroom door. He must have run the entire three blocks to Aunt Clem's.

I flushed the toilet even though I hadn't gone and came out.

Ed was leaning against the doorframe of the hall into the dining room, grinning at me.

"Ready?" he asked.

"Yep," I swallowed as he looked me up and down and winked.

"Half doily, half bed-spread. I can set my drink on the top half and go to bed on the bottom. Huh! Ahuh! Huh! Huh!" he laughed and his eyes grew wide and he reached out and grabbed my hand and pulled me through the house. "I been known to be out late," he called to Aunt Clem as he pulled me past the couch. "So it might be late when I get her back home."

"If it's that late, Baby, just spend the night at Mrs. Small's."

"Hear that Baby? You might as well spend the night. Does that dress turn into an actual bed and night table ensemble or do you need to pack a bag?"

My heart was ricocheting around in my chest as a million scary thoughts flew through my mind with one repeating image of being fed to the lions by my own aunt.

I looked at Aunt Clem to see if the loss of her mind would show up on her face under all her cold cream. She looked completely at ease as she gave Ed permission to keep me all night.

"See you Aunt Clem, goodnight, I'll...." I said as Ed yanked me out of the door and down the porch. Aunt Clem never even looked up from Lawrence Welk.

"Sweet Baby Blondie," Ed said to me as he raised my hand to his mouth and kissed my knuckles. "Sweet, sweet, heavenly, Baby Blondie," he said and turned my hand over and kissed my wrist and smiled at me and led me out into the humid June night.

"Are you really going out?" I asked him.

"No," he said and winked at me. "But look at those eyes! Those eyes, so dark and so serious. Work me over with those eyes, Baby, wrap me around your finger, make me yours, with those eyes," he commanded me as he brought his face close to mine.

    I ignored him and looked down because I didn't know what to do or say. Instead I asked, "How is Mrs. Small?"

    "Sick. Pukey. But for now, asleep."

    "Then who am I visiting and keeping company?"

    "Me." He looked at me and opened his eyes wide and my heart stopped and I gasped.

    Ed took me up on his front porch and stopped in front of the door without a word. I looked over at my Daddy's house but couldn't see much of it from up on the porch but I was still scared of my Daddy seeing me with Ed.

    "Ed?" I whispered and walked my hand up his arm and tugged the sleeve of his t-shirt as he just stood there on the porch for a minute.

    "What Sweet Blondie-Locks?" he asked and looked down at me with his eyes under heavy lids and his lips relaxed out in their natural pout and chills ran through me. I didn't answer Ed. I just stared up at his pale blue eyes. I forgot what I wanted to ask him. I forgot for the moment that it was important we get inside so my Daddy wouldn't see me out here with Ed. Ed wrapped his arm around my waist and pulled me to him right there on the porch and I was so surprised, I couldn't speak. I kept thinking; I am going to be here the whole night. The whole night.

Ed pulled me closer to him and I felt his hip bone press into my side as we stood pressed together.

"What's the matter, Sweet Baby?" I felt him kiss the top of my head. "Are you frightened, Baby?"

"Yes," I breathed out. "Very," I added importantly.

"Me too," Ed whispered and stroked my long hair that fell down to my waist.

I felt him walk his fingers up my arm to my collar bone. His fingers padded around my neck from one side of my throat to the other and back to the nape of my neck, under all my hair. A chill ran through me as I felt his other hand walk up my ribs. I looked beyond him, beyond the rails of the porch and up into the early evening night's sky and saw the moon with a yellow haze around it and heard the whippoorwills calling and the crickets singing and looked back up at Ed to see him with a slight smile on his lips as he looked down at me.

He pulled me close to him with his hand on the nape of my neck, his fingers entwining up in my hair, and his lips lit on mine in the dark summer night, not caring who saw us on his porch.

"Oh!" I gasped as he darted his tongue into my open mouth and licked the inside of my lips and made my knees melt.

"Ahh," he sighed and pulled me tight into him, his hand safely on my ribs and his other hand working its way through the underneath side of my hair and then down below my jaw.

His lips and his tongue played lazily with my lips. His tongue swept slowly in and out of my mouth, making me sway on my feet. My hands crept up the front of his shirt to rest on his chest and then on up to his wide shoulders to hold on to him and steady myself.

His lips met mine and drifted away above me and came back to meet mine, and pulled back away again in the dark. I stood on my tiptoes to try and keep his lips from breaking contact but he was much taller than me and could pull out of my reach. When his lips lit on mine again, my tongue sought to meet his own, sought his mouth, to keep him from pulling away from me. I felt him start at the unexpectedness of my tongue and instead of pulling out of my reach, this time he pulled my tongue into his mouth. As he kissed me deeper he entwined his fingers in my hair and pulled me tighter into his body.

"Ed," I whispered as his full lips sucked and pulled on my bottom lip.

"What, Sweet Baby Blondie?" he said as he traced his thumb across my bottom lip.

"I don't want you to go all the way, I don't want to go that far tonight," I breathed out as his other hand held me tight on my waist.

"Are you telling me to stop, Sweet Blondie-Locks?" he asked as his lips worked their way down my jaw. "Are you telling me no, sweet, heavenly Blondie?" he asked as he sucked and nibbled my neck, his beard scraping against my sensitive skin, as he lifted my hair away with one hand and began to knead the back of my neck while the hand on my waist squeezed me slowly.

"Sweet Baby?" Ed asked me as I ran my hands lightly across his shoulders and down his chest and pushed lightly against him.

"What?" I asked as I hoped he never stopped rubbing me on the back of the neck with his fingers. "What?" I asked again. I wanted him to stop talking so I could concentrate on the feeling.

"Baby, should I stop?" he asked with his lips against my collarbone, his finger now tracing dizzying circles up and down my throat.

"Yes," I groaned and ran my hands down his flat stomach and grabbed him by his belt. "Yes, please," I whispered as I pushed him away.

"Yes, what, Sweet Baby?"

"Yes, please, we should stop. I don't want to go that far, I don't want my Daddy to see me out here," I said and that seemed to bring Ed back to reality.

"Oh, you're right," he said and pulled me in the front door into the Small's living room and locked it behind us.

"Ed, is that you, dear?" Mrs. Small called from her bedroom when she heard the door.

"Yes, Mom, it's me," he said as he frowned down at me. "Shit mother fuck," he whispered and then asked me quietly, "you up for visiting Mom a bit?"

"Sure," I said and he squeezed my hand and pulled me through the house back to Mrs. Small's bedroom.

"Hello dear!" Mrs. Small brightened and smiled form where she sat propped up on several pillows on her bed next to Mr. Small's identical bed. His was no longer made up perfectly but showed the rumpled signs of somebody having napped on it recently.

Mrs. Small looked small in her white nightgown and white dressing robe. She had a pink and lime colored silk scarf wrapped around her perfectly round head and her hands went to it subconsciously and patted at it.

"Oh you look lovely, dear!" she cried out to me as I came in and sat on the edge of her bed and took hold of her frail hands. "I'm afraid I don't look so lovely dear," she said and took one of her hands away and touched her lips which were pale without her orange lipstick. "But you," she said and lightly stroked me on my arm and she rearranged my hair on my shoulder, "you look lovely as ever and such a beautiful dress. Lovingly made by one of your doting aunts, no doubt."

"Thank you Mrs. Small," I smiled at her.

"Ed, dear, sit down. Doesn't Baby look lovely, dear? Is she not just heavenly, dear?" she stroked my hair again and my eyes grew wide at her choice of words.

"Yes, Mom," Ed murmured and sat behind me on the bed.

"Such beautiful children you both are," she said as her eyes drifted shut. "Such beautiful children," she repeated and grew still.

I chanced a glance at Ed behind me, Ed with his long golden brown tangles and his dark tanned skin and his full beard like a mountain man. I looked at his pale eyes under his heavy lids and thought of how he was her son.

"Penny for your thoughts, Sweet Baby-Locks," he said and cocked his head.

"You are such a beautiful child," I said and reached out and touched his mouth with my thumb and then pulled his beard with just a small tug. He reached over to me and gently yanked a long hank of my hair.

**

"Blondie?" I heard Ed calling me from far away. "Blondie?" he called again. I felt a heavy weight in my lap and on my legs.

"Yes, Ed?" I reached out with my eyes closed and found his head in my lap and ran my hand through his hair.

"We should go to bed," he said as he kissed the web of my thumb.

I pried open my eyes to find myself in the Small's darkened living room. The tv was tuned to static and the sound was off. I was half propped up with my feet stretched out on the couch. Ed was lying between my legs with his head on the lap of my quilted skirt. It made me giggle to see him half asleep on my dress just as he said he would do.

"What's so funny?" he asked as his pale eyes flashed out from under his bruised lids.

"Nothing," I smiled and stroked his long hair.

"It's late, Sweet Blondie. Come to my bed with me."

I swallowed hard. "I should just stay out here on the couch, don't you think?" I asked Ed as he began to sit up.

"No," he said and tilted his forehead down at me as his eyebrow arched up.

"Ed," I breathed out and tried to wiggle the circulation back into my legs.

"Blondie Locks."

My eyes grew round and wide as I held my ground and refused to argue the point with him.

"Blondie, I promise. I won't touch one hair on your head. Well. Maybe one, you have so many," he smiled and reached over and ran his fingers through it like it was golden water. "Baby, please, those eyes. Those eyes are bottomless. Come on Baby, you're safe with me, promise," he said and stood up and held his hand out to me and I took it and let him pull me down the hall to his room.

"Shit mother eff, it's cold in here," he said as his big bare feet padded down the hall. "We'll turn the heat up on the waterbed. Mom keeps it too cold in here," he said as he opened his door.

Ed gave me a large, soft, v-neck t-shirt that was blue and yellow and said, "Ski the 'ridge!" and had orange mountains on the front.

"You can sleep in that, Sleepy-Locks. I'm gonna check on Mom." And he left me alone after he fiddled with a dial on his bed. I took off my dress and put on the clean and worn t-shirt that came to my knees and I stood dumbly in the middle of the room and waited for Ed to return. I looked around at his Pink Floyd posters and all his dirty clothes on the floor and remembered cleaning his room after he left the last time and swallowed a lump in my throat as I thought of him leaving at the end of the summer. I held the heart necklace on the leather cord I still wore, that said our names on it, between my fingers and wondered how I would survive Ed leaving again. I wondered if I would ever see him again and was working up being good and sad when he came back in the room and locked the door.

"Blondie? What's wrong?" Ed came to me and took me by the shoulders and pulled me into him. "Blondie, tell me what's wrong? You homesick?"

I wrapped my arms around him and rested my head on his chest.

"Nothing," I said, "just tired is all."

"Well let's get in bed. I promise to be good, Baby. If you tell me no, I'll stop," he said as he pulled back the plaid flannel comforter.

"Ed." I froze. "I already said," I trailed off.

"Just kidding," he whispered in my ear and kissed my hair. "Get on in bed, Blondie," he said and so I climbed in the rolling, warm waterbed and sunk back on a down pillow.

"I just gotta find something to sleep in," he said with his back to me as he dug in his dresser. "I don't reckon you'd let me sleep stark naked," he chuckled and pulled out a pair of never worn boxers. "Bingo." And he pulled off his t-shirt and stripped out of his tight jeans right in front of me as I yanked the comforter over my head. "Huh! Ahuh!" he laughed quietly and climbed in next to me. "Scoot over, Sleepy-Locks, I'm 'bout to freeze out here."

So I spent the night with Ed, in his warm, rolling waterbed, in the middle of summer, with his strong arms wrapped around me and his hairy leg thrown over mine.

"Ahh Baby, a man could get used to this," he sighed and kissed my hair.

"I wish I could sleep with you every night," I found myself saying.

"Uhmm," Ed grunted. "Someday," he said and he fell asleep breathing against my ear.

***

Saturday afternoon found me home alone, scrubbing dishes and cleaning the house while playing Fats Domino records.

I sang in the kitchen as I scrubbed the pots and pans and did my version of the stroll in front of the sink in my red and blue bandanna dress. The stereo was clear in my room but I had drug it to my doorway and turned it up loud.

I don't know what had gotten into me but I was in an amazing mood. Play practice was drawing to an end and that day's practice had been a full dress rehearsal with no stopping and had gone great.

Word had spread that Kai and I were no longer together but the troupe was much too preoccupied with rehearsals and the performance that was coming up to take sides or pry too much.

"I heard she mailed her ring back to him," I heard the girls gossiping as I skipped in my Peaseblossom costume to go practice somersaults with Cobweb and the other fairies and I slowed down to listen. I hadn't mailed my ring back. Far as I knew Ed still had my ring from when he'd taken it from me at the hospital almost a month ago.

"I heard she's seeing that guy that picks her up every night!"

"She's barely old enough to drive! How can she be with him?"

"How can he be with her?"

"Isn't that against the law?"

"What does he see in her? She's not even a woman yet!"

The girls were all in a hissy over me getting picked up by Ed most every night and how he almost always held my hand or plum carried me out of there in his arms or on his back. I hadn't talked to Kai since he'd pulled my hair and felt me up against my will. And I was thankful Ed no longer mentioned killing him. If Kai was at rehearsals, he stayed out of my sight and most importantly, out of Ed's.

Rehearsals were coming to an end and the play was in one week and I felt excited about it as I listened to Fats Domino records and paused to do the twist in the kitchen. I was in my own little world until I turned around and bumped right into Allen who was leaning in the doorway with his arms over his chest and a small smile on his face.

"Hi," I said out of breath from all my dancing about, and my shock of running into him down here in the kitchen.

I thought he took a hold of my hand to keep me from crashing into the wall but he led me out into the dining room where Ed was sitting on top of the table with his hands crossed over his chest and a small smile on his face as well. Allen pulled me in the dining room and put my hand up on his shoulder and my other hand in his, and he led me in a slow two-step as Blueberry Hill came on my record.

"Baby," Allen looked down at me with his big, dark blue eyes. His blond hair was curling out everywhere and his mustache was huge and needed a trim.

"Yes, Allen?" I asked as he spun me around and danced me around the table where Ed sat, dangling his long legs in his old jeans. "Seeing you this happy, makes me very happy."

"Well. Good." I didn't know what to say. I looked past Allen at Ed to see if he knew what was going on. Ed's eyes were half open and he grinned with his arms across his shirt-less chest as he sat there on the dining table, watching us dance around.

"Ed and I stood there and watched you dancing and singing and scrubbin' pots and pans and you never even noticed us there in the doorway watching you. You just went on dancin' and washin' and singin'. I'm just glad you're happy. I'm glad I haven't, well, that you haven't let me get you down."

I looked up at Allen as a sad smile played on his mouth as we continued to dance to Fats Domino.

"It's okay. Don't worry about it," I whispered to him and smiled at him as he gave me a quick squeeze and walked me over to Ed as the song came to an end. Allen offered my hand up to Ed to take. Ed took my hand and brushed my knuckles against his lips as he hopped down as the next song came on. Fats sang, "I want to walk you home," and Ed said, "How appropriate," as he took me by the waist. For some reason I felt like Allen had just given me to Ed, to have forever.

"I love the way you walk, I love to hear you talk," Ed sang down to me, his hair hanging long over his shoulders. I turned my face away from him singing so close to me but couldn't help but turn my eyes back up to him.

"There's those deep, beautiful eyes Blondie," he said. He two-stepped me around the table as Allen sat up where Ed had been and it was much different from when Ed had pursued me around the table, trying to get me to shriek to draw Allen out.

"I'm not tryin' to be smart, I'm not tryin' to break your heart," Ed sang and couldn't help but laugh as he looked down at me. I looked down at the small space between us and looked back up at him.

"Work me with those eyes, sweet Blondie, I don't mind," he said and batted his own dark lashes at me and smiled with all his white teeth against his dark beard.

"I never danced with a man with no shirt," I said and reached out and pinched his stomach.

"I wondered where all my hankies went," Ed said and he goosed me and then the record ended and we all three went out to the front porch.

"Allen," I said as he sat on the chair on the porch and Ed disappeared around the back of the house.

"Yeh Baby?"

"Will you come to my play Saturday night?"

I watched Allen as he swallowed hard and fidgeted with his hands as he kicked back on the two rear legs of the chair. I watched him as he looked for a way to tell me no and I heard Ed in my head saying over and over, work your magic, bring him out, if anyone can do it, it's you Baby Blondie. I was in a panic how to do that. Ed never really said how I was supposed to do that, though he was always telling me I did it to him.

Something about my eyes, but my eyes were just my eyes. Ed's eyes sometimes made me lose my breath and sometimes made me feel unable to think or move. What did mine do to Ed? And what did I want them to do to Allen?

I wanted to work him like Ed was always saying. I wanted to work him to my will, which was to get him to come to the play.

"Jeffrey and Lisa are coming," I said as I got up and walked over to him just as Ed came back to the front yard with the football in his hand. "Aunt Clem and Ed will be there too," I said to Allen.

"What about your Daddy?" Ed asked from down in the yard.

"Uhhh, I haven't told him about it yet."

"Baby, why not?" Ed asked.

"It's not his 'thing'."

"It's none of our 'things' but we're going cuz you're in it and you're our 'thing' and let's be honest; I'm going just to see you in your fleshy costume. Huh!" Ed laughed and threw the football at me hard and hit me right above my heart so hard my eyes shut as I struggled to get in a breath.

"Ed, you son of a," Allen stood up from his seat and limped towards the edge of the porch to go after Ed like he used to long ago. Ed started to run but stopped when he saw Allen wasn't coming after him after all. Ed gave me a pointed look and nodded at me as if I should continue doing something. Continue working Allen.

"Ed," I whined, "you hurt me," I said and held my hands over the middle of my breastbone where the football had hit me. "It's making a bruise that'll show up in the play!" I pouted as Ed darted his eyes at Allen. "Allen," I complained and I looked at my cousin and worked up a pitiful face. "Allen, Ed's too rough with me."

"Maybe if you have a good purple bruise it'll keep you from lookin' stark naked up there on that stage in your fleshy costume!" Ed chortled and came and got the football where it'd fallen on the porch. "Try and catch it this time, Sweet Blondie," he said and cocked his arm back to throw it at me again.

"Ed! No!" I flinched and cowered and covered my head with my arms and ran over to Allen, "Allen, make him stop, he throws too hard! He's just trying to hurt me!" I looked over at Ed who had a huge smile on his face underneath all his hair that had fallen in his eyes.

"Ed, you're too old to rough up Baby, anymore. For cryin' out loud, you're a grown man and she's just a kid."

"Then she should be good at playing," Ed said and pulled back his arm and threw it right at me, but threw it gently and I caught it.

"Huh! Ahuh! Blondie, now I get to tackle you!" he yelled and leapt up the steps after me.

"NO!" I hollered and ran right at him and knocked him down the steps backwards onto the grass.

"Good one, Baby," Allen said, getting up and limping down the steps to look at Ed who was sprawled out on his back in the grass, smiling and staring up at the sky.

I came over next to Allen and looked down at Ed too. His hair covered his face a little and his broad lips were split into a wide smile and he stared straight up at the sky.

"Is he dead?" I asked and poked him on the shoulder with my toe and his pale eyes flashed on mine and he smiled wider and quick as a cat he grabbed my ankle with both of his large, dry hands and said, "I see London, I see France, I see Blondie's…"

I pulled free and kicked him hard with my bare foot in the shoulder.

"Ow! Shit mother fuck!" Ed hollered and rubbed his shoulder.

"You two never change," Allen said and went back inside. As I watched him go inside Ed grabbed my ankle again and pulled my leg out from under me and made me fall on the grass next to him.

"You jerk!"

"I kind of like you better when you're cowering and helpless, Blondie, huh!" Ed laughed and reached over and pinched me on the arm.

CHAPTER EIGHTEEN

The day of the play the bottom dropped out of the weather. The temperature dropped and fast rolling clouds blew in and the wind cranked up in brief little blustery chuffs.

Ed took me out to the theatre and after walking through the woods, the prairie, and past the white tents to the stage without seeing Kai, he deposited me with Cobweb and ordered him to keep an eye on me.

"I'll see you much later, Blondie," he said and punched me softly on the chin. "Break a leg."

"Bring Allen."

"I'll try," he said as he walked backwards away from me in his tight jeans with a big smile on his face. "I'll try," he said again and winked at me.

I spent the afternoon relaxing with the rest of the fairies, stretching and running as we got loosened up for our gamboling and frolicking we'd be doing throughout the play.

When the curtain went up, when the sun went down, and the fairies and I had made our full transformations into our costumes; mine the peach and pink close fitting one with silk wings, and the boys in form-fitting and torn tights and no shirts, their hair spiked out here and there, their eyes lined with black and my own eyes lined in sparkly green and silver and my hair crimped and full of hundreds of green and white blossoms, we moved as one, the four of us overlapping one another, one cohesive unit of frolicking fairies.

The wind began to whip faster like the snap of a sheet on a clothesline as the curtain parted on the first scene. By the time I made my first appearance it began to sprinkle. We fairies frolicked and entertained the audience, Puck made me blush, the heavily made up older girls with the starring roles sulked as the star-crossed lovers and the Queen of the Amazon.

As we took our final bows the raindrops hung heavy on my false eyelashes and picked at my thin camisole. After the final curtain dropped and after all the cast hugged each other several times, I ran behind the stage to the white tents to look for my family and Ed but I only found Kai.

"Baby, come here," he said from the prop tent.

I stopped running and walked over to him, wondering what he wanted.

"Baby," he said as he pulled me into the dark tent, "Baby congratulations, you did such a great performance," he said in his lilted voice and handed me a bouquet of wild flowers.

"I've missed you so much. I've wanted to apologize for so long," he said as he took my hand. His hand was soft on mine and he rubbed my palm with his thumb.

"I can't stay," I said as I tried to see his face in the dark dusky tent. All I could see were his curls and his dark eyes.

"Please, Baby, let me apologize." He squeezed my hand.

"I have to find my family," I said and backed away from him towards the back of the tent. I pulled free of his grasp and held my hand in a fist close to my heart. .

"Please, Baby. I never meant to hurt you or scare you. I love you. Can't you see that?" I heard his voice waver with emotion as he held his hands out to me as I walked backwards from him.

"Kai," I held my hands out to him to keep him away. "You hurt me and you weren't very nice," I said as I continued to walk backwards from him. My false eyelashes felt heavy and my stage make-up was starting to feel hard and dry on my cheeks.

"Kai," I said with an edge to my voice as I backed into a tent-pole and tripped over a taut rope and fell backwards into the tent wall. Kai grabbed my upper arms and kept me from falling and pulled me towards him, away from the wall.

"Baby," he whispered and wrapped his arm around my back. "Baby, I've missed you so much." He caressed my face and I turned away from his fingers. When I looked back at him I could only see his mouth and the outline of his curls on his head as he pulled me into him. I put my hands on his chest and pushed at him.

"No, Kai," I said but was too late for his hand was once again on the back of my head as he slanted his mouth over mine and kissed me, his mouth greedy and tasting of mint. I beat against his chest and stepped backwards and tripped over the same rope and fell with Kai still holding me, his tongue searching my mouth as I pulled away and tried to shriek.

I fell with my back against the cold vinyl tent wall which snapped tight at my weight and Kai landed on top of me and together we slid down to the ground, my shoulder blades slamming into the earth and all of Kai's weight on top of me.

"Baby? Are you all right?" he asked me.

My head was pressed hard against the tent and my neck curved at an odd angle.

"No. Get off me." I shoved at him but he didn't move. My shoulder-blades felt bruised and my back ached from the fall.

"But Baby, I want to make up. Take me back. I can't live without you," he breathed into my face and I wriggled to be away from him but could not find escape. He stayed on me and he ran his fingers over my collarbone and down to my chest where he felt my breasts through my thin camisole, his fingers grazing me in my sensitive areas. I shrieked and bucked at the invasion of his fingers and his touch; I was frantic to get him off me, to make him stop.

"Get off me!" I flailed and struggled to smack at him but my arms could find no leverage.

"Baby," he whispered and kissed me again and grazed his palm on my breast. I smacked at his hand over and over and bucked and writhed under him in a panic, my back smashed up against the cold ground.

I pulled away and tilted my face towards the tent wall and yelled till my lungs burned, "Ed! Ed! Ed! Help me, Ed!" before Kai could clamp his hand on my mouth.

I bit the meaty part of his hand and when he released me, I pushed with all my might with my legs and popped my head under the tent and out into the rainy night.

"Ed! Help me!" I shrieked again.

I felt Kai trying to pull me back into the tent. He yanked at me with both of the strips of my wings. I felt them dig into my shoulders and burn and cut my skin and still the silk didn't tear and I gave another mighty push with my legs and got my shoulders clear of the bottom of the tent.

"Ed! Ed! Ed! Ed!" I shrieked up into the rainy black sky as my shoulders burrowed down into the mud and into all the little rivulets running underneath the tent. I felt Kai reaching under the tent and he grabbed my arms and scratched at my skin as he tried to yank me back under the tent.

"Ed! Ed! Where are you? Help me!" I screamed and I scratched frantically at Kai's fingers and I kicked out and with both my feet and I felt one foot glance a blow off his mouth.

"You kicked me!" Kai yelled and he grabbed me hard about my waist-band of my tights and began to pull me back through the mud, through all the little puddles of cold water, and back under the lip of the tent.

"You kicked me!" he said again and pulled me harder and I slid through the slick mud back under the tent up to my chin. He gave my waist-band another yank and I felt my tights begin to come down my hips. At that, panic shot through my heart and I reared my legs and kicked him again, this time in his chest.

"BABY!"

I turned my head in the mud and saw someone run around the corner of the tent in the dark.

"Baby!" he barked my name and ran towards me and I looked up at him upside-down, my eyelids weighed down with the false eyelashes and as I looked up at the falling rain I saw the blonde curly halo of Allen.

"Allen! Help me!" I croaked out as Kai gave my tights another yank and I almost disappeared under the tent. I shot my hand up to Allen who grabbed it up to my elbow and pulled me out of Kai's grasp, my limp body slithering in the mud under the tent. Allen pulled me clear of the tent and let me lie in the mud as he pulled something out of his pocket that glinted in the moonlight. He sliced the tent from top to bottom in one silent slice as if the vinyl tent were nothing more than a paper bag. Before I could even gather the strength to roll over in the cold mud I watched as Allen leaned down and hauled Kai to his feet by the neck of his shirt and backhanded him in the face with all his strength again and again and again until Kai drooped limp and unconscious. I winced at each smack; the violent sound of muscle and flesh coming to an abrupt collision against the fine bones of Kai's face.

I needed to move, to run but I was frozen to the ground in terror, my mouth open wide in a silent scream.

Allen dropped Kai in a small heap on the muddy ground and turned and looked at me but didn't say a word.

"Allen?" I breathed out.

He was silent as he came closer and leaned over me. I brought my hands up in front of my face and tensed in fear of him for in the moonlight with the rain all around he was unrecognizable to me.

"Allen?" I asked again as I peeked around my hands.

"How could you?" he asked, his voice like two pieces of paper rubbing each other. "How could you?" He breathed out again.

I couldn't see his face against the dark sky but I felt his anger burn against my face and I cringed away.

"I didn't," I stammered. "I didn't," I said and held my hands in front of my face as I lay back in the cold mud. He leaned over and wrapped his fingers around my neck and picked me off the ground and backhanded me on my cheek so hard my head snapped sideways on my neck and as I looked down at the many puddles in the mud, he struck me in the face again and again, each time harder than the last till he lost his grip on my neck and I slipped out of his grasp and landed in the mud on my side.

"Allen, no," I cried and began to crawl away, the rain running down my forehead, my hair heavy with mud. My face burned and stung as if doused in gas and lit on fire and my eyelid became too heavy to keep open. I tasted blood that ran from my nose and the corner of my mouth and I fought to breath through all the snot, the blood, the rain, and the swelling of my face. I found my knees as I heard him behind me and panic ran in my brain as I ordered my cold, assaulted body to move, move, move now!

"How could you, Qui Long?" he rasped to me.

"I don't know!" I shrieked. "I didn't!" I cried out as I found my feet one at a time and ran, leaving Kai unconscious in the mud and Allen behind me. "I didn't!" I sobbed out as I turned the corner and ran and ran blindly in the pouring rain towards the woods but the woods were dark and shadowy and frightened me and I skirted them and double-backed towards the stage and the open prairie, thinking if I made it out to the black top, past the audience prairie, I'd be safe and I could run all the way home. I ran and ran splashing through the tall prairie grass, the heather scratching at my bare feet.

"Blondie!" I heard and chanced a glance behind me and saw a tall dark figure running after me.

"No!" I cried and turned and ran through the deep prairie. "No! I didn't, I didn't, I never did!" I cried with tears and rain in my eyes, my chest bursting and my lungs exploding with exertion from all my sobbing and screaming. "I didn't!" I screamed out into the night as one of my hands cupped my injured cheek and the other turned into a claw and grabbed at the air as if to pull me along faster.

"Blondie!" I heard him bellow and it lit the fear in my heart and sped me on faster. My thick tights slid to my hip bones and began to sag between my legs and slow me down. I yanked at them as I leapt through the field as my leg muscles began to cramp in revolt against the cold and the exertion.

"Blondie! It's me! It's Ed!" I heard him yell and I faltered in my sprinting and turned to look at him in the moonlight. I saw a big mussed mane of hair and as I turned to get a better look, I stepped in a hole and twisted my ankle and went down hard and disappeared in the tall grass.

I lay there breathing in and out in burning gasps as I felt my ankle throb and my elbows scream with friction burns. My face felt frozen in makeup and my right cheek was swollen and drawing tighter and I noticed as I looked up at the night sky that my eye was only open a tiny crack and I couldn't see anything out of it at all.

"Blondie!" Ed gasped, his face above me, blocking out the rain. "Blondie! Jesus! Blondie, what happened?"

"Allen," I choked out as I held my hands above my face against being hit. I panted out as I peeked around my hands and saw it really was Ed; Ed with his glowing pale eyes and all his hair hanging down around his face. I reached for him to warn him, to shake him and make him understand, to protect him, for surely any moment Allen would catch up with us, with his knife, and beat us both and kill us both. As I grabbed at Ed's arms I began to quiver uncontrollably and felt as if any moment I would black out from sheer terror. Ed ran his arms under me and cradled me to him and picked me up and I wrapped my arms around his neck and hid in his hair.

"Ed," I panted, "if he sees us, he'll kill us. He has a big knife," I whispered in his ear.

"He'll do no such thing, Blondie," Ed promised as he looked all around. He had raindrops glistening in his hair and they looked like tiny lights in the moonlight. He walked us in silence past the white tents and I feared that any moment Allen would jump out behind us and kill Ed and me both. Just before we went into the forest Ed said, "Look," and nodded off to the left. "There he goes." And we could just barely see him limping across the county blacktop as a semi drove past, its lights making Allen glow momentarily; he looked very tiny and hunched over as he crossed the road.

"You're safe, Blondie," Ed almost growled.

"What about Kai?"

"He'll be ok," Ed shrugged and carried me to the Cutlass.

"I had flowers for you, Blondie," he said as he put me in the seat.

I thought of Kai's flowers and wondered where I'd dropped them.

"I had flowers for you and I waited for you but you never showed up," Ed said as he got in the front seat and shook and trembled as he started the car. He turned to me as we sat in the rumbling car as it rained around us. I instinctively locked my door.

Ed cocked his head at me, "Allen did this?" he asked as he reached towards my face and eye.

"Don't touch it!" I winced.

"I'm gonna have to pack you up and take you with me, Blondie. That's all there is to it," he whispered and reached out and kissed my forehead.

I collapsed on the seat as he put the car in gear and drove us home.

***

"Baby Blondie, ssshhh, you're safe now," Ed said to me as he stroked long strands of hair off my forehead.

"Where am I?" I asked. Fear rippled over my skin as I strained to see if we were still out in the dark prairie. I turned my head this way and that to look around and felt the thick down pillow under me.

"Shhh," he put his finger over my lips.

It was dark and I was stretched out on Ed's warm waterbed and had been asleep. Ed was lying next to me, fiddling with my hair that was tangled and twisted about my head. My face felt swollen and ached on the right side but it felt clean of all the hard makeup and my eyelashes were light again. The form fitting costume was gone and I had on soft boxer shorts and a huge t-shirt of Ed's.

Ed had one leg thrown over both of mine and he was half on top of me. I scooted closer to him and tried to get all the way under him until I heard him groan.

"Baby, what are you doing?" he asked in a low rumble.

"Nothing."

I focused on his face in the dark room and could only make out his eyebrows and eyelashes and his big lips. He'd shaved since he'd dropped me off at the theatre that afternoon before the play. I reached out and touched his chin and he smiled. I traced his jaw with my finger and felt the prickle of where he'd missed shaving.

"You were having a nightmare," he whispered and leaned over and kissed me on the forehead and then lightly brushed his lips against my swollen and stinging cheek.

"Did it really happen?" I asked him as I reached up with my fingers and lightly felt my closed eye that wouldn't open and my cheek that still blazed.

"Yes. I'm sorry, Baby. I'm sorry I wasn't there to stop it."

"Are you really here with me?"

"In the flesh, Sweet Baby Blondie," he said as he propped himself up on an elbow and gazed down at me. I felt him wriggle closer to me underneath the flannel comforter and I felt his waterbed roll in slow waves under us. I slid my arms around his neck and pulled him to me and nuzzled the uninjured side of my face in his hair.

"I brought you home with me," he whispered in my ear and kissed my hair as he eased himself all the way on top of me. His warm body enclosed me as we rolled up and down together on the waves of the bed and I relaxed and felt safe and could hardly keep my eyes open.

"What about Allen? What about Aunt Clem? Won't she worry about me?" I came to in a panic and asked out loud, suddenly remembering the details of the evening.

"Shhhh, Baby, you'll wake up Mom and get me in trouble. It's all taken care of," he whispered and kissed my ear.

"You have more hair than I do," he breathed in my ear a few minutes later as he ran his fingers through my hair. I unwound my arms from around his neck and pulled back just a little from under him to look at his face and could just see his eyes glowing silver under his heavy brows as he hovered just inches above me.

"I've never been with a girl who had more hair than me," he said as he smiled and ran his hand through all my hair that was fanned out on the pillow.

"I've never been with anyone," I whispered close to his lips and I kissed his bottom lip lightly as his eyes bored into mine. He put his long fingers on the side of my face that wasn't beaten and traced my jaw to my neck.

"And you're not going to be," he whispered and enveloped me with all of the weight of his body.

CHAPTER NINETEEN

"Daddy," I said as he opened the door of my old house, "Daddy, I'm moving back in," I said from where I stood on the front porch.

"Baby? Ed? Sweet God, what happened to your face?"

My Daddy stood in the door with his mouth open and stared from me to Ed and back to me. Ed was behind me with several boxes of my things; my clothes, my quilt from Aunt Clem, my Pink Floyd records and several books. All I owned boiled down to not much of anything valuable and could fit into a few boxes.

The day after Allen beat me, Ed and I slept in late until Mrs. Small peeked into Ed's room and saw us there and nearly had a stroke. Her high pitch whistle of a gasp woke us both. I had been sleeping with my uninjured cheek against Ed's shoulder and all my hair fanned out on top the comforter. He had his arm wrapped around me and his hand in my hair and his big leg thrown over me.

"Oh my, oh dear. Eddy," Mrs. Small whispered after she got her breath back.

"Hey Mom. Is there coffee still?" Ed asked her like nothing was amiss.

"No Eddy, its noon. But I'll make some more right away," she said and backed out of the room.

"She only calls me Eddy when she's flipped out but she'll get over it," he murmured in my ear as I was trying to burrow under the comforter and hide.

It was over coffee at the Small's while Mrs. Small inspected my eye that was black and swollen shut, and my cheek that was purple and green and tight, that I made my decision.

"I'm moving home today," I said out of the left side of my mouth and I looked at Ed while he read the Sunday funnies. He tilted his wide, slanted forehead down at me and furrowed his brows as he sipped his coffee and stared into my eyes. His eyelids looked bruised and he had dark rings under his pale eyes.

"I'm gonna need your help," I gulped. I was scared he'd tell me no or that he'd tell me it was a bad idea.

"Anything you want, Baby-Locks. I'm yours. Just ask."

Ed went with me to Aunt Clem's and he told her what Allen had done. He didn't falter or stop when she brought her fist to her mouth and sat down in the big chair with tears streaming out her eyes.

"So call Jeffrey, Mrs. Rawlins, or call the police but someone's got to find that boy. I'll not have him roughing up my Sweet Blondie ever again and she'll not be coming back here again. If Jeffrey or the cheese don't find him, you can bet Mr. Hunnicutt will and if he finds Allen, well, Allen's as good as dead," Ed said to her as she turned grey.

Her eyes flickered up to Ed. "You're telling Baby's Daddy?" Aunt Clem asked.

"Hell yes. She's his child, woman. He needs to know who beat his child."

Aunt Clem just stared at Ed as her lip quivered and as she wrung her hands in her lap.

"Please, Ed," she begged.

"Jesus Fucking Christ!" Ed yelled. "Look at Baby!" He pulled me in front of him. Now I was crying out of my one eye that could still cry.

"Jesus Christ. Look what he did to my Sweet Baby, woman," Ed yelled again, his voice wavering with anger. "I should find him and kill him myself," he growled between his clenched jaw as he squeezed my shoulders where the silk wings had torn at my skin.

"Ed," I pleaded and ducked from under him.

"She's moving out. Today," he said as he took me to my room.

And now we were on my Daddy's porch, waiting for him to let us in and waiting for him to stop looking from me to Ed and back again, trying to piece together what happened.

"Your daughter is moving back in, Mr. Hunnicutt. It's time for you to be her Daddy again," Ed said as he gently pushed me forward and I walked into my old house. "It's time for you to be her Daddy again because Allen didn't turn out to be so hot of one after all."

I sat on the couch as Ed and my Daddy carried my things up the steps to my old room. Daddy was absolutely mute the entire time. When they came back down Ed told him what happened.

"Allen flipped, Mr. Hunnicutt. Last night after Baby's play out in the country. He flipped," Ed hung his head and ran his fingers through his hair several times and cleared his throat before he could continue. "He flipped, Mr. Hunnicutt," Ed said again as he looked my Daddy in the eye, "He plum lost his mind and he beat her and she's lucky she got away." Ed looked at the floor and rubbed his lips with his fingers several times as a tear slid down his cheek and he shook his head in silence before he whispered, "I was too late. I was too late to stop him. I'm sorry. I'm sorry I didn't protect you better, Sweet Blondie," he said as he looked at me with his eyebrows wilted in and his pale eyes full of tears and his bottom lip out. Then he looked back up at my Daddy and steeled himself and said, "And now she's moving back home, where she'll be safe."

"Oh Baby," Daddy said as he took me in his arms. "I should have been there," he said as he held me to him.

"I should have told you, Daddy," I whispered into his plaid shirt and I breathed in his scent of Old Spice and sawdust. "I should have told you all about it and had you come out to see me."

"Shit mother, I was there and a lot good I was," Ed mumbled as he sat on the couch in a lump and bowed his head.

Moving back in with my Daddy was the first big decision I made about my life. I saw it as the first step I took towards growing up and becoming a woman.

The second decision I made in my life was a couple of days later when I told my Daddy that Ed wanted to take me to the fireworks at Rush Lake for the Fourth. I decided I didn't want to sneak around with Ed, and that I didn't want to miss out going with him either, I came right out and asked my Daddy.

"Is that ok, Daddy? Ed wants to be the one to take me to the Fourth." Maybe I couched it in a way that would make it look like Ed wanted to make up for not saving me from Allen soon enough, when really it wasn't Ed's fault at all. It was all Allen's.

It'd been so long since my Daddy had had to make a decision about me that he didn't know how to answer for several seconds.

"Well Baby, I guess that'd be fine," he finally said and I breathed a sigh of relief.

***

"Baby Hunnicutt, is that you?" I heard someone call to me while I was sitting on my Daddy's front porch reading the day after I'd moved in.

It was in the 90's outside and felt even hotter inside at just 10 in the morning so I'd brought out a jar of ice water and my old worn copy of Jane Austen's <u>Sense and Sensibility</u> to try to catch a breeze.

"Baby, by gosh it is you. So I guess the rumors are all true."

I looked up to see a brand new red muscle car had pulled in the drive across the street and a big guy in full La Rue High football gear was walking stiff legged across the street to come talk to me.

"Jimmy? Is that you?" I asked.

"Course it's me, silly," he said and smiled. "Who else would it be?"

"Where's your glasses?"

"I don't wear 'em to practice, Baby. They'd get busted up." He loped on tired legs over to me on the porch and knelt on one knee on the step below me and wolf whistled at me.

"So I guess it's true what they're sayin'."

"What's that?" I asked barely above a whisper. I suddenly found the breath knocked out of me and could barely talk. I wondered what people were saying.

"Well, for starters that your cousin, the one that went to Nam, busted up your face and Kai's too. And that there's a search for him and a warrant for him too, of course. And that you moved back in with your Daddy. And here you are." He said the last part like me being back at my Daddy's made up for, at least in his mind, all the other bad stuff that went down.

    Even though he was propped up on his knee on a step below mine, I still had to look up a little at him, he'd grown that tall. Without his glasses his eyes were big and deep-set and dark. He'd grown out his flat-top quite a bit, though it was still short and spiky and now it was shaped like a football helmet's insides. His jaw and his neck melted right into his shoulders or maybe it was just all his padding that came up to his neck.

    "Just came from practice," he said as if he heard my thoughts. "Water main's busted over that end of town, near the high school. No showers," he said as he put a big piece of bubble gum in his mouth.

    "Gum?" he asked and held out a square to me.

    "Oh, no thanks," I said and touched my right cheek without thinking. It hurt to chew on that side.

    "Baby," he breathed out as he chewed his wad of gum and shook his head back and forth, "I'm of the mind to go out with some of the guys and see if I cain't find your cousin who done this, myself. Look what he done," he sighed in almost a whistle. He looked down the road a bit and turned back to me and his face flushed scarlet as he looked down at my bare feet and back up to me again.

    "O' course, ahem, o' course you're still the prettiest girl at school," he said to me, the tips of his ears even turning red.

"Black eye and all, Baby, you're prettier than 'em all. Even all the pom pom girls," he said and looked down at my feet on the step near him. I curled my toes under and he looked back up at me. His dark, deep-set eyes roamed my face and I wondered if he could even see me without his glasses.

He licked his lips a couple of times and cleared his throat and said, "I got my driver's license last week."

"Really? You're already sixteen? You already learned how?"

"Well. Yeh. I got held back in kindergarten. You probably didn't know that. Year I met you was my second year at it. Anyway, being a year older pays off in football. I'm bigger than everyone on the team and then there's getting to learn to drive before y'all," he said and stood up all the way.

"Yeh, I see that."

"Yeh, so I got my license. And Dad got me that new Camaro. Just got it," he said and looked back down at my feet.

I pulled my legs up under me and tucked my dress under my feet and as I did, Jimmy's eyes rose up from my feet up to my face.

"So,uhh," he said, his face once more flushed red, "I want you to be the first girl I take out in my new car."

"Oh!" I didn't know how to answer and be polite. This was the first time Jimmy had ever really talked to me without trying to grab me somewhere.

"Oh, I don't know," I stammered and nervously touched my cheek.

"Oh, I know you don't want to go out till your face is healed up. But soon as it is, I'll take you out. I won't take out any other girls till then." He looked down again and flushed some more. "You're worth waitin' for, Baby Hunnicutt, you are," he gushed when he looked back up at me.

"Oh my," I whispered and covered my face out of embarrassment for us both.

"Well. I need to get home and shower. First day of summer practice and all. Quite a work out if you know what I mean."

I didn't know what he meant, but I didn't say anything.

He started to go but turned around and came back, clear up to where I was sitting and kneeled down right in front of me. Maybe the football team knelt down for all their huddles in practice and he was just used to huddling, but I'd never seen anyone kneel so much to talk to me.

"Baby?" he asked, his voice in a deep huff, like he was short of breath.

"Yes?" I asked and backed up a little from where I sat.

"Can I just have a kiss to hold me while I wait for our date?"

I backed up further and am sure if Ed were there he would have said something about my one good eye being big as a quarter.

"What?" I asked in a whisper.

"Just a kiss, Baby. It might be a long time till your face heals."

If God was good it would be.

I didn't answer, I was too dumfounded. I'm sure Petra would have had a million coy, smart-ass answers for him but I had none.

"Uh, I guess," I heard myself answer as if I were possessed.

Jimmy smiled and flushed some more and tilted my chin up and kissed me on my mouth. A nice, short, dry one.

"Thanks, Baby," he said and smiled and turned on his cleat and walked back across the street in all his football gear.

I licked my lips and got up and went back into the muggy house, leaving my book and my jar of water on the porch.

CHAPTER TWENTY

"Shit mother fuck, Blondie," Ed said to me a few minutes later from under the dining room table where I was laying on the floor, listening to a stack of records on the stereo. I'd forgotten how comforting it was to lay under the big dark table and listen to music; something I used to do when my Mama played the piano or records when I was small.

Ed had knocked and came on in and found me under there listening to Beethoven's Pastorale and he lay down under the table with me.

"Shit mother fuck," he said again. I rolled my head over to look at him.

"What?" I asked him.

He had on his worn out, too small jeans and a plain white t-shirt and he smelled like soap and his hair was still wet from the shower.

"Fuck, Blondie. I don't even know what to say," he looked at me with his bottom lip stuck out and his eyes closed. His lids looked dark and his lashes made perfect fans on his cheeks. I reached out and lightly touched one and caressed his cheekbone with the back of my fingers.

"How many boyfriends you got going on, Blondie?"

"I don't know what you mean. Jimmy was just asking me out, and the answer is obviously no, and then he asked for one kiss. It was nothing. Quit taking the mickey out of me for it."

"Is he going to be your next boyfriend?"

"Aren't you my boyfriend?" I asked quietly as I reached over and touched his dimple in his chin.

"I like to think I'm more than that," he said and looked me in the eye. I found it hard to keep his gaze and not look away from the intensity of his stare. His hair was stuck to his neck in long swirls where it was curly underneath near the back of his neck.

"What does that mean?" I asked him and gulped.

"It means," he said and looked up at the bottom of the table and licked his lips and tilted his head back far on the wood floor, "it means," he turned and looked at me with his pale eyes, "that I want more. I want much more than to just be your boyfriend."

All I could think of, that was beyond boyfriend, was husband and I couldn't imagine Ed wanting to marry me.

"Like, go steady?" I asked.

"Huh! Ahuh!" he laughed. "Do they even use that phrase anymore?"

"I don't know, Ed. I don't know what comes after boyfriend. I've only had Kai. I don't know."

"You didn't *have* Kai, did you, sweet Baby Blondie?" he asked and rolled over on his side to me. He raised his arm above his head and twirled a piece of my hair between his fingers.

"NO! Sheesh Ed!" I smacked his shoulder.

"So you're still a, uhhh, a virgin, sweet, heavenly, Blondie?" he asked me with a big smile on his face, his teeth white against his red lips.

Now I was flushing just like Jimmy.

"Of course, Ed. I'm saving that."

"For what?" he grinned with a sideways curl to his lip and he batted his eyes at me. "Or should I say, for whom? Hopefully not Mr. All-American." He squinted one eye at me and growled.

"I'm saving it, that's all," I said and pushed him away from me.

"What's that mean, exactly?" He came back closer to me.

"Ed!" I smacked at him again. He was trying to wear me down with all his questions and I told him just that.

"If I were trying to wear you down, Baby, I'd do this," he said and rolled over completely on top of me and cupped my chin in his hand and took my mouth with all of his, his tongue sweeping all the way into mine and out again and again. "Huh!" he laughed as he broke away a little bit. His lips left me breathless and his openly talking about my virginity made me feel flighty. He looked into my eyes as he waited for me to recover from his kiss and then he pushed my knees open with his legs and he kissed my bottom lip. He smelled soapy and fresh and he was clean shaven and tasted good like French toast.

"That's how I'd wear you down, sweet, virginal, Baby Blondie," he smiled and batted his eyelashes at me while on top of me. "I'd do that and I'd do this," he said and as he stared in to my eyes, he palmed my breast and squeezed me again and again and grazed my nipple with his palm through my thin dress and made me gasp. He grunted his approval at his effect on me and he pushed my legs further apart with both of his and pushed my dress up high on my thighs.

"Ahuh!" he smiled and kissed me quick and released my breast. "I should kill Allen for what he did to your eye, Baby. But I can still see that your eyes are both dark and deep as ever, but I know you're not scared of me, Baby. I know different, I know," he whispered in my ear, "that you're hot for me."

"Ed," I wanted to say something to him about getting off of me or stopping or something but I couldn't because he began licking my ear and I was unable to put two words together at all.

"If I wanted to wear you down, sweet Baby," he ran his hands under my hair, "I have a million ways to do it without asking questions or playing word games. No need for words. Use my mouth, yes, and my hands," he said between lapping my earlobe as he began to trace a circle with his finger around my breast through my sundress. He ran his finger over my nipple and then he began to squeeze and I felt him growing restless between my legs.

"Sweet God, if you never wear a bra it's fine with me, just don't let Joe Football near you," he growled and he took my mouth with his and continued to knead my breast in his hand over and over. His tongue swept in and out around mine in slow time to the Beethoven and I wrapped my fingers in his wet hair and was reminded of the first time he kissed me.

"Ohh, Baby, you still want me to try to wear you down my way?" he breathed on my neck as he ran his hands up my dress and began stroking me behind my knees.

"Yes, please," I breathed out, not knowing what I was agreeing to anymore, just knowing that I didn't want Ed to stop. My answer made him groan deep in his throat and he kissed me again as the record changed to Beethoven's La Pathetique.

"Ummmm," Ed groaned as I licked his full lips and squirmed under him and wrapped my legs around him tighter.

"Sweet God, right here under this table?" he asked.

I grabbed his jaw to kiss him for an answer and brought his mouth to mine and then I remembered my bruised face and stopped.

"Baby?" he panted. "Baby?" He nipped at my lips.

"Isn't my face horrible to look at, Ed," I asked and tried to turn away.

"Uhh," Ed groaned as he continued to caress me behind my knees and worked his hands down to the back of my thighs, stroking me in small circles. "Sweet heavens, your skin is like silk," he said and then he grabbed my butt through my panties. "Cotton panties," he huffed, "oh my God," he whispered and rubbed me there. "I love your tiny ass, sweet Blondie" and he pushed himself harder between my legs.

Just when I was beginning to think Ed didn't hear me ask about my face he said, as he kissed me on the cheek, "Your face is beautiful as always, even banged up, you can work me right over the edge, Blondie-Locks." Then he pulled my underpants off and began to stroke me with his fingers. "Sweet heavens, you're tight and so wet," he rasped. "You're beautiful as ever, and you're the tightest, sweetest thing ever."

"Ed, Ed, Ed, Ed, Ed," I panted out his name as he ran his fingers between my legs and I got closer and closer to losing control of myself.

"Yes?" he asked and kissed me. "Am I wearing you down now?" he asked with his hand between my legs.

"Yes, yes, yes, yes," I panted and grabbed his wrist to make sure he never moved his hand away. "Are you going to, Ed? Are you?" I dug my nails into his arm.

"I am. I am going to. Do you still want me to?"

"I think I am now, Ed!" I nearly yelled as Ed stroked me deeper and deeper.

"Shit mother fuck," he breathed as he unzipped his pants and pulled my dress up over my head and flung it. "Christ!" he said and pulled his own shirt off. I ran my hands all over his chest and stomach and it made his muscles all roll under his skin and made him quiver and groan as I felt as if I was going to lose complete control of myself any minute.

"Jesus woman, slow down, wait for me, shit mother," he smiled and grabbed the back of my hips.

***

"Sweet heavenly Blondie, do I even have hair left on my head?" Ed asked me as he rolled off me some minutes later.

"Why?" I asked and ran my hands through his hair as he lay there with his pants undone. I chanced a glance down there and was amazed at how much more hair he had there than me and how much darker it was than mine.

"Jesus God. I think I came my hair clear off my head or was that you pulling on it?"

I laughed and covered my mouth. It was me pulling on his hair like a horse's reigns.

He pulled his pants up and tucked everything back in and gave his zipper a yank. I was scared he'd get something stuck in it but I guess he'd been wearing his pants like that a long time and knew what he was doing.

"Sheesh, sweet virginal Blondie, you didn't put up much resistance," he laughed and smiled and rolled back over on top of me. "Sweet God, you're a piece of heaven right here. How will I ever be able to leave you behind?"

He reached under me and palmed my butt as he pressed his bare chest against mine.

"How Blondie?"

"Don't talk of leaving, Ed," I pleaded with him. "I don't want to think of it."

"How about we talk of wearing you down again? Huh! Ahuh!" he laughed and squeezed my butt with both hands. "Sweet heavens," he said with his big lips on my collarbone, "I've just had my sweet Blondie-Locks. Sweet Mother forgive me." He shut his eyes for a few seconds as if he was really saying a prayer.

"Do you need forgiveness for having me, Ed?" I asked as I ran my hands over his butt, but he had jeans on so it wasn't the same.

"By God, yes, Blondie Locks. Wearing you down, taking you, having you, coming my brains out in you," he shivered, "Jesus. Yes. All that. I'm sure to go to hell or jail or both at the same time, you only being seventeen."

"I'm sixteen, Ed."

"Good Lord, I'd do it again in a heartbeat," he said. "But, we'd better get off the floor and put you back together before my mom walks in or the whole fucking town or whoever and they string me up!" Ed ran his hands up and down my body a couple of times as if trying to memorize it and then said, "Go take a shower, Baby. I'll watch." He grinned like a maniac as I crawled out from under the table.

"You will not! You'll go home! Out the back door at that!"

"Just like old times," he laughed and left through the kitchen.

***

I was in the kitchen that evening getting a glass of iced tea for my Daddy when I heard someone at the front door. I froze near the library table in the hall outside the living room when I heard my Daddy say, "Ed, come on in." I froze and I rubbed the head of the little ceramic cocker spaniel out of habit as I took a chug of my Daddy's iced tea and listened.

"Mr. Hunnicutt, I need to talk to you about our Baby."

"Our Baby?"

"Yes, Mr. Hunnicutt. I'll be going back to Colorado before you know it and not be around to help keep an eye on her."

"Is that right?" I heard my Daddy ask as I took another sip of his tea.

"That's right, sir. And I have a feeling she's gonna need looked after, if you know what I mean."

"I'm afraid I don't know what you mean, Ed."

"Well. For instance, that kid across the street with the new sports car."

"Jimmy?"

"Yeh. Him. He's been harassing our Baby for years."

"I wasn't aware of that. I always thought he was a fine boy. Made varsity this year and only a sophomore."

"Yeh and he's got his eye on Baby. And I'm betting as soon as Baby's face is healed, he'll be asking her out. And I'm not gonna be here to help keep sweet Blondie, I mean, Baby, safe."

"What do you think I should do, Ed?" I heard my Daddy and it sounded like he was humoring Ed.

"Well, Mr. Hunnicutt, this is a serious matter. We're talking about your only daughter, here." I could hear Ed adding in his own mind, "and my own sweet love-child" and it made me smile to think I felt I knew him so well I could read his thoughts.

"What I think you ought to do, sir," Ed continued, "is put the fear of death in the boy."

"Don't you mean God, Ed? Fear of God?"

"No, I don't, sir. God forgives. Death don't."

"I see."

"Do you? Cuz I don't know that you do. That boy has a car now and he'll be wanting to take your sweet Baby places. Far out in the dark, country, sorts of places."

There was silence for a few seconds and I imagined my Daddy taking it all in.

"Is that what you think, Ed?"

"That's what I know, sir. Baby is innocent sir and she's just too sweet for her own good, sir. Too, I don't know, too eager to think the best of everyone and everyone's intentions and too ready to give everyone a second chance. She has no instincts sir. She's naïve as hell. I've known her a long time, and I know." I could picture Ed running his hands through his hair like he did when he got worked up about something.

"Do you now? You've known her a long time, you think?"

"Yessir. I have. I helped raise her, sir, over at Jeffrey and Allen's."

"Did you now?"

"Yessir."

"And what's that make me?"

"Excuse me?"

"What's that make me, letting a guy like you and those two twins raise my Baby?" I heard my Daddy getting angry and I heard him stand up.

"You did what you had to sir. I'm just looking out for Baby's safety before I leave."

"She was real safe with you out at the hippie get-together when her cousin beat her."

Silence again. I shifted from foot to foot in the dark hall.

"Mr. Hunnicutt, all I'm asking is that when that hot-rod driving punk from across the street asks to take your Baby out, that you reflect on her being hurt just recently, and you put the fear of death in that kid if he so much as touches one hair on her sweet head. I can do it myself before I leave town if you won't. But I thought I'd let you be the one."

"I'll talk to him if he ever asks her out. But he's a good, clean-cut kid. He's going places."

There was a tense silence and I imagined Ed grumbling in his mind about where Jimmy Collins was going. Then I heard Ed stand up and sigh and he said, "Well, I'm here to take Baby to the fireworks."

"And who's putting the fear of death in you, boy?" Daddy asked Ed just as I walked in with his tea.

"No one, sir," Ed answered and fixed his frosty eyes on my Daddy and then turned to me, "Ready Blondie?" he asked and winked at me.

CHAPTER TWENTY-ONE

Ed and I were lost in the dark amongst all the townsfolk from both La Rue and Rush who came together at Rush State Lake to watch the fireworks. Because it was dark, Ed said it was okay for me to sit on his lap as he sat Indian style on the plaid picnic blanket.

"Baby," he whispered to me as he wrapped his arms around my waist and pulled me close to him, "Baby, you wrapped me round your finger as soon as I came back to town." He kissed my hair, my ear, the side of my face.

"Ed, what if someone sees us?" I asked as I scooted closer to him.

"I don't care," he said with his lips in my hair. "Let them look."

I glanced around at all the spectators but no one was looking at us, they were all looking up at the sky, their faces lit up by the fireworks.

"Baby Blondie, come away with me, will you? Come away with me now," he said to me and lifted me up by my waist off his lap and pulled me away from everyone. He pulled me through the dark, through all the people sitting on lawn chairs and sprawled out on blankets. Sparklers and glo sticks flashed off to the sides of my eyes in a blur as fireworks sizzled and exploded overhead.

"Come with me, Blondie, faster!" Ed called to me as he pulled me faster and faster through the maze of bodies. I felt the jagged hem of my red and blue bandana dress whip about my knees and my hair trailed behind me and off my sticky back. I wondered what people thought to see Ed pull me away from the lake and the fireworks. Maybe in the dark they just thought we were the same age; two lovers leaving the fireworks to go have a moment alone, to go make love.

Sweat ran down my face from my hair and my heart beat a hard staccato in my chest as Ed pulled me into the dark woods.

"Where are you taking me?" I called to him, out of breath, as I watched his hair swing back and forth between his shoulder blades.

"Back this way to Settler's Beach."

Settler's Beach was the small beach used for canoe launching. It was surrounded on three sides by trees and was very dark. The air was even closer and damper back there; closed in by the trees and filled with the smoke of all the fireworks. Mosquitoes swarmed and buzzed about my head as Ed pulled me out of the woods and onto the sandy beach.

"Let's go for a swim. I'm meltin'."

I watched as Ed let go of my hand and he walked to the water. I wondered if he'd walk right in, in his skin tight new Wranglers, but he didn't. He stripped them off with his back to me. I was amazed at how wide and dark his shoulders were compared to how narrow and white his butt was. I watched all his muscles ripple just under his skin as he laid his pants on the sand and as all his hair fell over his shoulders I marveled at how white the back of his neck was compared to his bronzed back.

He stood up and twisted around to me and smiled in the moonlight.

"Penny for your thoughts, Blondie?" he asked and grinned. "Were you just now checking out my backside?" He turned all the way around to face me and I looked away a little.

"Blondie? Are you coming in with me or not?"

"Just turn around, Ed." I waved my hand at him that he should turn back around to the lake.

"Huh, ahuh!" he laughed quietly and startled a small bird that was sleeping near the water, its wings made soft, short chuffs as it flew out over the lake. "Baby," Ed called to me as he came back to me and I looked down at the sand at his long toes as they burrowed in the sand next to mine. "Baby, come swim with me, okay?" I felt his lips on my fingers as he took my hand to his mouth and then pulled me towards the water. "Come in with me, Blondie," he said and let go of my hand and he went right into the dark water.

Ed swam out a little ways and turned around to face me. I stood there with my toes anchored into the sand and stared right into his silvery eyes and remembered all the times Mama told me to stay away from him. I remembered how that made me want to be around him even more. As Ed watched me from the water, his broad lips parted in a wide smile and I untied the halter of my dress from around my neck and let it fall around my waist. Ed's eyes grew wide and his dimples popped out in his cheeks as he watched my bandana dress, my hankie dress, slide down to my feet, and I stepped out of it and walked into the lake and dived under the warm water.

"Sweet Blondie, swim out to me," Ed beckoned from where he tread water. I swam closer to him but stayed out of his reach.

"Blondie," he called and pooched his lips out in a pout, "come closer." He held his arms out to me as he lazily tread in the black water.

"No, Ed, I'll sink if I get too close."

"Why would you sink?" he laughed as he dipped his head backwards into the waves and soaked all of his hair as he grinned up at the night sky. When he came back up into the moonlight his head was sleek as an otter's.

"Besides, I'm naked," I said, and my mouth slipped under and I spat out the lake water when I came back up.

"Baby," Ed said and smirked at me.

"What?"

"I just saw you naked a second ago. Just get a little closer? So I don't have to shout."

I tread a few feet closer and he smiled and pulled me by my fingertips even closer to him.

"Sweet Baby Blondie," Ed said as he stayed afloat without much exertion. "would you rather I left tomorrow and came back at Christmas or left in two months and didn't come back for almost a year?" he asked as he pushed his wet hair off his forehead with both his hands.

I stopped circling my arms and went limp and began to sink under the water as I felt the bottom of my heart drop out. Quick as ever Ed had me below my armpits and pulled me into him. I wrapped my arms around his neck and my legs around his waist and felt his hand holding me up by my rear as his other arm made wide circles to keep us up.

"Baby?"

"Yes?" I asked with my face in his neck.

"Did you keep your underpants on?" he asked and I could hear his laughter just below the surface of his words.

"Yes," I said, embarrassed.

"You really are a child still, aren't you?" He sounded a hundred years older than me. He almost sounded like my Daddy disapproving of something I'd done.

"Yes," I whispered and kissed him below his ear.

"Jesus," he groaned and squeezed me on the butt. "My own true love-child," he tilted his head back up towards the starry sky and I kissed him on the throat.

I couldn't tell him goodbye. I couldn't get the words to come out so I gave him those two kisses as he held onto me in the deep, black water as the fireworks continued to explode out over the lake.

"Come back at Christmas," I whispered into his hair and squeezed against him tight.

"I will, Blondie, I will," he said and kissed my forehead. "Grow up some while I'm away. Make some decisions. Take control of things. I won't be here to wear ya down again, ahuh huh! But for God's sake don't let any other boy take control, please, Baby. You're still just a child and I'm sure to burn for what I've done to ya. But I don't want anyone else to have ya. I should just go away and not come back," he sighed. At that I let go of him and fell away from him a little. But he wouldn't let go of me and he pulled me into him again.

The warm water lapped at my back and my hair spread out on top of the water around me like a pale fan. When I looked up at Ed his eyes sparkled silver in the moonlight down at me.

"I'll want to hear from ya while I'm away, Baby. I'll want to know how you're growing up." His voice was gravelly and rough and I didn't have words to comfort him as I heard his voice catch. "Dammit, Blondie, what was I thinking getting mixed up with just a kid?" he asked. He pressed his lips against my forehead and kissed me above my eyebrow as he broke my heart and hurt my feelings with his words. "Dammit, Blondie, why'd you still have to be just a kid?" he asked as he nudged my chin up to look at him as I held onto his shoulders. I knew there were tears in my eyes just about to run over and I was doing all I could to not openly sob at the thought of losing Ed.

"Dammit," he said as he cupped my chin and slanted his mouth over mine and kissed me with the urgency we both felt with our time running out. I threaded my hands in his hair and wrapped my legs even tighter around him and kissed him back with all I could, wanting to remember the taste of him.

"What are we gonna do, sweet Blondie?" he asked as he kissed my throat and slid his hand down the back of my panties.

"Take me," I whispered, my lips in his hair.

"To Colorado?" he asked, somewhat shocked.

"No. Now." I ran my hands down his chest to his stomach.

"It's wrong, Blondie," he said as he squeezed me, "But I don't give a goddamn."

***

Ed and I made love on the beach just like in Here to Eternity as the smoke from the fireworks show rolled low over the lake on the humid air and disappeared in swirls in the woods.

"I love you, Blondie," Ed told me as he took my upper lip between his own full lips and sucked on it. "I love you, Blondie," he breathed as he ran his long fingers through my hair and kissed my eyelids and made love to me as slow as possible in the warm sand. "I love you, Blondie," he told me again and again as we moved together and as I clung to him and drew him as close to me as I could.

"I'll call you every week, Blondie, I promise," he said as he walked me to my front porch after driving us home. "I'll be back at Christmas, sweet Baby," he said as I wrapped my arms around his waist and I buried my face in his soft t-shirt and wondered how I could ever let go of him as the tears rolled down my cheeks.

"Say something, Blondie, say something," he told me as he took my chin and forced me to look up at him. His eyes were pale and brimming but I still felt the heat of their intensity as he stared into my own and I cried even harder when his tears spilled over as his eyebrows wilted in that old familiar expression that used to be a game to me when I was a child.

"You'll be gone forever, Ed," I whispered as we stood on my Daddy's porch.

"Not forever, Baby. Just till December."

Neither of us wanted to talk about him moving to Breckenridge when he was done with flight school. I wasn't even sure he'd be done with school in December.

"Feels like forever," I said as I gazed up at him in the dark.

""It's not, sweet Blondie, it's not."

He caressed the side of my face and I reached up and pushed his hair off his face and tucked it behind his ear. He took my wrist and kissed my pulse and grinned a crooked grin at me.

"Write me every week, Baby. I want to hear everything that your sweet little self is doing. I want all the details, Baby." He put my palm on his face and I felt his beard beginning to grow back and wondered how thick it'd be by December. I ran my hand over his jaw and I caressed his full lips as he kissed my fingers.

"Will you write me, Ed?"

"I'll call, Baby, I'll call you this time."

I stared into his eyes, not able to tell him goodbye.

"Get inside, Blondie, sweet Blondie. Don't watch me leave," he told me as he opened the door for me and pushed me through. "Go, Blondie, I love you," he whispered as he shut the door.

I leaned against the door and I thought of him walking across the yard back next door for the last time for a long time and realized I never told him I loved him.

"I love you, Ed Small," I whispered to the dark living room.

CHAPTER TWENTY-TWO

The month of July slid by and every day for the first two weeks I waited around the house for Ed to call. I got his PO Box from Mrs. Small and I wrote him a letter that very first day that he left on the bus. I told him I loved him and that that one month I had with him had been the best of my life and that I couldn't wait for him to call.

The second week of July rolled around and I mailed Ed a small greeting card with a drawing of a fuzzy white kitten on the front. All I wrote in it was, "I miss you. Your sweet Blondie."

By the third week I was growing more and more agitated so I went to visit Mrs. Small to see how she was and see if she'd heard from Ed.

"Oh yes, dear, Eddy's fine. I miss him very much," she said as she pulled out her pruning shears from a box in the basement. She had the shortest, tiniest curls growing out of her scalp and she tied a scarf on her head before putting her straw sun hat on.

"I feel good enough to putter out in the garden," she said and smiled and laced up her Keds. "Coming out with me, Baby?"

"Sure, Mrs. Small. So, Ed has called you, Mrs. Small?"

"Of course dear, I'm his mother," she said as she patted my hand and headed out the back door to the overrun garden.

"When did he call, Mrs. Small?" I called to her as I ran after her.

"Oh," she thought about it as she pulled her gloves on, "let's see, a couple of days after he got there. Now let's see what I can do today," she said as she walked through her wild and dried out bean field.

That night as I sat staring off while my Daddy watched Buck Owens on the tv, Jeffrey and Aunt Clem came over and told us Allen had been found and was in the VA Psychiatric Hospital up north. Daddy and Aunt Clem were distant with each other and only Jeffrey looked somewhat happy.

"Come outside with me Baby," he asked me as he pulled me off the couch. "I can still see where he hit you Baby," Jeffrey said as he caressed my cheek as we sat down on the top step of the porch. "I still can't believe he did that to you. I'm so sorry," Jeffrey said as he pulled me into his thin side.

"S'okay," I mumbled. I didn't want to talk about it. I was glad they'd found Allen and glad he was getting help. But I didn't know if I'd ever want to see him again.

"Heard from Ed at all?" Jeffrey asked.

"No," I shrugged as if it were nothing. I couldn't let anyone know how much it hurt me that it'd been three weeks and I'd not heard from Ed at all.

"Lisa and I have news," Jeffrey said and smiled at me.

"About Ed?"

"No, silly. Lisa's pregnant." His cheeks burned red as he smiled at me and stroked his russet goatee.

"Oh wow! That's wonderful. I almost feel like I'm gonna be an aunt but I guess I'm not, am I?"

"You can be our kid's aunt if you want to be, Baby," Jeffrey smiled and hugged me.

For some reason the news made me sad instead of happy and then I felt guilty for being so self-centered.

The fourth week of July I loitered around the house and I cried every day and still no word from Ed. I wrote him another letter telling him I hoped he was getting settled and that I hoped he'd call me soon. I added a PS: that said my face was finally healed up and looking normal. Normal enough that Jimmy had been over to ask me out. I didn't put that in the letter to Ed, but I hoped he got the hint.

The rest of July passed and August did too and still no call or letter from Ed.

"Ed is keeping very busy with his training," Mrs. Small told me the day before school started when I asked her if she'd heard from him while we were collecting sunflower heads to dry for their seeds. Their big, blazing heads reminded me of Ed and I felt ashamed of my pathetic self.

"So you talked to him recently?" I asked as I stood on the step ladder to cut down the heads as Mrs. Small pointed to the ones that were ready for drying.

"Oh yes. He called a couple of nights ago when I was watching tv. He's going to be a pilot, isn't that something Baby?

Oh how I worry about my Eddy flying up in those mountains," she said as she held out the paper sack for me to put the sunflower head into it.

**

"I'm thinking of joining the pom pom squad," I told Petra at her house the first Friday after school started back.

"Really?" she flipped around to face me from where she sat at her make-up table plucking her eyebrows. "Really?" she asked again, "oh, I'm so jealous of you. All I can do is be on the stupid pep squad." She reached down and touched her metal braces that buckled over her knees.

"So do it. You join the pep squad and I'll join poms," I told her. And that was the first time in a long time that we ever agreed on anything. "We can go to practice together and we both wear uniforms on the same day," I told her.

I figured joining the pom pom squad was one of the first decisions I made for myself since Ed left and after I made the squad, I sent him a card with a frog on the front. All I wrote inside was "I'm a paper-shaker now." And I didn't even sign it.

Weeks passed of me going to pom pom practice and Petra going to pep club and still no word from Ed. I went from sad and missing him to sad that he forgot me, to being mad and thinking he lied to me; that he didn't love me and that he never really intended on keeping in touch with me in the first place.

So with that in mind I said yes to Jimmy Collins and his new red Camaro and listened to a nonstop litany of football talk as he drove us all around the countryside on the curving blacktop. I got so bored one night I asked if he'd let me drive his car. I was still only sixteen but how hard could it be? So on our fourth date Jimmy let me behind the wheel and stopped talking football and taught me how to drive. It became a habit that we'd go out every Friday night to the Dairy Freeze where he'd buy me fries and a shake and then I'd drive us all over while he talked about bench presses and his muscles and plays and drills. He'd want me to feel his bicep while I drove and he'd want to know if it was bigger this week than last week but he never did anything out of line with me. He never tried anything at all as a matter of fact except for the same dried up old peck he gave me when he dropped me off at the end of our date. I loved driving that Camaro and I even liked going out with Jimmy because he was funny in an awkward way, and he kept his hands off me for once. But I missed Ed more than ever.

The end of September I wrote to Ed and said, "I'm dating a jock with a fast car," and "I bought a black bra," and "I cut my hair," and signed it "your sweet, heavenly, Blondie."

The truth was I was dating Jimmy only in words. We went out after every football game; me in my pom pom skirt and red La Rue Robin sweater and him freshly showered. But he never put any moves on me; we were a lot like two friends goofing, eating junk, dancing in the gym at the school dances, and hot rodding around in the country. I found it odd that he would talk a mile a minute while I drove his car around and I only half listened to him. He would sit there in the passenger seat holding his football and talking more about football than I ever imagined possible. At first I was wary of him and his hands because after all the years of him trying to grope me all the time. He never once put one hand on me and he never said anything out of line.

  I found it strange until Petra informed me that he was taking out an ever changing assortment of loose girls from the smoking section at school on nights he wasn't taking me out. This was who he was putting his hands on. Rumors flew at school that Jimmy was cheating on me, that I was naïve and being duped. But I didn't care. I ignored them and I enjoyed my time with him in his red car.

  I did buy a bra and I did wear it on a regular basis. My breasts felt like they grew over night just like Petra always said they would and they hurt when I did my pom pom routines without one on. I complained to Petra about it who thought it a great scandal for me to be the bra-less pom pom girl but she went with me all the same to help me pick one out. And it was she who was the one who talked me into cutting my hair. Though I didn't cut it like I wanted Ed to worry about. I had it cut in long layers and on game days I wore it in long, layered curls that bounced down my back.

The day after Halloween I woke up with the stomach flu and stayed home sick and was laying on the couch drinking 7-Up when the mailman brought me my first ever letter from Ed. "Sweet God, Blondie," he wrote in block letters on yellow lined paper, "do I need to come home or what?" I smiled as I heard his voice in my head. "I'd pay $100 for a picture of you and your sweet, sweet paper-shakers," he wrote and made me blush and shiver all over. "I cut my hair too," he said and he included a very long golden brown lock, secured on one end with a rubberband. "Oh my God, no," I cried as I held it next to my cheek. "I don't believe it," I said as nausea and chills ran over me.

Finally he wrote, "I miss you under me, sweet Blondie," and what made my heart pound nearly out of my chest, "I'm coming home for a visit sooner than expected. Yours, Ed."

Ohh, I thought, as another wave of nausea gripped me, that could be very soon, and I smiled as I ran to the toilet and threw up.

**

The big homecoming game the week before Thanksgiving took place in a snow storm as the bitterly cold weather turned a little warmer and the sky let loose huge, fast falling flakes on all of the football field.

The pom pom girls all decided to keep our jeans on under our skirts, it was so cold, and Petra scolded me from the bleachers where she sat with the pep squad, that I needed to get with the times and buy some Jordache or Calvin Kleins and ditch my second hand, low-rise bellbottoms whose cuffs swallowed up my saddle shoes. But they were the only ones that seemed to fit me anymore. Since Ed had gone, all the dates with Jimmy at the Dairy Freeze seemed to be putting the weight on me.

    Maybe it was because the game was so close and so exciting, or maybe it was because it was so cold and we spent the first half of the game cheering into the wind and snow, or maybe it was because just as we were getting ready to do our half-time routine and I turned around to wave at Petra, I saw him standing there. Standing there in front of the stands in a big dark brown suede coat with a sheep fur collar pulled up under his chin-length hair and his full beard, smiling at me with his ice blue eyes under his heavy lids.

    Maybe it was all of that combined, that sent me right over the edge. I turned and I saw Ed in front of the stands, with snow in his hair, grinning with his eyes on me in my red pom pom uniform with the La Rue Robin on the chest, with all my hair in windblown curls down my back and I felt as if my heart would beat itself crazy and then I felt as if it would completely stop.

    Someone turned off all the sound on the game and suddenly there was so much snow all around me that the whole world went all white and soft. I was confused as I felt something pull hard deep inside my chest and I watched the smile drop off

Ed's face as my knees buckled under me. I watched as he pulled his hands out of his pockets and ran to me in slow motion, as everything around me, and in me, suddenly ceased to be.

CHAPTER TWENTY-THREE

I came to flat on my back, my eyes shut. Someone was gently brushing my hair and working real hard at getting it to part on the wrong side. It felt so odd to have it parted on that side and I wondered if I came to flip flopped, with everything that had been on the left, now on the right, and the thought made my head hurt and I almost went back into the dark again. Then I felt quick nimble fingers and heard the pop as a barrette was snapped into place and I woke all the way up.

"Ed," I whispered and there was no doubt in my mind that it was him and not my Mama cradling my head.

"Blondie, sweet God, finally."

My throat hurt and I had tubes in my nose and the pain in my chest ached so deep it felt like I'd been broken in half and stapled back together.

"Ed," I whispered again but couldn't open my eyes.

"I'm here, sweet Blondie, I'm here," he said and I felt his fingers on my right hand and they felt very warm to me.

"I love you, Ed Small," I rasped out.

"I know," he said and kissed me on the eyebrow.

The urge to see him willed me to open my eyes.

"Hi," he said and his lips curved into a tight smile when I looked at him.

His eyebrows dented down over his cool blue eyes and his lips were tensed out into a worried pout as his eyes roamed my face. I smiled at him to try to ease his worries.

My throat ached to speak to him but my chest hurt too much for me to draw enough air just then to say much of anything. I tried to point with my left hand at my chest but my left hand was strapped to the bedrail. I turned and saw it had an IV sticking out of it. My right hand was free so I pointed at my chest and looked at Ed for an explanation to why I hurt so bad there.

"Your heart stopped," he whispered. "It just stopped. Just like your mama's."

I frowned at him meaning, what else?

"I had to start it back up for ya, sweet, heavenly Blondie." He kissed my knuckles and looked down for a long time. I squeezed his fingers and he looked back up at me with sad eyes, his mouth turned down. "Blondie?" he asked, his voice barely a whisper. "Was there something else you wanted to tell me in your letters? Something you left out?" He didn't wait for my answer. He shut his eyes and I saw that his lashes were wet. When he opened them and looked back at me I shook my head, No. I didn't know what he was talking about.

"No, Blondie?" He came closer to my face. I shook my head no again as my Daddy came in.

"She's awake!" he shouted and came around to the other side of my bed and held the fingers of my hand that was strapped down. I wiggled them at him and whispered, "Take it off."

"Baby, I don't think I'm supposed to."

"Off," I said, my throat dry.

"She's awake, sir, you can undo it now." Ed looked grave at my dad.

My Daddy looked at Ed with his face blank and unstrapped my hand with the IV and took my fingers in his as I shut my eyes and sighed.

"Ed," I heard my Daddy whisper but I kept my eyes closed. "You tried to warn me about Jimmy Collins," he trailed off.

The room was silent so long I nearly fell back asleep but I just lay there with my eyes shut as Ed held one hand and Daddy held the other.

"Ed," Daddy said again. "You tried to tell me."

"Sir, I don't think now is the time." I could imagine Ed furrowing his brows at my Daddy, his voice sounded so powerful.

"But you were right, Ed. I didn't listen to your warning about him. But you were right all along. If I would have listened to you, then, part of this might not have happened."

"Mr. Hunnicutt. Sir. That baby wasn't Jimmy Collins'," I heard Ed say as clear as could be as he squeezed my hand. "That baby was mine."

My eyes popped open and I looked from Ed to my father and back to Ed, confused. Ed's eyebrows were dented in and his bottom lip was poked out far as he looked at my Daddy. Daddy's face was red and his lips were mashed in a line. He squeezed his eyes into a bulging glare as he looked over me at Ed.

"Your baby?" Daddy asked Ed.

"Mine."

"What baby?" I croaked.

Ed leaned down to me and licked his lips in concentration and stared into my eyes and said, "You had to know you were pregnant, Blondie."

"No," I gasped.

"Baby, you were pretty far along." Ed looked long and deep into my eyes. What I saw there was all my denial. All my refusal to believe. All my desperation to hear from him. All my waiting for him to call so I could tell him I thought something was very wrong. I could not put those fears into words in a card with a kitten on the front. I couldn't tell him what I was scared was happening to my body, in a letter. If he didn't care enough to call like he said he would, how could I tell him what had happened?

"You never called. I wasn't sure. I didn't think it could be," I said, my mind reeling. There was no way I could tell my Daddy, or Petra or anyone. And now they all knew. "I couldn't tell you in a letter, but I can tell you now, I think I'm pregnant." I felt relieved to finally tell Ed.

"What you did is against the law," Daddy growled at Ed. I squeezed Ed's palm to get his attention; to get him to stop glaring at my Daddy like he was going to sock him in the jaw any moment.

"Ed, I'm pregnant," I said again and squeezed his hand again.

"No, Blondie. You lost him," he whispered and leaned down and put his forehead on mine. "He's gone, Blondie. He didn't make it." His rested his warm lips on my forehead.

"Him?" I breathed out. I felt the air catching in my throat.

"Him. A son."

I looked up at my Daddy with tears in my eyes. A son. I was going to have a son. But not now. Now he was gone.

"Where is he?"

"He's being buried next to your dear Mama, Baby." My Daddy said.

"No. He's not," Ed said to my Daddy and then to me, "We're going to bury him next to my brother."

"Over my dead body, boy! You'll be in jail! You'll have no say in it!"

"I've already arranged it, sir. He's my son."

"Your son, ha." My Daddy was now the color of chalk and he let go of my hand and began to storm out of the room.

"He'll be buried next to Dale, Daddy! You hear me?" I called out even though it took every last bit of strength and hurt my throat and chest to yell it.

"You know about Dale, Blondie?" Ed leaned down to me and held the back of my hand against his beard and kissed the back of my fingers. I nodded my head and fell asleep as Ed held my hand and Aunt Clem and Jeffrey came in with flowers.

***

What a strange Thanksgiving we had that year. Daddy told Aunt Frances and Frieda and Uncle Fritz and all the Hunnicutt cousins we wouldn't be having Thanksgiving that year; that I didn't feel up to having everyone over. That I was still healing from the surgery to repair my heart. I was also still healing from losing my little baby. We named him Dan and Daddy, Aunt Clem, Lisa and Jeffrey, and Mrs. Small all went to the cemetery with Ed and me when we buried him next to Dale, way out in the country just a few plots away from my Mama. We put flowers on her grave that morning too. My Daddy seemed drained of all angry words and was quiet and thoughtful and held my hand on one side of me while Ed held my other one and Jeffrey stood behind me. I missed Allen. Mostly I missed the Allen I once knew.

Instead of the Hunnicutts, Daddy had MRs. Small, Ed, Jeffrey, Lisa and Aunt Clem back to the house for Thanksgiving. It was the first time he'd invited all of them over for the holiday. I spent most of the holiday on the couch with Ed. I had a red scar going from the top of my chest down to the top of my stomach where they had fixed my heart and I was sore and weak and not allowed to help with the dinner preparations at all.

Daddy chose to forgive Ed's transgressions with me and he even glared openly at Jimmy Collins as if it were still his fault that I'd gotten pregnant, when he stopped by with flowers to see how I was. Of course no one outside of the family knew about the baby Ed and I lost.

"Jimmy never even tried one move on me, all those times I went out with him, you know?" I said to Ed as he unbuttoned my peasant blouse and kissed the top of my scar after Jimmy cut his visit short and everyone else went back in the kitchen to help with the turkey and fixings.

"Ed, what if Daddy comes in," I whispered and threaded my fingers in his hair as he delicately kissed me on my bruised chest.

"I don't care," he said but he stopped a minute and looked around the living room and listened to the sounds coming from the kitchen.

"You ever wonder why he didn't try to touch you, Baby?" Ed asked as he kissed me there again with his big soft lips and his whiskers caressed me and gave me the shivers.

"Why?" I asked him. He was grinning from ear to ear. I couldn't help but touch his dimple in his chin and his dimple in his cheek.

"I told him I'd lop his wiener off if he laid one finger on you, sweet, sweet, Blondie. I told him you were mine and he'd better keep you safe and if he couldn't think of anything to talk about, to talk about football."

That sent me into hysterical giggle fits that made me ache. So that was why Jimmy talked nonstop about football and seemed so nervous with me.

"I thought he'd bore you to death and you'd stop going out with him, huh ahuh!" Ed laughed and buttoned my blouse back up and wrapped his arms around me on the couch.

We shared knowing smiles over dinner as we remembered our first time together under the dining room table. As I wondered if it was when we made little Dan, my eyes sought Ed's and I could see he was wondering the same thing and we shared a sad smile.

"Blondie," Ed said and drew my name out long and deep. We were sitting together on the couch after dinner while Daddy and Aunt Clem did the dishes. Mrs. Small and Lisa sat at the piano together trying to play Claire de Lune in the dining room.

Lisa's belly was swelled out round with their new baby growing inside and I had seen Ed glance at it a few times before dinner. Jeffrey had gone outside on the front porch to have a smoke and Ed and I were alone on the couch.

"Blondie," Ed said again and pulled me all the way up on his lap.

"Ed?" I asked as I snuggled into him and looked into his pale eyes.

"Lay your head on me, Blondie," he told me and pushed my head on his shoulder. "How do you feel, Blondie-Locks?"

"Okay," I sighed. "I'm sorry about the baby. I was too scared to face it, I guess."

"Baby," Ed whispered and kissed me next to my eye. "Baby," he said again and ran his hands through my hair and sighed. I felt his thick fingers crawl over the top of my hair and heard the familiar pop as he took out my barrette and I heard his soft chuckle. "I love you, Blondie. You shouldn't a had to face that alone," he said as he tilted my head back in his arms and kissed me on the mouth. "I love you," he said as he held my jaw and kissed me again. "There'll be more," he told me as he looked me in the eye.

"More?" I asked.

"Babies, Blondie. We're gonna have dozens," he said and broke into a huge smile. "When you're a little older, Blondie. It'll kill me to wait. But I will." He hung his head down for a second and then looked up at me through all his hair and then kissed me again. He didn't stop kissing me until we heard my Daddy come in the room and clear his throat.

"Ahem. Just what are you doin', Ed Small?" Daddy demanded from where he stood in the doorway with his hands on his hips.

"Kissing Blondie, sir." Ed winked at me and gave me a crooked grin.

"Ed. That's my Baby for cryin' out loud." My Daddy's sharp mustache nearly crackled with his frustration to intimidate Ed.

"I know, sir," Ed said and kissed my hair. "I'm well aware of who I'm holdin', sir. I'm well aware. Believe me, sir," he said and opened his pale eyes wide.

"Try to show some respect, son!" My Daddy barked.

"You hear that, sweet, heavenly Blondie?"

"What Ed?" I asked as I lay my head back on his shoulder and snuggled into him.

"He called me 'son'. I heard him. It's like I'm part of the family already," Ed said and laughed, "Huh! Ahuh!" as Aunt Clem, Mrs. Small, and Lisa came in the living room and Jeffrey came back in from having a smoke.

CHAPTER TWENTY-FOUR

"What is it you want, sweet Blondie?" Ed asked me the next afternoon. I'd snuck over to his house while my Daddy took Mrs. Small Christmas shopping an hour away at the new shopping center in Rush.

"Right now?" I asked Ed as I watched dust motes swirl in the sunlight of his bedroom. We were laying on his waterbed with the heat turned up on it. He was being very gentle with me and was resisting his urge to climb on top of me. My incision and surgery was definitely not ready for that.

"Do you want dozens, Baby?" he asked me as he traced my lips with his thick finger.

"Of what?" I asked him, and I turned to him and smiled to let him know I was teasing.

"Do you, Baby?" he asked with his eyebrows furrowed down at me. As he leaned over his hair all fell in his eyes. Now that it was shorter it wouldn't stay tucked behind his ears. He pushed it back several times and he finally gave up and just held it back out his eyes with his hands as he bobbed up and down on the waves of the waterbed.

"You mean babies, right?" I asked him. He didn't answer. His mouth opened slightly and his eyelids drooped as he waited for my answer. I looked at his mouth and as I did he pooched out his big lips at me in that age old habit he had. Then I looked up at his clear blue eyes that were half hidden under his bruised lids and his long lashes.

"Blondie," he said, "Those eyes of yours," he breathed out in a deep chuff, "work me right over," he groaned and he touched my eyebrow with his thumb. "Blondie, those eyes," he shut his own and turned away from me and grinned. "Sweet God, I'll be glad when you're healed up," he shook his head. "So, Blondie?" he asked as he leaned over me, his face very close to mine. It was all he could do to not climb on top of me and I smiled at how hard it was for him to resist me. "Babies? Will you have my babies, sweet, heavenly, Baby Blondie-Locks?"

"Can I finish high school first?" I asked and grinned at him as he stroked my hair off my face and down my arm.

"Maybe," he said and smiled and flashed his ice blue pale eyes on me and made me squirm as he leaned down to kiss me and growled, "maybe not."

EPILOGUE

One and a half years later on my eighteenth birthday

"Do you sweet, heavenly Blondie-Locks promise to love me with long hair or none, with bare feet and my shirt off, with my smart ass mouth and my giving you dutch rubs on the back of your head from this day forward?" Ed asked me as we stood on the sand of Settler's Beach at Rush State Lake, as he rubbed his big, tan hand over my round belly and felt our baby kick at him through my white eyelet, strapless prom dress I never got to wear to prom.

"I do, Ed Small, I do. I loved you since the day my Mama told me to not look into your crazy, pale, hippie eyes, Ed Small," I told him as I stood up on tiptoe and traced my thumb over his pooched out bottom lip. He leaned down and winked at me before he kissed me with all his might in front my twin cousins, Jeffrey and Allen who raised me, and in front of my Aunt Clem who loved me, and in front of crying Petra who was my very best friend, and in front of my Daddy who was offering up a prayer to my poor, dead Mama, to forgive him for not keeping me away from Ed.

I kissed him with everything I had and I ran my hand through his golden brown tangles that had been shampooed just that morning and were now blowing all around his head and as they caught in both our mouths, he pulled them away and mouthed to me with his eyes wide, shit mother fuck.

THE END

DEDICATION

With much love and never-ending thanks to my husband Craig and my sons for giving me time to write this.

And to Bethany for reading all the chapters right off the press and always giving me your opinion with much grace.

A big hug to all my followers on my blog who kept me encouraged after all the rejections.

And last but not least, to Roger Waters, and to Pink Floyd for your amazing music that I listened to while writing every word.

I Heart Ed Small

Printed in Great Britain
by Amazon.co.uk, Ltd.,
Marston Gate.